PRAISE FOR

THE REVOLUTION OF
BIRDIE RANDOLPH

A Chicago Public Library Best Teen Fiction Pick

An ALA Best Fiction for Young Adults Pick

An ALA Quick Picks for Reluctant Young Adult Readers Pick

"Touching and **uplifting**." —*Entertainment Weekly*

"A **beautiful and necessary** read." —Buzzfeed

"There are **few authors in contemporary YA today who write with Colbert's quiet power and nuance**, and her fourth novel is a perfect example."
—*Barnes & Noble Teen Blog*

★ "Colbert's latest novel **brilliantly delves into first loves, forbidden romance, rebellion, and family expectations—all of which teens will strongly relate to**." —*Booklist*, starred review

★ "*The Revolution of Birdie Randolph* crescendos with **an unexpected, masterful plot twist** and an extremely satisfying ending." —*Shelf Awareness*, starred review

★ "This **thrilling tale of first love** explores what it means to be held to an impossible standard and still learn to live an authentic life."
—*Publishers Weekly*, starred review

"The book **may actually help struggling teens** realize that they are not alone in whatever hardships they may face."
—*School Library Connection*

"**A great addition to teen collections everywhere**."—*SLJ*

"An **emotionally gripping tale** about family and young love and how they can be your entire world while still being worlds apart." —*Kirkus Reviews*

THE REVOLUTION OF BIRDIE RANDOLPH

ALSO BY BRANDY COLBERT

POINTE

LITTLE & LION

FINDING YVONNE

THE REVOLUTION OF BIRDIE RANDOLPH

BY BRANDY COLBERT

LITTLE, BROWN AND COMPANY

New York Boston

Copyright © 2019 by Brandy Colbert
Excerpt from *Finding Yvonne* copyright © 2018 by Brandy Colbert

Cover art copyright © 2019 by Erin Robinson. Cover design by Marcie Lawrence. Cover copyright © 2019 by Hachette Book Group, Inc.

Little, Brown and Company
Hachette Book Group
1290 Avenue of the Americas, New York, NY 10104
Visit us at LBYR.com

Originally published in hardcover and ebook by Little, Brown and Company in August 2019
First Trade Paperback Edition: August 2020

Little, Brown and Company is a division of Hachette Book Group, Inc. The Little, Brown name and logo are trademarks of Hachette Book Group, Inc.

The publisher is not responsible for websites (or their content) that are not owned by the publisher.

The Library of Congress has cataloged the hardcover edition as follows:
Names: Colbert, Brandy, author.
Title: The revolution of Birdie Randolph / by Brandy Colbert.
Description: First edition. | New York; Boston: Little, Brown and Company, 2019. | Summary: Sixteen-year-old Dove "Birdie" Randolph's close bond with her parents is threatened by a family secret, and by hiding her relationship with Booker, who has been in juvenile detention.
Identifiers: LCCN 2018022809| ISBN 9780316448567 (hardcover) | ISBN 9780316448574 (ebook) | ISBN 9780316448550 (library edition ebook)
Subjects: | CYAC: Family life—Illinois—Chicago—Fiction. | Secrets—Fiction. | Dating (Social customs)—Fiction. | Identity—Fiction. | African Americans—Fiction. | Chicago (Ill.)—Fiction.
Classification: LCC PZ7.C66998 Rev 2019 | DDC [Fic]—dc23
LC record available at https://lccn.loc.gov/2018022809

ISBNs: 978-0-316-44854-3 (pbk.), 978-0-316-44857-4 (ebook)

Printed in the United States of America

LSC-C

10 9 8 7 6 5 4 3 2 1

For Mom
Thank you for being you and for letting me be me
Your Lovey loves you

A STRANGE WOMAN IS SMOKING ON MY FRONT STOOP.

Actually, it's the stoop of my mother's hair salon. We live in the apartment upstairs. But my mom and Ayanna make their clients go down the street to smoke—none of them would ever sit right here in front of the door.

Maybe she just needs a place to sit. This is Chicago. We're in Logan Square, near the California Blue Line stop—people are walking by constantly.

She takes a drag just as she notices me standing a few feet away, watching her. She exhales and smiles and lifts her hand in greeting. I give her a tight smile—this is Chicago—and quickly squeeze past her on the stoop, shutting the door to our stairway firmly behind me.

I'm in the kitchen getting a drink of water when I hear

footsteps on the stairs and, a few moments later, the front door opening. It's too early for my father to be home. I guess Mom needed to run up for something.

"Dove?"

I freeze. That's not my mother. How could I have forgotten to lock the front door?

And then I turn around and see the woman from the stoop standing in the doorway, and I drop my glass. It shatters at my feet. Water splashes over my ankles and the tops of my school loafers. I back up, pressing myself against the kitchen sink. I don't look at it, but I'm very aware that my hand is within reach of the knife block.

"Oh." She takes in my frightened face. Holds up her hands. "It's okay. You're Dove, right? I'm Carlene."

I stare at her, wondering if my mother would be able to hear me scream downstairs over the music and blow-dryers and incessant chatter of the shop. How does this woman know my name?

"I'm your aunt."

I frown and then my mouth drops open as I remember that my mother has a sister. She's her only sibling, and I haven't seen her in so long I'd forgotten I have an aunt on that side. Mom doesn't talk about her much. Never, really.

"Aunt Carlene?"

She smiles, and I wonder if I'll see my mother in

it, but I don't. Thick, black Marley twists hang past my aunt's shoulders. Her eyes are tired but friendly. "Remember me?"

"Um…just barely."

Her smile fades a little. "Well, it's been a long time. You've grown so much," she says almost wondrously, her eyes roaming over me as if she's trying to match the Dove she used to know with the one standing in front of her.

I want to ask her exactly how long it's been, but something in her eyes tells me not to. Instead, I say, "I'm sixteen. I only have two more days left of sophomore year."

My hands are still clenched into fists, even though I'm pretty sure she is who she says she is.

"I know." She takes a couple of steps forward so she's standing fully in the kitchen. The cigarette smoke clings to her clothes or her fingers or maybe both, and it's not a good smell, but I try to pretend like it doesn't bother me. "Seventeen next February, right?"

"Right." I smile back at her, but I'm surprised she remembers. I didn't think she knew any more about me than I know about her, which is pretty much nothing. "Are you visiting for a while?"

"I am." She pauses then says, "I don't know how long. But I'm hoping your mother will let me work in the salon while I'm here."

"You know how to do hair?"

"Girl, who do you think taught your mama?"

Just then, I hear feet on the stairs again: thundering up. The front door bursts open and then my mother's voice: "Birdie?"

"Birdie?" my aunt echoes.

"We're in the kitchen," I call back. Then, to Aunt Carlene, "That's her nickname for me. You know...a play on the whole Dove thing."

Mom stops abruptly in the doorway.

"What's wrong?" I ask, staring at the worry lines etched into her forehead.

"Nothing." She lets out a long breath as she looks back and forth between us. "I was just—it's been a while since you've seen Carlene, so I wanted to make sure everything is okay." Then she spies the broken glass in front of my feet. "What happened?"

"I wasn't expecting anyone to come in and...I got freaked out."

Mom presses her lips together as she heads across the room to grab the broom and dustpan. "I wanted to let you know before you got home, but Carlene showed up unannounced in the middle of an appointment. I couldn't get away."

"It's a broken glass," Aunt Carlene says, raising an eyebrow. "Nobody died."

She tries to take the broom from my mother, but

Mom shakes her head and motions for me to get out of the way as she sweeps up the wet shards.

I don't think they've seen each other in years, either, but they don't look so happy to be reunited. They're not close; maybe my aunt doesn't know her well enough to understand how much Mom values planning and order.

"Don't walk barefoot in here for a while," my mother says after crouching to make sure she's gotten every piece that she can see. She tosses the broken glass into the trash can and leans the broom against the wall. She looks at Aunt Carlene. "I also wanted to make sure you're settling in okay. Should I have Raymond stop anywhere on the way home?"

"I'm settling in just fine. I don't need anything," Aunt Carlene says. "I'm actually going to lie down for a while— I had a long day on the train."

My mother's lips are still pursed, but some of the tension leaves her body. "We'll wake you for dinner."

"Wake me up in time to help," my aunt says over her shoulder.

I get a fresh glass from the cupboard and pour more water, then sit down at the kitchen table. Once the door to Mimi's room clicks closed, Mom joins me.

She sighs, running a hand over her twistout. "I didn't know she was coming."

"Yeah, I kind of gathered that." I watch her. "Are you okay?"

"Oh, I'm fine, Birdie. Just tired." She pats my hand. "You okay with her staying here for a while?"

"Sure." I shrug. "I don't remember her at all, but she seems okay. And Mimi's not coming home this summer, right?"

"Right. Okay. Good." Mom smiles.

"She's going to work in the shop?"

"We could use another braider, but she has to be licensed, and that takes a lot of hours. I don't know if she'll be here that long."

"She said she taught you everything you know about hair."

Mom's face drops so fast it makes me laugh. "Oh, she did? We'll see how much she remembers after—"

"What?" I prompt her.

She shakes her head. "Nothing. She's just been out of the game for a while."

"Mom?"

"Hmm?"

"Are *you* okay with her being here?"

"Carlene is family," she says in a voice that doesn't match her face. "Of course I am."

⸿

My father comes home loaded down with bags of Thai takeout and a tired smile. He's a team physician for the Chicago Bulls, but his main job is at Rush University, where he sees regular patients for sports medicine. He is always busy and always tired, but he tries to be around as much as he can be.

I'm in the living room, texting with Booker. At least I don't have to pretend to have my nose stuck in a textbook every second of the evening now that final exams are over. There was plenty of studying over the past few weeks, but there was plenty of texting Booker Stratton in between.

I set my phone facedown on the couch and hop up to kiss Dad on the cheek. "Did you get lard nar?"

"I even got extra tonight since you ate it all last time."

"Not my fault you and Mom are slow eaters."

He shakes his head, laughing as he carries the bags into the kitchen.

My phone buzzes. I keep expecting this delicious, warm feeling to go away the more I hear from Booker, but the truth is that it only increases. Mitchell never made me feel this way, and we were together for a year and a half.

When can I see you again?

I pause, my fingers hovering over the phone as I think about this. It was easy to push away the question when I was in the thick of finals. Or even before that, since I go to a pretty demanding private school; academics take up the majority of my time during the year. But summer approaching means even more parties are approaching, and I'm not sure how long I'll be able to escape the fact that my parents have my whole life planned out for me.

Maybe this weekend?

I don't admit that the only way Mom and Dad will let me go out with him is if I introduce him first. I don't know if either of us is ready for that yet.

The smell of Thai food floats into the living room, making my mouth water. I tell Booker I'll text him later and head into the kitchen to help unpack the bags.

My parents are talking in low tones, their words sharp and pointed at the edges. Dad is pulling cartons from one of the bags, and I don't even know how it's possible for them to already be having such an involved conversation.

They stop as soon as I walk into the room. Mom looks over and smiles. "I was just telling your father he got so much food we'll be eating leftovers for weeks."

She clearly was doing nothing of the sort, but I'm too confused to challenge her. My parents rarely argue, and when they do, it's behind closed doors, after they think I've fallen asleep.

"Well, we have company," Dad says. "Gotta make sure everyone has enough to eat."

I glance toward the hallway. "Should I go wake Aunt Carlene?"

"No, sweetie, I'll get her," Mom says. "You help your dad."

It takes an extraordinarily long time for my mother to get my aunt. We've unpacked all the food and set the dining room table, and I'm grabbing the pitcher of water by the time they walk into the kitchen.

Aunt Carlene smiles at me before her eyes shift to my father, who is washing his hands at the sink. "Hi, Ray."

He takes a moment to turn around, and when he does, there's a strange look on his face. Almost like he's seen a ghost. Which doesn't make sense; he knew she was here. "Carlene. It's been a real long time."

"Indeed. You look good, Ray."

"You too." But it sounds like someone forced him to say it. I'm starting to wonder if anyone besides me is actually okay with my aunt staying here.

She looks over his shoulder at the food. "Chinese?"

"Thai."

"Oh, I love Thai food."

"Good," Mom says. "Eat up. We have enough to feed the whole block."

Aunt Carlene asks a lot of questions at dinner, but only to me. I end up talking the most, which I guess is okay because my parents are so quiet it's unnerving.

"What are you up to this summer, Dove? Hanging with your friends?"

"A little bit, I guess."

She frowns. "What else is summer for?"

"I'm taking some college prep courses," I say, avoiding my mother's eyes. "And working at the shop some."

"That sounds...structured," my aunt says, her eyes landing right on my mother.

"I like being at the shop." And then I shove noodles and chicken into my mouth so I won't be tempted to say what I really think about the college prep courses.

"Birdie is focused," Mom says. "Both our girls are."

Aunt Carlene takes a sip of water. "Focused is good. Lord knows our mother wouldn't stand for anything else. Which is why we fought like we did." She looks off into the distance, as if she's remembering scenes from her childhood. Then she looks at me. "You know, Dove, your mother was always the overachiever. I didn't stand a chance."

"I suppose I always thought overachieving was better than the alternative."

Even my father, who has barely said a word since we sat down and seems lost in his own world, looks in surprise at my mother. That sentence had claws.

Mom glances at us and exhales loudly. "Sorry. It's been a long day."

But she doesn't even look at her sister when she apologizes. Aunt Carlene stares down at her food.

I glance around the table as we finish the meal in silence, but their faces give away nothing. It's times like this that I really miss my sister. I'm still not used to navigating this family stuff alone.

∽๏

I like to text Booker before I go to sleep.

I like having someone to say good night to after my parents, and remembering his texts as soon as I open my eyes in the morning. I like knowing someone is thinking of me before they drift off, too.

Tonight, I get under the covers and text him as usual, but I wonder if I should be listening at my parents' bedroom door. Maybe I'd hear the telltale murmurs of a disagreement—some clue as to what was really going on at dinner. He texts back:

> Don't know if I can wait
> much longer to see you

My cheeks flush with heat. We've kissed only a couple of times, but I remember it well, the feeling of Booker's thick, soft lips on mine. One hand cupped around my face, the other palm pressed to the brick wall of Laz's building behind me.

> I think you have to? No going out
> on school nights over here

There's a knock at my door just as his next message comes through:

> You could always sneak out

"Come in." I shove the phone under my pillow.

My mother closes the door behind her and perches on the edge of the bed next to me. "I can't believe my baby is finishing her sophomore year in a couple of days. And that you'll be taking the SATs in a few months!"

"Me either," I say.

Mimi has done everything before me, so I know what my life is supposed to look like. I'm supposed to graduate at the top of my class and go to a good college where I will study something respectable that will get me an impressive, high-paying job. But it's still weird to be doing all the things I watched her do, as if I never really thought they'd happen to me.

"I know it'll be a busy one, but are you looking forward to the summer?"

"Mom." I don't like small talk in general, and I especially don't like it with my mother. Also, we said good night earlier, so I'm not sure why she's in here talking about my summer. "What's going on?"

She takes a deep breath. Gives me an uncomfortable smile. "So we didn't do a good job of pretending everything is normal?"

"Uh, not quite."

My mother plays with her wedding ring, twisting it around and around her finger. "There's no graceful way to say this.... Your aunt is fresh off a stint in rehab. Her longest one yet."

My eyebrows go up. "Rehab? For alcohol?"

"For...a lot of things." She pauses. "I don't feel comfortable telling Carlene's story for her, but I didn't want you to be in the dark since she's staying here."

"Is that why I haven't seen her in so many years?"

Mom nods.

"How long? Since I've seen her?"

"You would've been young...really young," my mother says, looking down at her hands.

"You said 'her longest one yet.' How many times has she been in and out of rehab?"

"I'm not sure, Birdie. She's been dealing with substance abuse issues for a while."

"How long?" I feel like a broken record.

Mom pauses and doesn't look at me when she says, "Since she was your age."

I didn't know anyone in our family had addiction issues. Isn't that supposed to run in families? My parents aren't big drinkers, but they often have a glass of wine with dinner or to relax afterward. And my father always has a beer with his Thai food. Except I remember that he didn't tonight.

I don't drink. Like my mother, my ex-boyfriend, Mitchell, didn't like parties, so we never went to any—not the ones thrown by kids at our school nor at Laz's. Mitchell always said we were too smart to hang out with people who deliberately got wasted on the weekends, and I never challenged him because it was easier to stay quiet.

"Like I said, it's not my place to tell her story," Mom says, and I wonder if my emotions are cycling across my face as rapidly as they're traveling through my head. "But you're old enough to know."

I nod. And I'm secretly pleased that my mother thinks I'm old enough to be let in on what has been a family secret up until now. I wonder if Mimi knows. The part of me that never gets to experience anything first takes pleasure in maybe knowing before her, but I doubt that's the case. Mimi knows everything.

Mom kisses me good night for the second time this evening and closes the door softly behind her.

I turn off my lamp and close my eyes, but I'm not tired at all. Especially not now. I can't get my mother's tone out of my head. She was trying to sound neutral, but it landed somewhere between judgmental and disappointed. If she feels that way about her own sister, how would she feel if I told her about Booker? *All* about him. As much as I've tried to tell myself she might surprise me, I don't think she would.

So I can't say anything. Not yet.

I look at my phone to see if he's texted again, but he hasn't. His last message is still there on the lock screen, marked as unread.

You could always sneak out

I don't want to leave him hanging until tomorrow. But I don't want to say the wrong thing. If I keep giving excuses for why I can't meet up with him, he might stop asking to see me.

I take a deep breath, type as fast as I can, and send the text before I can think too much about it:

How about tomorrow?

THE PERSON WHO KNOWS ME BEST IN THIS WORLD IS MIMI, BUT SINCE SHE'S my sister, that's always seemed like a bit of a default. Of course we don't have to be close just because we're related—my mom and Aunt Carlene are proof of that—but it's always been easier to work with her than against her.

There was a noticeable gap in my life when Mimi went away to school in Wisconsin just before I started my freshman year. We still text and video chat, and e-mail sometimes, too—but it's not the same as having her here every day. We didn't even get to be at high school together.

Thank god for Laz. He's the one I *choose* to let know me best, and I don't know what I'd do without him. We've been best friends since second grade when his mom, Ayanna, went into business with my mother to open the hair salon. They met in cosmetology school and became fast friends, both working at other salons for a few years before they decided to take the plunge and go into business for themselves. Laz and I circled each other curiously the first couple of times we were both at the salon, and after we got over our shyness, we could barely stand to be apart.

He goes to another school, so we only get to see each other on weekends and afternoons sometimes. Laz is on the water polo team, which always takes up a lot of his spring semester. Stowing our books and breaking from practice is always the sign that summer has officially begun. And it means that we finally get to see each other when we want to during the week.

I text him the morning after my aunt arrives to tell him I need his help seeing Booker.

He takes a while to respond. I picture him emerging from his crumpled bedsheets, blackout shades blocking the sun so the phone's glow is the only light in his room.

> Tell me what you need to me to do

> Too tired to think

I tell him I want to sneak out and need to say that I'm with him. I finish making my bed as I wait for him to wake up, pulling the sheets tight over the mattress and fluffing the pillows like I've been doing every morning since I can remember.

> Can't wait till this weekend?
> Easier for you to get out then

I slip on my loafers and hook my bookbag over my shoulder as I text him back:

> I can't wait

There's a long pause before his next text, and I tap my foot against the rug, hoping Laz isn't falling back to sleep. He likes Booker, but I don't think he ever expected us to get involved. I know he didn't. He's introduced me to lots of his friends and I've never been interested in any of them. Even after Mitchell broke up with me a few months ago, I didn't think I'd meet anyone new. Not so soon, anyway. Maybe it's more that I couldn't trust myself to know what I really wanted. I thought I wanted Mitchell for the year and a half we were together, but now I think maybe I just liked the way we looked on paper. Or maybe I liked the idea of someone who told me they wanted me, even if his actions didn't always match his words.

K, let me know what our fake plans are

I never do things like this, and I can't believe how good it feels.

I smile so big that my mother asks why I'm so happy when I head out to school.

⌒ℚ

The day is long and uneventful, and I'm counting down the minutes until I can see Booker as I sit down to dinner.

We decided to meet at the library. It's foolproof. Laz and I study together sometimes, and it's a place my parents are comfortable letting me go by myself at night. But that excuse won't work this summer. Not even people who are great at school want to spend time studying when it's out of session. Not even those of us who happen to be enrolled in SAT prep courses.

I saw my aunt at breakfast this morning and I braced myself for another awkward meal, but my father had already left for work and my mother seemed more relaxed than last night. Maybe she's getting used to Aunt Carlene being here. Mom made her eggs, and when she set the plate in front of her sister, my aunt looked up with raised eyebrows and said, "Just the way I like them." Mom shrugged and said, "Who else likes their eggs so runny?" But there was a comfort between them that put me at ease.

My aunt is nowhere to be found when dinner is

served, though. I wonder if this will please Mom, but she is anxious again. Maybe more so than when Aunt Carlene arrived unannounced. She keeps tapping the tines of her fork against her plate absentmindedly, barely touching her pasta.

When Dad is halfway through his meal, he gets up and goes to the fridge and pulls out a beer. Mom doesn't notice until he sits back down, and I don't miss the sharp look she gives him.

"Raymond, we talked about this."

His fingers are squeezed around the bottle cap, but he doesn't open it. "She's not here. And what difference does it make? The beer has been in there since last night. She's the sober one, Kitty, not me."

It's always been strange to me that my mother goes by the name Kitty. She's the only person who calls me Birdie, but everyone calls her Kitty. Short for Katrina, which I guess makes sense. Still, she's too serious to have such a cutesy nickname.

I take a drink of water, and both their eyes slide to me. Now that I'm old enough to know this sort of business, I wonder if they'll keep talking. I wonder if I will be around when my mother proposes to no longer keep alcohol in the house, because I'm pretty sure that's where this is headed. And I'm pretty sure my father is going to put up a fight.

She changes the subject. "Where is it you're going with Laz tonight, Birdie?"

"Just the library."

"Extra credit?" She frowns, running over her mental snapshot of my calendar, color-coded by classes. Which is front and center on the fridge, just in case she forgets.

"No, I've turned in everything. But Laz has two more weeks. He has to study for exams and I figured I'd help him, since I'm still technically in school."

"That's nice of you," she says. Approvingly, but not surprised.

Across the table, Dad pops the top on his beer with a fizz.

⁓ℓ

I change out of my school uniform after dinner. I want to look good for Booker, but I don't want to dress too nicely since I'm supposed to be meeting Laz. Mom already seems on high alert with Aunt Carlene—I don't want to give her a reason to start watching me, too.

I decide on a gray sundress with pink and white flowers, and cover my shoulders with my denim jacket. My aunt still isn't home when I kiss my mother goodbye, and I can tell she's starting to get worried.

At the station, I walk to the far end of the train platform, and when the "L" arrives, I get into the first car, just like my mom always tells me to do if I'm riding alone. She says at least that way I'm as close to the conductor as possible if something goes wrong. The car is nearly empty when I get on.

My palms sweat as I think about Booker. I feel braver the farther I am from him. Not in what I say, but in what I think, too. It's as if the closer the train takes me to him, the better he will be able to read my thoughts. Like how I think about touching him all the time, and that's new for me. Everything I did with Mitchell felt like we were checking off boxes on a high school relationship chart from the 1950s. Chaste and uninspired.

Booker and I do meet at the library, but we have no intentions of going in. I exit the train and cross the street and see him leaning against the wall in front of the doors. Even in the twilight, I can tell that it's him. Booker is a large guy—stocky and strong with broad shoulders and big hands.

He stands up straight when he sees me coming. I clutch the strap of my bookbag tight against my chest as I walk. My heart speeds as I get closer and make out his features—his lips curving into a wide smile, the tight curls of his chunky Afro illuminated by the halo of light he's stepped into.

"You really did it," he says when I'm standing in front of him, smiling like he can't believe I'm actually here.

"I told you I would."

We don't touch, but we're just inches away from each other. All I've been thinking about since the last time I saw him is touching him, and now that I'm here, I can't. Not first, anyway. I become a little less shy each time I see him, but this is only the third time. And it's the first without Laz acting as our accidental chaperone.

Booker reaches toward me just as the heavy library door bursts open. A mom walks out with two young kids bouncing behind her, each holding a stack of picture books high above their heads. We step out of the way, out of the light, and watch them go, Booker's hand at my elbow.

When their silhouettes are just indiscernible spots in the distance, Booker's fingers make their way from my elbow and up the back of my arm, rubbing lightly. My stomach flips and my limbs fill with heat and I wonder if anyone will ever make me feel the way Booker makes me feel. There is still so much we haven't done, but I am sure this is special.

He kisses me, and just like each time before, I am surprised at how good he is at this. I only have Mitchell to compare him to, but nothing we ever did made me feel so deliciously weak. Truly, it's like my arms and legs have forgotten how to move, sustained only by the warmth of Booker's touch.

I stumble. Not a lot, but enough to make him catch me softly by the shoulders and ask if I'm okay.

I nod. "I'm just—" I stop, feeling silly.

"What?" he asks, looking at me as if he can't make it through the night without knowing my thoughts.

"I'm just happy. Here. With you."

Booker smiles a soft smile. "I'm happy with you, too." Then he pauses and licks his lips like he's nervous, and I ready myself for the *but*. Only there isn't one. "Do you want to come over? My dad works graveyard. Won't be home till morning."

The look on his face is so hopeful, so sweet I wish I could give him the answer he wants. But I know myself. The nerves from lying to my parents are still pulsing beneath my skin like electric currents. If I take this deception any further, I might actually explode.

I shake my head. "I can't."

"Not even if I promise to have you back by curfew?"

"I only have a couple of hours and . . ." I pause, tugging at the hem of his T-shirt. "It was a big deal for me to get out of the house. I'm afraid to jinx it."

"Your folks super religious or something?"

"No, just . . . protective. They have a lot of rules," I say. "About who I can spend time with, and where. They're not super accepting of people they haven't known for a while."

"Oh," he says. "Will it help that I've known Laz for a couple of years now?"

"Can we not talk about my parents? I'd rather get frozen yogurt."

He laughs, a full one that emerges from deep inside. "Frozen yogurt, huh? You are a rebel, Dove."

"I don't know when it became cool to start hating on frozen yogurt, but I'm not crossing over to the dark side."

"When was it ever *cool* to like frozen yogurt?"

I poke him in the shoulder. He leans down to kiss me.

Booker rides the train home with me after frozen yogurt. I tell him he doesn't have to, that I can get home by myself, but he insists. I hope it's because he doesn't want to say goodbye. Does he get that same yearning that lingers in me? As if a part of my brain is already thinking about having to leave him as soon as we meet? Maybe he is just lonely, with his father working all night.

Or maybe it's a little bit of both.

"There's a party this weekend," he says, lightly tapping my knee. "Saturday night. You should come."

My heart speeds, but it's not all excitement. Of course I'm happy that he asked me—that he wants to see me again even after I declined to go back to his house. He still likes me even though the only thing we did was sit in a frozen yogurt shop and talk.

But parties are off-limits—unless my mother knows the parents and knows that one of them will be there. It's always been like that, and it was never an issue with Mitchell because he never wanted to go to any of the unsupervised ones in the first place.

"Yeah," I say. "Sure. Maybe."

I'm sitting as close to him as I can without sitting *on* him, and I feel him deflate. Just a bit, but his body sags, the same way it did when I told him I couldn't go to his house. I hate disappointing him, especially since I want to go more than he knows.

"It's just...my parents. But I'll figure something out, okay?"

"Okay," he says, and I try not to think about how I might have to disappoint him no matter how much I try not to.

I wonder what Booker and I look like to other people. As if we go together? Like we should call each other boyfriend and girlfriend? I slip my hand into his and watch my deep brown skin disappear beneath the smooth dark brown of his fingers.

"Tell me how you got your name," I say, hoping the subject change will boost the mood.

"You really want to hear this?"

"You're the only person I know with a more confusing name than mine."

He laughs. "All right. So it was a big fight between my parents. My old man wanted to name me something like Jonathan or Matthew, but Mom wasn't having it. Said she wanted to give me a special name. Something that'd set me apart."

Booker rolls his eyes, but I say, "Keep going."

"I mean, that's it, right? Like Booker T. Washington." He shrugs. "People love it."

"But why Booker?"

He hesitates, and I hope I haven't pushed him too far. Maybe he doesn't want to talk about his mother.

I squeeze his hand. "It's okay. We don't have to—"

"She liked that he put education first. She said she knew the minute she was pregnant with me that someday I'd 'effect some real change.' Her words, not mine." Booker smiles a little. "And that was that. Imagine, having a baby named Booker."

"I bet you were a cute baby."

He grins now. "I was all right."

The train whirs along the tracks, and I think how strange it is to feel comfortable with someone new. And how it is stranger to have someone else in my social circle besides Laz. Mitchell was there for a good while, but I haven't seen him outside of school for months now. Do two people even count as a social circle? Well, it's a triangle now.

"It was worth it," I say when we are one stop from mine.

Booker looks at me. "What?"

"Sneaking out to meet you. It was worth it."

"Yeah?" he says.

"Yeah."

I hold tight to his hand, trying not to think about how I probably won't be able to see him many more times.

Not once my parents find out he's been in juvenile detention.

I WAKE UP PARCHED AT ONE IN THE MORNING.

I've kept a glass of water next to my bed every night since fourth grade, but I forgot this evening. I felt like I was floating when I walked into the apartment. I'd spent the last ten minutes before curfew kissing Booker on the next block over. All I wanted was to fall into bed so I could close my eyes—to relive his lips pressing hungrily against mine, his fingers grazing the small of my back.

I tiptoe down the hall to the kitchen and start to creep across the room to the cabinet when I see a shadow at the table. I recognize it's Aunt Carlene and stop myself from screaming. Just barely.

"Girl, you are jumpy," she says, her voice calm. I'm light on my feet, but I guess she heard me coming.

I flip on the light. "Sorry. Most people don't sit here in the dark in the middle of the night."

She smiles and sips from the mug in front of her. I wonder what's in it, but I don't look.

I fill a glass with water and linger near the table. It's late and I have school tomorrow, but this is the first time I've been alone with my aunt since she arrived. And I'm not actually that sleepy now that I'm up. I can't stop thinking about Booker. But maybe she wants to be alone. She *was* sitting in the dark.

"Have a seat," she says, which should make me feel weird since this is my kitchen, not hers—but it doesn't.

I sit.

She's wearing a bathrobe that looked white in the dark but turns out to be powder blue under the bright kitchen lights. The elbows of it are particularly worn, like she's spent a long time leaning on them. She smells faintly of cigarettes, and by now I'm guessing my mom has asked her to smoke down the street and not in front of the salon.

"Are you always so skittish, or is it just because I'm here?"

I pause. "I don't know."

"This apartment is too big," she says. "Easy to sneak up on people. Did you know your mom and I shared a room when we were growing up? And we had no proper dining room, just a kitchen, where we all squeezed in to eat. This place is probably twice the size of our old home."

I've never thought of our apartment as *too* big—more like just right for us. It's three bedrooms, and there's a full bathroom in my parents' room plus one in the hallway, a proper dining room and large living room, and a kitchen big enough for all of us to comfortably eat in. There's a decent-size mudroom in the back, off the kitchen, and a rooftop deck that we don't use as much as we should. My parents did a pretty big remodel when they bought the building, and we moved up here about a year after the shop opened all those years ago.

"You shared a room with Mom?" Seeing the two of them with each other now, I can't imagine that was ever peaceful.

She shrugs. "I wasn't around a whole lot when we were your age."

I nod, thinking of what my mother told me but not wanting to let on how much I know.

I wish I could walk into my mother's room as easily as she came into mine the other night. Just spill everything about Booker—everything I know, that is—and trust that she'd believe the guy I like is a good guy, even with a past she'd call "undesirable."

I feel Aunt Carlene staring at me, and when I look over, she's squinting. Like she's trying to see deep into my soul. "You're not really here."

"What?" I blink at her.

She taps a finger against her temple. "Your mind. It's somewhere else."

It's with Booker, but I can't tell her that. Booker isn't supposed to exist. Not without my parents knowing about him.

She doesn't give up. "I know that look. You're thinking about someone."

I don't know how she's read me so well when she barely knows me, but it freaks me out. I shake my head. "I'm just tired. Ready for school to be out."

"I don't know why you're so ready for summer when Kitty's making you study the whole time."

I shrug. "What else am I going to do? I don't really have anyone to hang out with besides Laz."

"Ayanna's kid?"

I nod. "Yeah, he's my best friend. But he's the only person I really see now."

Aunt Carlene takes a sip from her mug. I look when she sets it down. White liquid: warm milk. "Why is that?"

"I sort of lost touch with all my old friends when I stopped playing soccer."

That's not true: I *totally* lost touch. I think we all just assumed we'd be friends for the long haul, but we didn't realize how essential soccer practices and games were to our friendships. Now they're virtual strangers; smiles passing by in the hallways and cafeteria. It's hard to believe I used to spend nearly every afternoon with them on the field, running and sweating and practicing drills, and weekends where we didn't talk about soccer at all. Mitchell's friends were around when I was dating him, but they were dull and seemed to only tolerate having me around because I was his girlfriend.

"Now you look sad," my aunt says, and I wonder if she is going to analyze my mood like this for the rest of the time she's here.

In the back of the apartment, I hear my parents' bedroom door open. Aunt Carlene and I sit in silence as my mother's soft footsteps pad down the hall.

Mom leans against the doorframe, yawning. She scratches at a spot on her satin headscarf. "What are you two doing up?"

"I got thirsty," I say.

"I was already up," my aunt says. "Sorry if we woke you."

"You should go to bed, Birdie," Mom says. "You've still got school in the morning."

I finish my water and take the glass to the sink. When I turn around, my mother is trying and failing to slyly sneak a peek at what her sister is drinking.

Aunt Carlene tips back her mug to finish the rest and stands. "It was milk," she says without looking at my mother. "With honey. To help me sleep, Kitty."

"I didn't say—"

"You didn't have to." She rinses the mug and places it next to my glass in the sink. Touches my arm on her way to the hall. "Night, Dove."

"Good night, Aunt Carlene."

"Just call me Carlene," she says over her shoulder. She ignores my mother as she passes her in the doorway.

Mom kisses my forehead before I leave the kitchen. I wait for her to switch off the light and follow me down the hall, but she goes to the sink.

Says, "I'm just going to put these in the dishwasher."

I hear her, but she says it under her breath—almost mumbles. As if she is trying to convince herself that her motivation is honest.

ONE OF MY FAVORITE PARTS ABOUT SUMMER HAS ALWAYS BEEN SPENDING more time in the salon.

I don't know how to do hair. Mom has tried to teach me several times, but I guess she didn't pass down that talent. My fingers bumble over a simple French braid, and I can never seem to get the little things right, like how to secure my curls into a proper bun or evenly section off my hair for twists. Mimi is actually good at doing hair but doesn't like it, and thankfully Mom never pressured either of us to keep practicing. So when I'm in the shop, they put me to work sweeping the floors and wiping down stations while the stylists grab a break or quick lunch between appointments.

The salon can be too loud, mostly when regular clients are there. They talk over one another and gossip with abandon and discuss things that make my mother shush them and nod toward me, in case they forgot I was in the room. I hate that she still does that. She acts like I don't know what sex is or have never heard a curse word, let alone said one.

Regardless of how much they're forced to censor themselves, I like being around all the chatter—the cheerful energy that crackles through the air as people get their hair permed and braided and faded and cut. It's the opposite of the quiet, respectful apartment upstairs.

Laz meets me there after school. I'm still jittery from last night and I want to pepper him with questions about Booker. Did he seem extra happy today? Did he mention seeing me? Laz won't volunteer that information himself, so I'll have to get him alone and badger him.

The bell above the door jingles as he walks in. Necks crane and multiple sets of eyes look to the mirrors to check out who's arrived. When they see it's him, a round of hearty "Hey, baby" and "Hey there, Laz" and "Afternoon, Lazarus" rings out in tandem, making his buttery brown skin flush as he steps inside.

He takes too long to say something, though, and from across the room, Ayanna calls out, "I know you didn't just forget your manners, mister."

"Hey, everyone," he says, dipping his head as he lifts a

hand in greeting. He walks swiftly across the room to give his mother a loose-armed hug. She smacks a loud kiss on his cheek in return.

"How was school?" I hear her ask as the salon powers back to life with overlapping discussions. I'm posted a few feet away at the cabinets in back, folding freshly laundered towels and trying to pretend like I didn't just hear Mrs. Johnson say she's thinking of trying marijuana for the first time at age fifty-five. Mom heard it, too, and gives her a pursed-lip look in the mirror.

"All right," Laz says to his mother. "Ready to be done."

"Tell me something new." Ayanna ruffles his thick dark curls before walking over to check the time on Ms. Evans's dryer.

Laz's hair has always been a hot topic of conversation around here. His dad is Mexican American and Ayanna is black, and his hair is gorgeous. The older women always talk about how he has "that good hair" and Ayanna always tsks at them, saying he'll get a big head from all their fawning.

He makes his way back to me, dropping his backpack at his feet. "Thanks for helping me study last night," he says in a voice that's too loud.

I pretend not to notice that I'm stepping on his foot as I reach for another towel from the pile. "Would you stop? You sound like you're reading from a script," I mutter.

He grins. "Gotta keep you on your toes."

Laz helps me finish folding the towels, then we gather up a batch of dirty smocks and tell our mothers we're heading to the laundromat around the corner. I let out a long breath as we step onto the sidewalk, trading the intimate noise of the shop for the city commotion outside: lumbering buses and rock music blasting from open car windows and loud conversations dripping with Chicago accents.

"Did you see Booker today?" I ask after we start walking.

"I see him every day." Laz swings the canvas bag of dirty laundry between us, falling into step behind me when we meet someone on the sidewalk.

"Did he..." My words trail off because I don't even know what I want to ask. But it feels that if I don't talk about him as much as possible, he will disappear when I'm not paying attention.

"He likes you, Dove. Not much else to say." Laz looks over, his eyes tired. The water polo team made it to the playoffs this year, and as soon as that ended, he had to launch right into prepping for final projects and exams.

I miss juggling completely different activities. When I was playing soccer, I felt balanced; on the field I could stop worrying about tests and grades and just lose myself in the game, and when I was in the classroom I didn't have to worry about strategies for upcoming matches.

Laz doesn't complain, but all I have to do is look at him to know when he's overwhelmed.

"Is it weird that we like each other?" I ask.

Down the street, the train stops at the California Blue Line station. Faintly, I hear the brakes squeal and the doors fly open and the automated voice announcing the stop.

Laz shakes his head. "I didn't expect it, but it's good to see you like this."

"Like what?"

He opens the door of the laundromat, motioning for me to go in ahead of him. The neat rows of stainless steel machines steadily hum and gurgle while the TV on the back wall blares a rowdy judge show. The woman who manages in the afternoons nods at us as she straightens a row of wheeled wire carts.

I plop the plastic tub of detergent on top of an empty machine. "Like what?" I prompt when he doesn't answer me.

Laz takes his time emptying the smocks into the washer, then he drops the bag in with them. "Like...happy."

"How am I normally?" I think of my conversation with my aunt last night. Even she seemed to think there was a palpable change in me, and we haven't seen each other in forever.

39

Laz considers this as we sink into the chairs by the vending machines. He digs into his pocket and pulls out a couple of dollars. "Focused," he finally answers.

Focused. The same word my mother used to describe Mimi and me. A word that described Mom when she was my age, according to Carlene. I wonder if there was ever a time Mom wanted to wild out—just completely break all her own mother's rules.

"I've never seen you let anything distract you like this before," Laz continues.

"I've never met anyone like Booker, I guess."

"You *guess*? Mitchell was boring as hell."

"Yeah, well." I shrug. "I get that now. And there's nothing boring about Booker."

Laz makes a face. It's slight—just a twist of his lips—but I notice immediately.

"What?" I say.

He feeds his money into the machine, and a bottle of soda tumbles out seconds later. "I just wonder . . . how long do you think this can go on?"

His words stab at the bubble of happiness I've been gliding around in since last night. I shove him when he sits back down. "What the hell, Laz?"

"I'm not trying to be an asshole. I'm just being realistic. So you keep seeing him and you keep liking him more and more....If you're already sneaking out now, your mom's gonna find out."

"Maybe she won't if we don't *tell* her."

"Or she'll find out about everything like she always does and then you'll be grounded all summer."

Laz is right. There is something disturbingly clairvoyant about my mother. She's so intuitive it makes me wonder if she can see something in me that even I can't at times.

"My aunt seems so different from my mom. She's really chill." I bring my knees up and wrap my arms around them.

"Isn't everyone chiller than your mom?"

He has a point. My mother is so invested in making everything about our lives look good and respectable that she's always on edge.

"Okay, what's your best-case scenario with this whole thing?" he asks.

"That I introduce him and she likes him and we can go out without sneaking around."

"Right," Laz says, and it makes me smile, to think of things going so easily with my mother. Until: "But then that all goes to shit when she finds out he's been in jail."

"It wasn't *jail*," I say quickly. "It was juvie. There's a difference."

"Have you met your mom? The only thing she's gonna care about is that Cook County had its hands on him."

The happy bubble officially bursts. I know Laz isn't saying this to be mean. He's never been more right about anything. Even if my mother did like Booker, she'd never let me date someone with a past like his. It doesn't fit in with her plan.

I'd be lying if I said I wasn't surprised when I heard he'd been in trouble. But I think sometimes people judge situations too quickly without considering the people behind them. The more I know Booker, the more I like him.

"I'm not saying you shouldn't see him." Laz twists open his bottle of soda. "I just don't think your mom's gonna be cool with it."

I stare at the judge show on TV, where a white woman with watery brown eyes is pleading her case.

"There's a party this weekend," Laz says slowly. "Sort of a last hurrah before we have to give up our lives for exams."

"I know," I say. "Booker told me."

"You should come."

"How am I going to get out of the house for that? You know she'll find out right away that no parents are going to be there."

Laz pauses. Says, "Tell her we're going to a movie or something. I've got your back."

"Really?"

"You're my best friend. Of course I do."

"Thank you," I say. He doesn't have to help me out with this. I know it puts him in an awkward position; Ayanna wouldn't be very happy if she learned he was helping me sneak out to places I'm not supposed to be. I don't want to create any unnecessary tension between her and my mother...but I also want to have a life.

I used to worry that Laz and I would grow apart once he started getting more involved in sports and I devoted all my time to academics. It's hard enough not going to the same school. But every time I think we might be growing apart, he does something to show me he cares.

I nudge him when he takes a break from chugging his soda. "What are we gonna get into this summer?"

"Definitely the beach," he says, and I nod right away. Summer isn't summer without at least a handful of trips to Montrose Beach. "I want to hit up Ribfest this year. And the lineup for Ruido Fest is crazy good, but I gotta get a loan from my mom. Tickets are ridiculous. What's on your list?"

"Um, I don't know," I say. "I guess I haven't really thought about it."

Laz gives me a look, a smile teasing at the corners of his mouth. "The only thing you're thinking about is seeing Booker."

"Busted."

It's true. I'm still on my Booker high. Not as much as before I talked to Laz, but it's still there. I can't let go of this…whatever it is with Booker.

Not yet.

I'M SITTING IN THE KITCHEN SATURDAY MORNING, EATING A LATE BREAK-fast alone, when my phone rings.

Mimi.

I answer it right away—even though it's a video chat and I'm still in my pajamas, my black curls pulled into a lazy Afro puff.

"Good *morning*," Mimi trills like she's starring in a princess movie. She used to wake me up that way some-times when I'd pressed snooze too long and we were going to be late for school. Even when she was younger, she liked to be up earlier than everyone else.

"Let me guess—you've already been to the farmers market and showered and made breakfast?"

"Yeah, I ate, like, two hours ago," she says. "It's almost noon."

"It's Saturday."

"Stop being cranky, Dovie. Wasn't yesterday your last day?"

Behind her, I see the unfamiliar walls of her new apartment. She just moved in a couple of weeks ago, when her semester ended. Dad offered to drive up to Milwaukee and help her, but Mimi said she and her friends had it covered. It feels strange for her to be out of the dorms and living somewhere I've never seen.

"Yeah, and I get to spend half my summer in SAT prep," I say. "Can't wait."

Mimi sighs. "I know. But she's not going to get off your back unless you just do it. Suck it up, kick ass on the test, and then the summer before your senior year is free."

That seems so far away. Another year of prep and testing and serious discussions about college applications before I can rest. All the lead-up is exhausting, but I'm actually looking forward to college. I'm not positive what I want to study, though I'm leaning toward civil engineering. I've always been fascinated by how the train tracks and bridges and streets are built and operate (almost) seamlessly. Or maybe architecture because I've been in love with the beautiful buildings around Chicago since

I was a little kid. Tribune Tower and the Civic Opera House are my very favorites.

"Didn't it seem like this would never end when you were my age?" I ask. Because Mimi studied just as much as I did, if not more.

The first time Mimi came home after she'd been away at college, she showed up sporting a low fade with a side part. My mother looked like somebody had slapped her. They have a barber at the shop, but Mimi had always kept her hair long and natural and braided, occasionally straightening it when my mother fussed over things like graduation and prom. Mimi said the new cut felt more like her. It took me a minute to get used to it, but the more I looked at her, the more I liked it. Mimi is super pretty with creamy brown skin and the same big, clear brown eyes as Mom.

"Yes, and it sucked," she says.

"It would suck a lot less if I were playing right now."

Her voice softens. "You really miss it that much?"

"I do."

It is soccer, and I started playing in competitive youth leagues when I was in third grade. I was on the middle school team, too, and I loved it. All the running that we complained about during practice was suddenly fun when we were on the field. Sweating through my jersey made me feel like I was working hard, and shit-talking the other teams when our coaches couldn't hear was one of the most rebellious things I've ever done. I felt uncontained when I was on the field. Free.

"Well." Mimi stops because she knows firsthand there isn't much she can say to make me feel better about the decision my mother has made for me. "Maybe you can play in college."

"I'm not good enough, Meems."

That was the reason Mom decided it would be best for me to stop playing and focus on extracurriculars like quiz bowl and the environment club. Her logic is that schools wouldn't necessarily be impressed by my athleticism unless I was good enough to be scouted. The fact that soccer made me happy wasn't enough.

"Sorry," Mimi says, and she looks away from the screen, but not before I see a flash of regret in her eyes. She had to give up cheerleading. She was really good—a lot better than I am at soccer. "But you have to get through it. And then you'll go away like I did and you can do whatever you want."

"College doesn't sound easy, though."

"Of course it's not. But I've gotten through my first two years, even with my hellish load." Mimi is premed, which makes both of our parents extraordinarily happy. She thinks she wants to go into dermatology. "And it's a lot better to deal with the pressure here than there." She scratches the tip of her nose. "Dad said Aunt Carlene is staying with you guys?"

I nod.

"How is she?"

"She's good." I don't know if she's here, but even if she is in Mimi's room, I don't think she can hear us.

"She was always nice when she came around."

"You remember her?"

"A little bit," Mimi says. "She sent us toys a couple of times, and Mom used to get all weird about it. Like she had to know where they came from, and she'd make sure they were age-appropriate before she let us play with them instead of just accepting a gift like a normal person."

Our mother is definitely downstairs in the salon by now, maybe even finishing up with her first client.

Still, I lower my voice as I say, "Mom *is* weird around her. She's keeping tabs on her and, like, sniffing her mugs to make sure she isn't drinking."

And then I remember. It hits me suddenly—the last time I saw my aunt. It was after the shop opened, but before we'd moved in up here, so I couldn't have been older than eight. She was a skinny woman I didn't recognize, and as soon as she stumbled into the shop, Mom hustled her through the salon and out the back door and into the alley. The woman kept trying to look behind her, and at one point she met my eye and stared.

I noticed how the dull roar of the shop had quieted to a hum, and how Ayanna was looking worriedly toward the back. I slowly inched closer and closer to the door, trying to hear what they were saying. Trying to figure out who the woman was.

I couldn't hear anything as I peeked through the screen door, but I could see them. My mother tossing her arms in the air and frowning, the woman raking her hands through her disheveled hair and pleading. My mother shook her head again and again, and I saw the first tear fall down the woman's cheek before Ayanna was there, yanking me away.

"Who is that?" I asked as she deposited me by her station, where she was pressing someone's hair.

Ayanna looked around the shop as if searching for anyone else who could give me the answer. Then she sighed and studied me, her eyes soft as she said, "Your mother's sister. Carlene."

"Her sister...My aunt?" I didn't know anything about my aunt, and I wanted to get a better look at her. I started to run back to the door, but Ayanna caught me by the arm before I could go.

"You stay right here, Dove. They need privacy."

"I just want to see her," I whined, but I shut my mouth when Ayanna gave me the universal Black Mom Look. I knew not to argue with that.

When my mother came back in, she closed both doors firmly behind her and locked them. Carlene wasn't with her. Mom disappeared into the tiny break room for a while, and even I didn't have to be told not to bother her until she came out.

I consider asking Mimi about this—where was *she* that day? Am I remembering this correctly or is my brain making up stories?—but for some reason, I want to keep the memory to myself for now.

My sister sinks down onto her bed and rolls her eyes. "Of course Mom is keeping tabs on her. Takes some of the heat off you, though. Right?"

I shrug. "It's not so bad."

But we both know I'm lying, and Mimi doesn't let it go. "Bullshit, Dove. You're her precious treasure. Do you know she didn't even offer to come help me move?"

"Dad did."

"Yeah, of course. But do you really think she would let you move into an apartment on your own without her explicit approval of the place before you signed the lease? She hasn't even asked to see pictures."

"She just thinks I'm more fragile than you are."

Mimi snorts. "Or maybe she just loves you more."

"That's not true."

"Okay, this feels like telling you Santa Claus isn't real

all over again, but you know that's a thing, right? Parents can't love all their kids equally. It's just not realistic."

"And *I'm* the one who's cranky?"

But her words make me uneasy because a part of me believes she might be right. I don't know if my mother loves me more, but she pays more attention to me. She always has, and I've always tried not to notice.

The front door opens, and a few moments later my aunt walks into the kitchen, stretching an arm across the front of her body. She's wearing a loose tank top, a sports bra, and running shorts, her skin damp with sweat. She waves as she heads to the cabinet to grab a glass.

"I'm talking to Mimi," I say, and she smiles and has me hand the phone to her.

They chat easily and, not for the first time, I wish Mimi were coming home this summer. It will be strange without her, even with Carlene here to fill her space. I expected her to be a little homesick, to say how much she would miss being away from Chicago the whole year for the first time. But she looks happy to be away and on her own. I wonder if I will be, too, when it's my turn to go.

I say goodbye to Mimi a few minutes later. I wanted to talk to her about Booker, about how I am seeing him tonight. How I'm so nervous that I wonder if he will sense it as soon as I'm with him. But I'd have to start from the beginning because she doesn't know anything about him. And I don't know if I can trust Carlene yet.

My aunt downed her first glass of water, and she stands at the sink taking her time with the second one.

"Your sister is so grown-up now," she says. "I love the hair."

"It looks good on her."

"She has a boyfriend?"

"No." I take a bite of my toast, even though it's too cold to be good at this point. "She's not seeing anyone right now, but she dates girls."

Carlene raises her eyebrows. "Exclusively?"

"Yeah. She's gay."

"Funny that your mother never mentioned it when I asked about her," she says in a way that means she doesn't think it's funny at all.

"She's...still getting used to it." That's the nicest way to say that my mother accepts that Mimi likes girls, but she's still visibly uncomfortable discussing it, as if she will accidentally say something offensive.

"Well, I hate to say that it might not get any better. Your mother is still getting used to me," Carlene says.

I look at her. "You mean...?"

"I like women, too," my aunt says. "I've liked some men, but mostly women. I always have, and Kitty flipped out when I told her I'd kissed a girl for the first time. I was sixteen and she was fourteen, and she thought my life was over. That nobody would ever accept me."

"She was wrong, right?" I say.

Carlene sets the glass on the counter. "Well, yes. You accept me, don't you?"

"Of course. I just…I guess I worry about Mimi, too, sometimes. I hear the things people say when they think no one cares, and they can be really shitty."

"I didn't say it's been easy, but my life was far from over. Still is."

I pop the last bite of hard-boiled egg into my mouth and chew, watching Carlene stretch in front of the sink. "Do you like running?"

"No," she says simply. "And the smoking doesn't help. But I try to go for a run every day."

"Why do you do it if you don't like it?"

"Because I've been doing it ever since I got clean and I figure it can't hurt my cause," she says, shrugging.

"Oh." I look down at my plate. We haven't discussed her rehab or sobriety, though she must know that I know after the way she and my mother danced around it the other night.

Carlene drains her glass of water. "I'm going to wash off this city dirt. You need the bathroom before I jump in the shower?"

"No, take your time," I say, not quite meeting her eye.

She pauses in the doorway. "You know, I'm not proud of some of the things I've done, but I'm not ashamed of trying to stay sober," she says in a clear, kind voice. "It's okay to talk about it."

I don't know how to say that I'm not ashamed but that we don't openly discuss a lot of things around here. I think being uncomfortable makes my mother feel out of control.

My aunt lingers in the doorway, only heading down the hall after I look at her and nod.

BOOKER'S ARMS ARE WRAPPED AROUND MY WAIST, HIS CHIN HOOKED OVER my shoulder.

I'm sitting on his lap at the kitchen table and he's holding cards in front of us for the drinking game that's in session. I am the most sober person in the room, by far. I've had a couple of sips from Booker's cup throughout the night—my first taste of alcohol. It was pretty anticlimactic and it tasted just as bad as I thought it would. Booker was two drinks in by the time Laz and I showed up an hour ago, but he doesn't seem any different than when he's sober.

Booker plays a card, and I guess it's a good one because everyone else groans and takes a drink from their bottle or can or cup.

This is my first party with alcohol and where at least one parent isn't around. I expected to feel more out of place, but it's surprisingly natural. Booker pulled me into an empty corner as soon as I arrived and kissed me. He hasn't left my side for more than a couple of minutes, and I always thought that sounded so suffocating, someone not giving you space. But it makes all the difference in the world when you want to be near them, too.

"You smell good," he whispers in my ear.

His warm breath and soft words send a long shiver down my back, and I shift on his lap. I want to turn around and kiss him, but as comfortable as I feel, I'm not so sure I'm okay with public displays of affection. Even when he pulled me aside earlier, I kept opening my eyes to make sure no one was looking. Mitchell would never have dreamed of being affectionate with other people around—we barely did anything when we were alone. I'm still trying to get used to being with someone new and I don't want anyone to watch me. What if I'm doing everything wrong? What if I've always been doing everything wrong and that's why Mitchell dumped me?

"Fuck," says the guy with curly blond hair sitting to our right. "My cards are shit. I'm out."

He starts a chain reaction; one by one, people set down their cards and pick up their drinks. Half the table disperses.

"Let's go somewhere," Booker says.

"Where?" I ask, still not turning all the way around to look at him head-on.

He shrugs. "Somewhere without all these people."

"Maybe I should get a drink first," I suggest, stalling for time.

If Booker notices, he doesn't let on. He pushes the chair back from the table so I can stand up, his hands sliding over my hips as I leave his lap.

Laz is on the other side of the kitchen, leaning against the counter with his phone in hand. He watches as I open the refrigerator and search the shelves.

"You're drinking?"

"I was thinking about it."

I always thought I was too nervous before, but maybe that was Mitchell's anxieties transferring to me. Since he didn't want to go to parties, it seemed easier to tell myself I didn't want to, either. But now that I'm here, I wonder what I've been missing out on. My mom would, of course, be furious if she knew. Especially after what she told me about Carlene. But I'm not Carlene, I'm Dove. And I know my sister drinks sometimes—I want to try it, too.

But I don't know where to start. Light beer or dark? Or should I mix something like Laz and Booker are drinking, with soda and liquor?

"Am I going to have to take care of you the rest of the night?"

"I'm not going to get drunk. I just want a drink. *One.* Will you help me?"

Laz peels himself off the counter and sets about making me a drink, ice and all. When he's done, he turns around to hand it to me and says, "Let me know if it's too strong."

And then he stops. Stares over my shoulder. I turn around, expecting to see Booker, but it's not him. This guy is short and skinny and white.

He glances at me before his eyes rest on Laz again. "Playing bartender?"

"Just making weak drinks for newbies over here." The corner of Laz's mouth turns up in an almost imperceptible grin.

"Make me one?"

"Can't promise it'll be weak."

I look back and forth between them, and it takes only a moment for me to understand that this is *him.* The guy Laz briefly mentioned and has been too shy to talk about ever since.

The color in his cheeks deepens. "Greg, this is my friend Dove," he mumbles.

"His *best* friend," I clarify.

"Your name is Dove?"

"Just like the bird."

Greg smiles at me and I decide I like him right away. He has a nice smile, with a couple of crooked teeth on bottom and a dimple in one cheek. "Nice to meet you, Dove."

"You too. Thanks for the drink, Laz," I say, starting to walk back toward Booker.

"Is it too strong?"

I take a sip and I can't even taste any alcohol. Just cola and ice. I shake my head and hand it back to him. "More, please."

"Seriously?"

"I watched you make it," I say. "You barely even put any liquor in there."

"You don't sound like a newbie to me," Greg says, still smiling.

Laz gives me a warning look like *You'd better not get too fucked up tonight*, but he obliges me and splashes in a bit more of the alcohol. *Rum*, the bottle says.

I taste the drink again. The rum hits my tongue instantly, and I think it might actually be too strong now, but I try not to let him see this as I say, "Much better. Thanks, Lazarus."

"Lazarus, huh?" Greg says, turning his grin on Laz now.

I scoot away before Laz can yell at me for using his full name.

Booker is sitting at the table in the same spot. He stands when he sees me. Takes my hand and says, "Come on."

We move through the crowded rooms of the house, passing through the dining room and living room, where people are playing more games and dancing and generally acting like school is already out for them. I guess the parties at my school look like this—I wouldn't know.

I feel safe with my hand tucked in Booker's, but my heart pounds a bit faster as we walk. My hand holding the cup starts to sweat, mingling with the condensation, and I tighten my grip. We go up the staircase, carefully weaving through people lounging on the landing and two girls who are making out on the steps.

"I take it you've been here before," I say when Booker heads straight down the hall and stops in front of a door.

"It's my boy Jackson's house." He turns the handle. "I used to play football with him."

The room is dark, but moonlight spills in freely through the windowpanes, the curtain panels pushed to the sides. It's small: a little kid's room with a toy chest in the corner, a twin bed, and a bureau on one end. Booker sits on the edge of the bed, his cup still in hand.

"Where is his family anyway?" I ask, standing by the still-open door. Stalling again.

"They went to see his grandma in Indiana, but he complained about needing to study so much, they let him stay." He shakes his head. "Let me try to throw a party when my dad is out of town...."

"Is he strict?"

"Not too much, but he keeps tabs. Him taking this graveyard shift was a big deal. He's still worried—" Booker stops and looks at me. "Why are you standing all the way over there?"

I haven't budged from the doorway. I open my mouth and close it. When I open it again, I say, "I can't have sex with you tonight."

He laughs that deep belly laugh of his that I love, though I don't know how to feel about it right now. Is he laughing *at* me?

"Sorry," he says when he sees my face. "I just like how serious you are. How you say whatever you're feeling."

"I'm not like that with everyone." I'm not like that with most people. I do say whatever I'm thinking with Mimi and Laz, but definitely not my parents.

"I like that you're that way with me. And we don't have to do anything you don't want to do, Dove. We don't have to do *anything*.... I just want to spend time with you."

I take a long sip of my drink, shudder, and then take another one before I close the door and join Booker on the end of the bed. "I want that, too."

"Good," he says with a small smile.

"Can I ask you something?" My drink is strong

enough that I feel it almost immediately, feel my body and mind relaxing bit by bit. The alcohol makes me hazy but brave.

Booker nods.

"What did you do to get in trouble?"

"Oh." He swallows a long drink and looks down at the cup. "I was going to tell you, it just hasn't seemed like a good time to bring it up."

"Laz told me you went to juvie, but I don't know what happened."

Booker started to say something once—the second time we met up, when it was clear that we liked each other. We'd been hanging out with Laz, and we were finally alone for a few minutes. I could see how difficult it was for him to get it out, so I told him it was okay. Laz had briefly mentioned something after I first met Booker, so I knew he'd been in trouble, but I told him he didn't have to go on.

I need to hear it from him now, though. All of it, not just vague details from Laz.

"I've been this size since I was twelve," he says, gesturing to his solid form. "The football coaches went after me hard as soon as I got to middle school. The first year, sixth grade, was good. Coach Reed was our main coach and he was always cool to me. He worked me hard, but it felt like he did it because he just wanted me to be better. But then I got to seventh grade and had to play under Coach Gibson, too.... He hated me from the minute he saw me. I could just tell."

A bad feeling settles in the pit of my stomach like a seed. All Laz told me is that Booker was expelled from his old school and served time in a juvenile detention center.

"When you're as big as I am, some people are intimidated, but other people like to fuck with you, just to see how far they can push you. Gibson was like that. He yelled at everyone, but he'd scream his fucking head off at me. Every practice, every game. Like he was trying to break me." Booker clears his throat and doesn't quite look at me, but turns his head, just a bit, as if it's the best he can do in lieu of eye contact. "My mom got sick and I started playing like shit and everyone noticed. Coach Reed could tell something was wrong, but when I didn't say what, he was cool with it. Just told me I should take a break if I needed to. But Gibson wanted to get to state that year—real bad. And he thought they could do it for the first time in years with me on the team."

I didn't know his mom had been sick. I just knew that he lived with his dad and she wasn't around. Now that my eyes have adjusted to the dark, I look at his face, try to find the emotion in his big chocolate-brown eyes or in the angle of his mouth. But I see nothing—just his blank gaze focused on the rug.

"One week, Gibson was really riding me…just saying whatever he could to get my mind back on the field. Brutal. I wanted to kill him, but I just kept playing because at least if I was playing, I wasn't thinking about how my mom wasn't getting better. Then, for some reason… Coach Reed…he never usually went there, but one of the guys had pissed him off and he just started screaming at whoever he could see. He said something—he didn't know my mom was sick. I didn't tell anyone. Not until… But he said something like, *Bet your pansy-ass mom could play better than the shit you're pulling out there, Stratton.* And I fucking lost it. Everything went red. I don't remember any of it."

"What did you do?" I ask, trying not to cringe. I am the one who asked him to tell me, after all. "I mean, what did they say you did?"

"I tore away from the game and went right up to him and punched him in the face. Over and over and over. Then I blacked out." He runs a hand over his face, over his eyes, as if trying to remove the image from his memory. "I broke his jaw and a couple of his ribs and—shit." His voice breaks and he stops.

His words feel out of place in this room around all the little-kid furniture—and around me. I like how sturdy Booker is. How, even though I don't know him very well,

I have never thought he would use his size against me. But this doesn't sound like your average fight. It sounds like an attack.

Still, as much as what he's saying scares me, I feel like it's scaring him, too. The memories. Slowly, I put my hand on his arm, and he looks at me for the first time since he started talking.

"It's like it wasn't me. Like it was someone else. And when I realized what I'd done..." Booker shakes his head. "I just couldn't believe it until I looked down at my hands. At my shoes. Coach Reed's blood was on them. And I just kept looking back and forth between him and Gibson, wondering how I snapped on the wrong one. Coach Reed forgave me, but Gibson...he was so pissed that his chance at state was shot, and it wasn't enough for me to be expelled. He got the school to press assault charges and I ended up in juvie the last few months of seventh grade."

"I'm sorry, Booker."

"It was my old man's fucking nightmare. All my life, I'd grown up hearing him talk about how nobody wanted to be sent to the Audy Home. How teachers and parents used to scare the shit out of him and other kids by saying they'd have to go there if they fucked up."

My parents grew up in Chicago, too, and they've said the same things about the Audy Home. It's not officially called that anymore, but I've heard the stories, and whatever the name is, nobody wants to go there.

"I'll get it if this is too much," he says when I don't say anything. "If you don't—"

He doesn't continue.

A part of me, the one that's so sheltered it fights against everything that breaks the rules, like lying about where I am and drinking rum-laced Coke, thinks it is too much. That I should be with someone who has a clean record, like Mitchell. Someone who never gets in trouble. Like me.

But the other part is stronger. The one that wants to touch Booker and kiss Booker and maybe even one day *be* with Booker. The part that reminds me he has only ever been gentle around me.

He blinks. "I went to anger management, too. My dad made me quit playing football because he read a bunch of articles and thinks getting hit so much fucks up everyone's brains. That CTE thing. And I haven't done anything like that again. I promise I wouldn't—I'd never hurt you, Dove."

"I know," I say quickly, giving in to the strong part. "It's not too much."

"It's not?"

I nod and he smiles and I move my hand from his arm to his shoulder, big and muscled. He flexes involuntarily, then relaxes against my hand. He's looking at me and now his eyes are full of feeling: softness and sadness and what I am sure is a bit of relief.

He touches his forehead to mine.

I lift my hand to his face, and I lean forward and kiss him first. His emotions transfer to his kiss. The sadness is in the urgent way he presses his mouth to mine, as if he's never needed anything so badly. The softness is in how he coaxes my lips apart, slow and almost questioning.

I wonder if he can taste the alcohol on my tongue like I can taste his or if it has all mingled together in the sweetness of this kiss.

I wonder if this feels a bit dangerous to him, too, after his confession, or if it is just the other part of me thinking that. The sheltered, weak part.

My phone vibrates and I pull away briefly to make sure it isn't my mother. The movie I'm supposedly seeing should be wrapping up about now.

It's Laz.

> Still here? Should head out soon if you want to make it home by curfew

"Sorry. It's Laz," I say to Booker as I quickly text back. I don't want him to leave without me.

> Ten more minutes. Meet
> you downstairs

A few moments later, his reply comes.

> Your mom, your funeral

But what he doesn't understand is that for once in my life—maybe for the first time—I am not worried about what she thinks.

I am finally living.

7

I TURN MY KEY IN THE FRONT DOOR TWO MINUTES BEFORE CURFEW.

My mother is sitting in the living room, pretending like she's heavily invested in a true crime documentary and isn't watching the clock instead.

She pauses the TV and smiles when I walk in. "How was the movie?"

"Good. Longer than I thought, and then Laz and I ran into one of his friends on the way out."

The lie rolls off my tongue, sweet and easy. I sit with it for a moment, but it never turns sour.

I yawn. "I'm going to get ready for bed."

Laz and I got a ride home from Greg, and I fell asleep in the car, even though I tried to stay awake to spy on them from the back seat. I've never seen Laz with anyone he likes. Ayanna doesn't have rules like my mother, but he's afraid that she won't love him if he's honest about who he's into. Greg and Laz were talking about their physics final as my eyes closed; Laz had to shake me awake when we pulled up in front of my building.

Carlene waves from the dining room. She's hunched over a table full of paperwork, a pair of chunky black-framed glasses perched on the edge of her nose.

"What are you doing?" I ask.

"I have to apply to schools for the hair-braiding license since your mother won't let me set foot in her shop until I have my three hundred hours."

"That's not true, Carlene." Mom sighs. "You're welcome to come down every day and help me out around the salon. But I can't break the law. I'm not letting you get us shut down because you're desperate to do a set of box braids."

Carlene's lips pull tight, but she remains quiet. She must have known long before me that it's almost never worth fighting with my mother when she's made up her mind. I think back to that day long ago, when they were arguing out back. I didn't make it up—I'm sure of that.

Still, it's nice to see them spending time together. Mimi and I practically became one when we were relaxing— our arms and legs draped across each other as we watched movies and shared bowls of popcorn, huddling together under blankets on frigid winter nights. This is the first time I've seen my mom and her sister anywhere near each other when they weren't in the kitchen, and it feels good, like maybe they don't actually hate each other.

"You can practice on me," I say to Carlene, pushing a hand into my curls.

"I have to go through a school for it to be official, but you let me know anytime you want me to hook you up, Dove." She smiles.

"Good night," I say to them both, and I've almost reached the hallway when Mom stops me.

"Too old for a good-night hug?" she says.

I'm not too old, just tired, but I walk back over. Drop down on the couch next to her, and fold myself into her arms. She squeezes me and kisses my hair and says, "Sleep tight, Birdie."

Then she freezes.

Pulls back and looks at me with disbelief. "What's that smell?"

Fuck.

She sniffs at me. "Is that *alcohol*?"

I don't respond. I stare at the smooth skin of her never-been-pierced earlobe.

"Open your mouth," Mom says. "Breathe out."

Her voice is scary quiet, and when she sounds like

that, I follow her instructions without thinking. Greg gave me a piece of minty gum to chew on the way home, but it doesn't mask the sips of rum and Coke I drank when I was with Booker.

She stands and walks a few feet to the window that overlooks the street below. When she turns around, the look of disbelief is back. "You were out *drinking*? What in the world would possess you to do something like that?"

From the corner of my eye, I see Carlene shift in her seat. When I don't say anything, my mother continues.

"Have I not made it *very* clear that you're to stay away from alcohol? You're *sixteen*. You have plenty of time to try it when you're older. When you're of age. When you know how to handle yourself."

"I only had a couple of sips." But now that I've felt what it's like to let myself relax—to let go, even just a bit— I wonder what I'd be like if I'd finished my drink. I wonder what I would be like with Booker.

"What has gotten into you, Dove?" My mother shakes her head at me, and I realize that I've stumped her. Mimi never broke her rules, and I haven't, either—until now.

I stand, too, because I don't like looking up at her from the couch. It makes me feel small. "It's summer," I say. "I got a perfect GPA this year. Same as last year."

"This isn't the time to get lazy." She exhales so loudly

the sound fills the entire room. "We make these rules for a reason. You need to stay motivated this summer. The SATs are practically around the corner and—"

"Mom—"

"Give me your phone."

"What?" I stare at her, so shocked by the demand that I forget to be afraid.

She holds out her hand. "I want your phone."

"How am I supposed to talk to anyone?" Anyone is just Laz and Booker, but that doesn't make it any less important.

"That's exactly the point. You're grounded. From hanging out with Laz, and from your phone."

"Why do you need to take it? My phone is private."

"Maybe privacy is what got you into this mess."

I frown at her. "What mess? Mom, I'm *fine*. Look at me."

My aunt's chair pushes back, scraping against the hardwood floor. "Come on, Kitty. Her phone? Don't you think that's a little harsh?"

Mom's head whips toward her. "Stay out of this." Then back to me. "Phone."

"No."

I don't know where I get the courage. I didn't have enough of that drink to feel *this* brave. But the thought of my mother looking through my texts with Booker and scrolling through my pictures makes me queasy. I am so good for her all the time; I shouldn't have to negotiate my privacy.

Her mouth drops open. "I don't know who you think you're talking to, but—"

"Kitty, you need to chill. Having a few sips doesn't make her a drunk. She's a teenager."

"Yeah? Well, so were you." My mother's voice could chisel ice. "And if I were going to ask for parenting advice, it certainly wouldn't be from you, Carlene."

The room is so quiet I can hear my mother's breathing. Then, downstairs, the door to the building opens and closes behind my father. He's just back from working a Saturday night Bulls game at United Center, which always makes him tired. He trudges up the exterior hallway stairs and then he's inside. Finds the three of us standing in the two front rooms, perfectly still.

He looks at each of our faces, trying to piece together what's happening without upsetting us further. Slowly, he latches the apartment door closed and sets down his medical bag. "Everything okay here?"

"Oh, sure," Mom says with a sharp laugh. "Your daughter has been drinking and my sister thinks it's perfectly normal."

"Kitty, I did *not* say—"

"Can you give us some space?" my mother cuts her

off. "This is between the three of us. We don't need any more input."

My aunt glares at her but says nothing. She slides on her sandals. Picks up her pack of cigarettes. And seconds later, she's out the same way my father came.

～〇～

I am grounded, for a month, but Dad persuades Mom to let me keep my phone when I tell them I was with Laz the whole time. Being in trouble with Laz isn't good, but it's better than trouble with someone they don't know. I text to tell him what happened; say that I'm sorry and I'll make it up to him. I know Mom will give Ayanna an earful, who will pass that on to Laz.

I consider it a small triumph. I've thought about defying her so many times, but I was never brave enough.

Like when she made me quit soccer; it wasn't just that she made me quit, it was the way she did it. I got a B-plus on a social studies test and she freaked out—even though I was in eighth grade and it was an honors class. The next day she made me wash and turn in my uniform and gave my cleats away to Goodwill without telling me. All before the season was over.

Or how she wouldn't let me go to Lollapalooza with Mimi and her friend Ariel two summers ago, even though they got a ticket just for me, because she said I was too young to be "in a place like that" with "those people"—whatever that's supposed to mean.

But I think what I hate most is the tiny, everyday injustices: like how I can't eat at the diner around the corner because she thinks it's unsanitary. And how she stops me from giving money to the homeless people in our neighborhood because she believes it's better to donate to shelters and food banks. I'm so used to her snatching my hand back, stage-whispering, "They're just going to spend it on drugs and alcohol anyway," that I hesitate now before I part with my spare change even when I'm alone.

This isn't the greatest act of resistance I could've carried out, but it's something. I think Mimi would be proud of me.

Having my phone is probably the only way I'll survive the next month. Being confined to the apartment and salon is going to be torture: listening to the same marginally funny jokes Ayanna has been telling since I've known her; watching Mom's prim-and-proper routine dampen the good cheer of the salon; studying for the stupid SATs when I should be lying on the beach with Laz.

If I can't see Booker, at least I can talk to him. What would have happened if I'd just disappeared on him, if his texts went unanswered? Laz would tell him I was grounded, but what if he didn't believe him? I wouldn't want him to think I'd changed my mind—that he was too much for me after all.

A half hour after I hear my parents shut off all the lights and go to their room, I slip out to the hallway, taking care not to step on the squeaky part of the floor beneath the runner. The strip of space under Mimi's door is dark; Carlene returned to the apartment after I'd already gone to my room. I hold my breath and get as close as I can to my parents' bedroom door.

They aren't whispering. Not really. Their voices are lower but not contained. Dad sounds exhausted.

"I don't know what you want me to do, Kitty. She's your sister. If you don't want her here, you need to tell her yourself."

"So then I kick her out and what? Where does she go, Raymond? I don't want to be blamed if she relapses."

My father sighs. "I think the most important thing is that she doesn't relapse, not who takes the blame."

"I'm just saying, I don't think it's a coincidence that Birdie starts acting out days after she shows up."

There's a long pause and I lean closer, waiting.

Then: "Carlene deserves to know her, Kitty."

"And I've worked too hard to have her ruin everything we've built. She's a good girl, our Birdie."

"Yes, she is," my father says, his voice softening. "And you have to trust that."

I NEVER THOUGHT I'D LOOK FORWARD TO SAT PREP, BUT ANY CONTACT WITH the outside world is welcome after my first week of being grounded. There's only so much time I can spend in the salon, and I think my mother has been telling everyone they have to be on their best behavior because there's not even a hint of a juicy conversation when I'm around.

Mom drives me to the first study session.

"You don't have to do this," I say as I buckle myself into the passenger seat. "I could've taken the train."

"I want to make sure you get started off right," she says, but what she really means is that she wants to make sure I go. I mess up one time and she's convinced I'm the most rebellious teenager in Chicago. She says she'll be back to pick me up when I'm done.

As soon as I step out of the car, I feel like I'm breathing for the first time in weeks. I gulp in air through my mouth. I don't get much of a break having to be at the shop so often—and with my mom just one floor below me when I'm not there. I've been going up to the roof more, to get some space of my own when the apartment feels particularly suffocating. But it's not enough. I miss seeing people—one person in particular.

I'm early, so only a handful of people are sitting in the room when I walk in. My eyes scan the space, finally landing on—oh, *fuck.*

Mitchell Simmons.

My ex.

He looks up and his mouth drops open, but only for a moment. He quickly closes it, nods almost indiscernibly, and looks back down at his desk where his workbook is already open.

The last time I saw him was the last day of school, and I didn't expect to see him again until we start junior year. Seriously, out of all the SAT courses in the city, he had to end up in this room?

I choose the seat farthest from him, my heart beating too fast. I don't have feelings for him anymore; we had a clean break. It's just jarring to see him when I wasn't expecting him. We went from talking every day and hanging out every weekend to acting like we'd never known each other at all.

The instructor walks in then. A white guy who looks like he's in his late twenties with round metal-framed glasses and pink cheeks. He nods at us and plops his messenger bag on the table up front.

I slowly pull my workbook from my bag, thinking of the first time I went out with Mitchell. We spent a Sunday afternoon at Navy Pier, which I hated but didn't say because I didn't know him very well and everyone seemed so excited that we were going out. By everyone, I mean our parents. Mitchell's mom is a surgeon at Rush and shares patients with my dad sometimes. When they found out we were at the same high school, our families went out for dinner and we've been pushed together ever since.

"How was it?" Mom asked when I returned.

I was full of cheese-and-caramel popcorn, which was honestly the best part of the day. Mitchell looked terrified the entire time we were on the Ferris wheel and sat as far away from me as possible. He only confessed to being afraid of heights after we were safely off. He looked bored the rest of the time and I was surprised when, at the end of the date, he said he'd text me later.

"Fine," I said to my mother, shrugging. I couldn't think of anything else to say. That was it. Nothing about it had been exciting or extra terrible or anything out of the ordinary. It was just *fine*.

"It's your first date, Birdie." Mom cupped my face in her hand, smiling. "You'll remember this forever."

No, I probably won't, I thought. And then I wanted to say that just because she and Dad had been high school sweethearts, that didn't mean Mitchell and I would be together forever. But what I said was "It wasn't a date."

We didn't hold hands. We didn't kiss. And I could tell he wasn't trying to hold back from doing either. I had better chemistry with our toaster than Mitchell Simmons. I didn't think he liked me at all, but he texted me that evening, as promised. And the next day and the day after that, even when we'd seen each other at school. Then I started sitting with him at lunch, ditching my old soccer friends, and that's how we fell into a relationship.

I slide a pencil onto my desk and try not to look at Mitchell's dark hair and the backs of his olive-skinned arms. I try not to think about how my mother will never accept Booker the way she accepted Mitchell, and that it has nothing to do with the fact that our families aren't friends.

The instructor leans against the podium and holds up his hand. His name is Jared, and his voice is shockingly deep as he says we're going to be concentrating on reading, writing, and math concepts this summer to help us with the test in a few months.

Mitchell taps a rhythm against his workbook with a mechanical pencil as Jared talks. Not just any mechanical pencil—the vintage Cartier his mother got him for his birthday last year, engraved with his initials.

Jared says we'll start out talking about numbers and operations, and I'm actually happy when he passes out worksheets. Relieved that I'll have something to focus on besides the awkwardness of being across the room from my ex-boyfriend.

I keep my head down as I'm packing up my things after class. Still, I can feel when Mitchell passes my row. I think he pauses, like he wants to say hi, but he keeps moving and when I look up, I see the back of him walking out the door.

Mom is waiting outside when I walk out a minute later, double-parked beside a car with her flashers on.

"How was it?" she asks as I slide in.

"Fine." I pause, because I usually regret telling her anything about my life. But she's one of the few people I see on a daily basis now. I'm feeling desperate. "Mitchell is in my class."

She can't even keep the smile off her face. "Oh, that's so great, Birdie!"

"Great? Did you hear what I said? *Mitchell* is in my class. My ex."

"I thought your breakup was cordial."

"I guess." If you consider cordial being that it came out of nowhere and he did it on a Saturday night, after we'd sat through dinner and a movie.

She turns off the hazards and flips on her blinker, watching the street in her side mirror before she starts driving. "Well, sometimes we have to be around people we don't necessarily want to be. And honestly, I don't know why you two broke up in the first place. You were such a good couple."

"But we weren't, or we'd still be together," I say. What we had was boring and nothing special, even though I tried hard to be a good girlfriend to him. But I was mortified when he dumped me first. I wondered if people thought that meant I liked him more than he liked me.

"All I'm saying is we were all sorry to see you two split up." Mom sighs like she always does when I talk about Mitchell: wistfully. "And you never know, Birdie. Maybe you'll get back together sometime in the future."

"Definitely not."

I liked Mitchell's brain best of all. Loved how he knew a little bit about everything and how quickly he retained facts. One of my favorite things was to test him by throwing out a random topic and seeing what he knew off the top of his head. He rarely disappointed.

The kissing wasn't *bad*, exactly. It's just that he never seemed that into it. More like he was going through the motions. It's even more obvious now that I know what it's like to be *really* kissed, by Booker.

Mom turns to me after she's stopped at a red light. "Okay, Birdie," she says, nodding.

But it bugs me how amused she looks, like eventually I will come to my senses and agree with everything she's saying.

It annoys me that she thinks she knows everything about my life when she doesn't know what I want at all.

When we get home, Mom parks and goes straight back to the shop for her next appointment. I'm headed upstairs, maybe to sit on the roof for a while, when I see Carlene walking toward the building. She's with someone—a man I don't know. He's tall and thin with dark skin, and he walks stooped over, like he's much older than he looks. They're both smoking, and they stop a couple of doors down, so deep in conversation that I don't think she even sees me.

I sit on the stoop and wait, soaking in the sun. It's hot now, but the nasty, stifling humidity of Chicago summer still hasn't kicked in. I watch Carlene and the man. They stop talking and take long, silent drags from their cigarettes. Then they put them out under their shoes, exchange a few more words, and hug before he walks away.

She slips her cigarette pack into the pocket of her shorts

and makes her way toward the stoop. She smiles when she sees me.

"You look happy," she says.

I shrug. "I'm not."

"Well, you at least look like getting out of this prison did you some good." She motions for me to scoot over so she can sit next to me. I scoot. "How was your class?"

"Fine. Boring." I think about mentioning Mitchell, but I don't think I want to get into that again.

"Well, at least it was a different kind of boring than sitting around here."

"I guess. Who was that guy?" He's disappeared from our view, but I nod in the direction he walked.

"Emmett? He goes to my meetings. AA," she clarifies.

It still surprises me how open she is about her recovery. "Is he your sponsor?"

"No," she says, looking amused that I know the terminology. "But he's trying really hard, like me. We help keep each other accountable."

I wonder how often she thinks about having a drink, but I don't ask. I don't want her to think I'm rude, even if she is so honest about her life. I am still just getting to know her, though I already feel more comfortable around her than my mother.

"What are you going to do now?" I feel a bit like when I was younger and always asked Mimi what she was doing.

But Laz isn't around the shop today, and I don't feel like being in there without him.

"Go for a run," she says. "Want to come?"

Running was always a challenge when I played soccer. It kept me in shape to do my best on the field, but it never got easier. Doesn't sound so bad now, though. I guess most things don't when you're grounded.

"I can't," I say. "The whole punishment thing."

"Oh. Right." She squints out at the traffic for a moment, then stands. "I'll be back. Stay here."

Where am I going to go? I watch Carlene walk into the shop, the screen door slamming and voices floating out behind her. She returns a couple of minutes later, a grin lighting up her face.

"The warden will allow it."

I raise an eyebrow. "That easy, huh?"

"I'm still her older sister," Carlene says. "And I know how much she hates looking bad in front of people, so I made sure to ask loudly in front of her client."

I laugh out loud, truly joyful for the first time in a week.

⌒ℓ

Running through our neighborhood is different with my aunt by my side.

First of all, she's already on a friendly basis with people I've seen my whole life but never spoken to. She waves at the old man who owns the convenience store around the corner; he's smoking a cigarette out front and calls out, "Afternoon, Miss Carlene!"

A few minutes later, my aunt drops a couple of damp dollars into the cup of the woman who sits near the entrance of the train station. The woman doesn't look up, but she presses her grimy fingers to her lips and blows a kiss in our direction. My face burns with guilt when I think about all the times I've ignored her, pushing down my own instinct to help someone who needs it. All because of my mother's rules.

"How do you already know everyone?" I huff next to my aunt. I can tell that I'm slowing her down, but she doesn't complain, just silently adjusts her speed.

She laughs. "That always used to bother your mom, how easily I made friends. She said I had no standards."

"Was Mom ever nice to you?" Mimi and I have our moments, but she's thoughtful about her words.

Carlene doesn't answer for a while, not until we stop at a red light halfway down the block. She turns to me, still lightly jogging as we wait on the corner. "Your mom's always been kind of…curt."

No kidding.

"But she shows her love in other ways. She remembers things about me that no one else knows. She's giving me a place to stay. Even our mom gave up on me before she died, but Kitty…she's still here, you know? I don't need her to be nice. And to be fair, I have gotten caught up with some people I had no business being around."

Our feet pound against the pavement in rhythm as we move, the light wind rushing in my ears and mixing with the sound of my breath. It actually feels good to run. The fresh air flowing through my nose and burning my lungs, my legs pushing forward with purpose. It's still not easy, and I'm drenched with sweat, but I wonder why I stopped. Quitting soccer didn't mean I had to quit everything connected to it.

We head south, cutting through Humboldt Park so we can take in the lagoon and the majestic red-brick field house. We're surrounded by kids playing and people running and walking with their dogs, and I feel so free that for a moment I forget I'm grounded.

We run until we retrace our steps to the corner of our block. I'm exhausted but sad to be back home already. I felt so comfortable next to my aunt, like when I'm with Mimi. Like I don't need to fill every moment of silence. Like it was okay to just be me.

"Hey, kid," she says after we catch our breath. "How many times have you been grounded before?"

I bite my lip as I think. "Twice. Once for lying about having done my homework so I could go to a sleepover, and the other time because I took the bus to Laz's without telling my mom. She thought ten was too young to ride by myself."

Carlene twists her lips to the side, thinking. "Ten is kind of young now. We rode it alone at that age, though. I was ten and your mom was eight."

"I thought Grandma was strict like Mom."

"Oh, she was lax when it benefited her," Carlene says, laughing. "She worked a lot, and since our father wasn't around, I had to be the one who looked out for Kitty. So we rode the bus, went grocery shopping, made dinner most nights. We were living like little adults before we got to junior high."

I can't imagine her taking care of my mother. Especially since my mom seems like the older one now.

"I think that's why she was hit so hard by who I turned out to be." Carlene's voice isn't happy or sad. Just stating the facts. "Both of them were. I used to be so responsible and then—well, then Kitty and I basically switched roles."

My aunt peels off her tank top, pressing it against her forehead and then around her sports bra to soak up the sweat. She walks ahead of me when we meet someone on the sidewalk and I notice a tattoo peeking out from the bottom of her sports bra.

"What's that?" I point to her ribs.

"Oh." She stops and lifts the bra a couple of inches. It's the outline of a bird in flight, small and faded but detailed in its shading. "I've had this forever. Probably about time to get it touched up."

I squint at her. "Does our whole family have an obsession with birds or something?"

"Seems like it, huh?" She dabs her shirt against her chest and keeps walking. "I got a bird, my friend got a butterfly. We were young. And we were both so high, we barely remember it."

"Oh," I say.

"What about you? Any ink?"

I shake my head quickly. "I could never sneak that by my mom. And I haven't thought about it. It doesn't seem like me."

She grins. "No. It doesn't seem like you at all."

I'M NOT SURE WHAT'S GOTTEN INTO MY MOTHER, BUT A COUPLE OF DAYS later she says I can go to Laz's house.

"I don't want you going anywhere else," she warns.

I say okay, and I don't know why she's being so lenient with my punishment—did my aunt have something to do with this?—but I shower and get out of the apartment before she can change her mind.

Laz lives on the other side of the expressway, northeast of us in Roscoe Village. Everything seems cuter in his neighborhood. Quaint and sweeter than Logan Square—almost like the suburbs, but not as boring. He and his mom live on the left side of a duplex on a quiet street thick with trees. White people look at us crazy in both of our neighborhoods, like they think every single black person in Chicago should be living on the South Side, but they mostly leave us alone.

I open the screen door, letting myself in like I've been doing for years.

"Hi," I call out so he knows I'm here.

"Hey, Dove," his voice comes from the back of the house. "Be out in a sec."

I plop onto the couch and look around. His mother is always changing up the front room—rearranging the furniture or slapping fresh coats of vibrant paint on the walls or swapping out the framed prints that line them. Today there's a new rug, thick chartreuse stripes lined up against gray and white. The room smells like incense, even though none of the sticks from Ayanna's extensive collection are burning.

Laz appears in the doorway, barefoot and shaggy haired. He's finally done with school and I think he's been spending most of his free time catching up on sleep. I haven't seen him at the salon much.

"Want something to eat?"

"Sure." I follow him to the kitchen. It's only eleven thirty, earlier than I normally eat lunch, but all I had for breakfast was fruit.

He stands in front of the open fridge. "Grilled cheese okay?"

"Can I have tomato in mine?"

"Yup." He pulls out butter and cheese. "So your mom didn't say why she let you out of the house?"

I put a skillet on the stove to heat, then lean against the island, watching him. "Nope. Maybe she's going soft on me."

"She's probably just glad you haven't snuck out again." He pauses as he reaches for the bread. "So am I."

"What's that supposed to mean?"

"It *means* you know my mom wasn't happy about me being with you that night," he says, giving me the raised-eyebrow, cocked-head combination of a disappointed parent. A look I know all too well now. "She didn't ground me, but I wish she had after the way she went off."

"I'm sorry," I say, not for the first time.

He reaches around me to grab a tomato from the bowl on the counter, purposely elbowing me in the side. "I know." He's quiet as he slices into it, then, with his back still to me, he says, "I went out with Greg last night."

"*Out* out? Like on a date?"

He shrugs. "Yeah, I guess. We went to see the new Marvel movie. Then we got some food."

"And?" He still doesn't face me, so I swoop over to stare at him, standing uncomfortably close.

"God, you're annoying," he says, but he laughs. "And... we hooked up some. In his car, under the Metra tracks."

I flush, thinking of when I kissed Booker on the next

street over from mine. I want to see him. To touch him and feel his warm fingers grooved between mine again. "It was good?"

"Yeah." He turns his head, but not before I see that smile. I know it because it's the same way I feel when I think about Booker. "It was good. I like him."

I watch Laz butter two pieces of bread and fill them generously with slices of American cheese and tomato. "Do you like him enough to tell your mom about him?"

"She's not like your parents. She doesn't need to know everything I'm doing."

"But maybe she'd be happy that you found someone who makes you happy."

He presses the sandwich into the skillet, his back to me. The buttered bread sizzles in the pan. "You know it's not that easy, Dove."

"You're not your dad," I say softly.

He sighs. "Can we please drop it?"

I nod, even though he can't see me.

My phone buzzes with a text just as we're finishing our sandwiches. I pop a string of melted cheese into my mouth and look down at my phone. It's Booker. He says he's bored and asks what I'm doing. We've been texting every night and sometimes during the day, but we are both frustrated that we haven't figured out a way to see each other.

I'm starting to type out a response when I freeze. "Laz, is your mom at the shop all day?"

"Think so." He glances at my phone suspiciously. "Why?"

"Can Booker come over?"

He groans, sliding down in his chair.

"I miss him," I say. "And that's not why I came over." It's not, but I can't believe I didn't think of it until now.

And there it is, the new, unfamiliar part of me that cropped up the other night when I was with Booker. The one that ignores all the good decisions I've made in the past and gives in to the pure, uninhibited craving that twines through me when I see or think about him.

"Fine," Laz says, "but remember how much I said my mom yelled at me? You're on your own if you fuck this up, too."

"Uh-huh." I'm barely listening to him as I text Booker and anxiously wait for his reply. And then it comes:

> Be there soon

Laz rolls his eyes on cue at my squeal, but he can't hold back his smile when he sees me so happy.

I cheerfully punch him in the arm. "I love you so fucking much, Lazarus Ramos."

Maybe it's because I haven't seen him in a while, but

Booker looks better than I remember. He feels better, too. His arms are tighter around me as we hug, his lips softer as they brush against mine in greeting.

"I'm glad you're here," he whispers in my ear.

I turn around to see if Laz is watching us, but he's crouched in front of the TV, fiddling with his video game controllers.

"I'm glad I'm here, too," I whisper back.

I want to kiss him again—for real—but I'm afraid I won't stop. And by the way Booker's eyes are nearly sparkling at me, I think he feels the same way. I lean my body into his and he wraps an arm around my waist, pulling me closer.

Booker and Laz have some never-ending *Call of Duty* rivalry and apparently abide by an unspoken rule that they have to play it whenever they're here. Which means I have to spend the next hour watching them shoot at anything that crosses the screen. Laz parks himself on the new rug while I sit next to Booker on the couch. He looks over to smile at me every few minutes, occasionally touching my arm or knee.

Laz finally drops his controller and stands, stretching his arms to the ceiling. "Going out for snacks. What do you guys want?"

"You have a full pantry in the kitch—" I stop when I realize both Laz and Booker are staring at me. Laz bursts out laughing and Booker's lips twitch, clearly trying to hold his in. "Oh."

I am so bad at not following the rules.

"Back in a bit," Laz says, and at least I have the sense not to ask why he's taking his backpack.

As soon as the screen door slams, Booker and I turn to each other. He's still smiling, but he looks a little shyer now that we're alone, and I'm relieved. No matter how much we text, I am still nervous when we're together, because I feel strong and free when I'm around him, and no one has ever made me feel those two things at once.

"I was worried you might be mad at me," he says, biting the corner of his lip.

"Why would I be mad?"

"Because I got you grounded for a month?"

"That wasn't your fault." I shrug. "I was sloppy. I'm not good at being bad."

"Bad is overrated," he says as he leans in to kiss me.

Everything feels heightened, more dramatic since I've been grounded—like I'm experiencing every single bit of freedom for the first time. But I swear, this kiss with Booker lasts forever. And it is perfect. I've thought about kissing him a lot over the last week, but all my daydreams pale in comparison to his lips on mine and his hands in my curls and the way he breathes my name when we finally pull away.

"Damn." He runs his palm softly over my cheek. "I missed you."

"I missed you." I pause. "But is that weird? That we miss each other? We're not…"

His thumb moves down to trace my lips. "We're not what?"

"I'm not your girlfriend," I blurt, looking away. "But this all feels…real. Realer than an actual relationship I was in for a year and a half."

"Yeah?"

"He had so many rules about what we could and couldn't do."

"What kind of dude has rules for his girl?" Booker frowns.

"Maybe *rules* isn't the right word. It's just that he had a plan. For everything," I say, wondering if I shouldn't have mentioned Mitchell. Booker looks peeved. "And he was only ever happy if things went his way and—sorry."

Booker's frown melts away. "For what?"

"I don't want to talk about Mitchell." I slip my hand in his. "How are you? When do you start at the garage?"

"Next week."

"You don't sound excited."

He sighs. "I don't mind working. My uncle Les is all right, and I like the other guys who work at his garage. I just hate that my old man's planned my whole summer. He didn't used to be like this, but with my mom and juvie, he's on my ass all the time. Feels like I can't decide anything for myself anymore."

"Do you like him?" I ask.

"My old man?" He shrugs. "He's okay. We got along better when my mom was around. She died a few months before eighth grade. Maybe Laz told you." He clears his throat.

I shake my head. I knew something had happened, but Laz never told me.

"It's not easy to talk about without depressing the shit out of everyone, so I just...don't." Booker swallows.

"You can talk to me about it. About her," I say. "You're not going to depress me."

He inhales, spreading his big hands in front of him. "She got breast cancer. The chemo worked, and then the cancer came back and the chemo didn't work. I miss her. I...I didn't think I was going to get to say goodbye to her. She was getting worse and worse while I was locked up, and—she died a couple of weeks after I got out. It sucked. It still sucks. Every single day. And I don't think my pops is ever gonna go back to the person he was when she was here."

"I'm sorry," I say. As much as my mother annoys and even infuriates me at times, I can't imagine her not being around. I don't know how I could just get up and go on with everything like normal, day after day, knowing someone so important was gone. Carlene hasn't even been here a month and I'm already starting to get so used to her that I wonder if my life will feel different when she leaves.

"I have to see someone every week because of the trouble I got into. A counselor. He wants my dad to come in so we can talk to him together. But *my* pops? Nah. He's an old-school black dude from the South Side. Therapy's not in his vocabulary."

"I can't see my dad going to therapy, either. Not unless my mom made him." But I don't think my mother would ever suggest therapy because she's too afraid of people knowing we're not perfect.

"Do you like your old man?" Booker turns my question back on me.

"He works a lot. He's quiet. But he's a good dad. He's always trying to keep everyone happy."

"Your family sounds nice." *Picture perfect* is what he doesn't say, but I see it in his eyes.

I don't know how to explain that even though everything looks good, it always feels like something is simmering under the surface. Like there's information just under my nose that everyone is aware of except for me. I've always felt this way, and maybe it's worse because I'm getting older—becoming less naive.

I can't figure out a good response, so I kiss him again.

Being with him—kissing and touching him—is a special kind of good. Soft and warm and comfortable. I forget that we are at Laz's house and that I'm on borrowed time and that I don't know when I'll be able to see him again. I slip onto my back and Booker hovers over me on the couch, his lips planting tiny kisses down my throat. I wrap my arms around his broad back, pulling him closer. I like the weight of him, a reminder that he's real and not just someone who lives in my phone.

Laz makes a lot of noise as he comes up the walk and opens the door, giving us enough time to break apart and straighten our clothes and smooth our hands over our hair. He appraises us with a raised eyebrow as he sets a plastic bag of potato chips, gummy bears, and Gatorade on the coffee table.

My mother summons me home a few minutes later.

"I don't want to go," I say to Booker when he walks me to the bus stop.

"I don't want you to go," he says.

He doesn't ask when he'll see me again—I think it makes us both a little sad that we don't know when. I have less than three weeks left of my punishment, but even after I'm no longer grounded, my mother will be watching to make sure I don't mess up again.

The bus pulls up. Booker kisses me as the people exit, then he kisses me again when I'm on the first step, until the bus driver clears his throat and says we can get on or off, but we have to keep moving.

MOM DRIVES ME TO MY SECOND SAT SESSION, DESPITE MY PROTEST.

I still don't understand why she let me hang out with Laz the other day, because she hasn't lifted or lightened my punishment. She's been spacey lately, like she's not quite herself.

She and Carlene are getting along a little better. Carlene has been keeping busy with AA meetings, braiding classes, and running. She's with us for most breakfasts and dinners, and thankfully, the tension during mealtimes has started to evaporate. Carlene doesn't seem any different, but I can tell Mom is trying hard to be pleasant and less critical of her sister. Less vocally critical, anyway. I still catch the way she looks at her sometimes, like she doesn't trust her not to run off with the silverware.

I say goodbye to my mother, and when I get inside I'm happy to see I'm the first person in the room. No Mitchell. Maybe he dropped the class. I sit in the same seat as last time and take out my workbook, glancing at the sections on quadratic equations and ratios that we were supposed to go over. I've become so good at studying during the school year—making up schedules and methods and sticking to them—that I didn't expect to have any trouble this summer. But it's hard to concentrate, even though I have all the time in the world.

I don't look up as people begin coming in. I don't want to accidentally make eye contact with Mitchell. It's awkward, being in the same room and not talking. But knowing we have nothing to say to each other, anyway.

Eventually someone plops down into the seat next to me. I look over and startle when I realize it's him.

"I know you hate me," Mitchell says, staring down at the desk, backpack still hooked over his shoulders. "But if we're going to be in the same class all summer, maybe we can at least say hey?"

"I don't hate you." My voice is quiet as I look around to see if everyone else is looking. Nobody is looking. "You're the one who broke up with me."

"It's not like you were sad about it."

I frown. "We were together for a year and a half. The breakup came out of nowhere, and it seemed so...so..."

I feel him looking at me, but now I don't want to meet his eyes.

"It seemed so what, Dove?"

We make eye contact for the first time in months. And I'm surprised to see, for the first time, Mitchell looking at me like he really wants to hear me. Like he cares what I have to say. The arrogance that always tinged his features is gone for the first time in a long time.

"It seemed like part of your life plan," I say, finally managing to get out what's been bothering me for the past four months. "Like you'd written down how things were going to work. Go out with Dove for exactly a year and six months, take her out to a nice dinner and a movie, break up with her outside the Blue Line station. Like I was a checkmark on your to-do list."

He is quiet for so long that I look over. His dark eyebrows are raised, his eyes wide. "Wow. You really think that's how it was?"

"I *know* that's how it was. You weren't upset at all. You—it felt like you used me just to keep your parents happy. To have someone around you could call your girlfriend who you liked just fine, but not enough."

And I just kept going along with it and never said anything.

Jared, our instructor, walks in then, his cheeks seemingly pinker than last week.

Next to me, Mitchell is stunned into silence. He finally slips off his backpack and takes out his workbook and Cartier pencil. I concentrate on Jared, whose baritone I still can't get over. It doesn't fit his slim frame and boyish features, and I spend the rest of the session concentrating on his voice instead of our math lesson.

After class I get up immediately, stuffing my things back into my bag. Mitchell takes his time, and I am relieved he's not going to follow me out.

"Hey," he says, and then I have to look at him.

"I promise you, it wasn't like that," he says. "I thought you were cool, Dove. Way too cool to be going out with someone like me. The whole time, I thought...I thought *you* were just going out with me to make *your* parents happy. Because yours *and* mine really seemed to like us together, and I figured there was no other reason you'd ever want to be with me."

I open and then close my mouth, not sure how to respond. Part of the reason I never thought about breaking up with him myself *was* because I knew how happy our relationship made my parents. They felt I was safe when I was with Mitchell, and it was nice knowing there was someone besides Laz they trusted me to be around when they weren't there. But he thought I was going out with him for the same reason, which means it could look like I was using him, too. I never thought of it that way.

"Look, we don't have to be friends," Mitchell says, standing up. "We never really were good friends to each other, huh? I just don't want you to think I was trying to use you. Because I wasn't."

"And I…I'm sorry if you thought that's what I was doing, too," I say. "I guess I never felt good enough for you. Like I wasn't smart enough or disciplined enough, and I kept wanting to prove myself the longer we were together."

He nods, and I think both of us are somewhat appeased and confused by our sudden openness. We never talked about what we were when we were actually together. We didn't talk about much besides school, what we were going to do on the weekends, and our parents' expectations.

I'm almost to the door when I turn around and look at him again. "Thanks," I say.

"For what?" Mitchell shrugs. "I was just being honest."

"Exactly," I say before I walk out of the room.

⬞

Later that evening, my parents do something so rare it makes my eyes pop in surprise—they go on a date.

I sit cross-legged on their bed while my mother is

getting ready. She's perched at the vanity, brushing rouge over her cheeks. It's weird to see her wearing makeup. She doesn't, usually, not besides mascara. But tonight she's all done up, her lips stained plum and her eyelids lined.

"What's the occasion?" I know their anniversary isn't until October because my father always panics about what to get her right around a week before Halloween, frantically combing through the list of traditional anniversary gifts with Mimi and me.

"No occasion. We haven't seen much of each other lately."

"Where are you going?"

"A new Italian restaurant that opened in the West Loop. Your father saw a review in the *Tribune* and said he had to take me." She blots her lips and examines her reflection.

"You look pretty, Mom."

She smiles at me in the mirror. "Thank you, Birdie. You'll be okay here with Carlene? I'll leave some money for pizza, or maybe she can go pick up something for you two."

"We'll be fine. I like her."

I can feel my mother still watching me, even after I look away.

"What?" I finally say when she's been quiet too long.

"Nothing." She smiles again, her lips a bit tighter this time. "That's good, Birdie. Carlene likes you, too."

Carlene is tired and hungry, which makes her cranky. Today she went to braiding class and then an AA meeting when she got back to this side of town. We try to order a pizza, but there's a Cubs game tonight and every place around us is slammed.

"They won't be able to deliver it for almost two hours," she says after she hangs up with the third place.

"Mom said you could go get something for us," I suggest, feeling like I'm six years old.

Carlene rolls her eyes. "And then it'll be cold by the time I get back, and we'll have a completely unsatisfying meal for no good reason."

"I guess we could make something." I look nervously toward the kitchen.

"Let's go out."

"I can't." I hate being grounded.

"They'll never know you were gone. Come on." Carlene is already sliding her shoes on. "We'll go to that diner a couple of blocks away. Easy in, easy out, and we'll have a good, hot meal."

I get the feeling this isn't up for debate, so I grab my phone and the money off the table and follow her out the door.

The sign at the front of the diner says to seat ourselves. Carlene and I scan the dining room, which is busier than I thought it would be. We find a booth next to the windows.

"What's good here?" my aunt asks after someone drops menus on the table.

"I've never actually been in here," I say, opening the plastic menu.

"You're kidding me. This is practically in your backyard."

"Mom always said it looked filthy." And, actually, I can't help noticing the grime around the windows and the chipped, faded tabletop.

"Of course she did."

We're still studying the menus when the diner door jingles open. The man who walks inside looks familiar, and it takes me a moment to realize it's his shoulders. I'd recognize that stooped posture anywhere.

"Your friend is here," I say.

Carlene turns around, her face lighting up as she spots him. "Emmett!"

He turns almost suspiciously at his name, then his scowl drops when he sees us. My aunt waves him over, and he pauses for just a moment before he walks our way, hands deep in his pants pockets.

"How y'all doing?" He's skinny, and his voice is deeper than I expected—and raspy from cigarettes.

"We're okay," Carlene says. "How are you? What's wrong?"

Emmett sighs. "My girl—"

She shakes her head at him. "You aren't supposed to be thinking about her right now."

"I know, but damn, Carl. I miss the shit out of her and—" He stops and glances at me. "Sorry. Hey, I'm gonna grab that table over there before—"

"Nope. I'm not letting you sit alone when you're like this." She scoots across the booth and pats the seat next to her. "Join us."

He looks back and forth from her to me. "I don't want to impose on y'all."

"You're not imposing. We're just having a quick dinner." She nods toward me. "This is Dove. My niece."

"Hi." I raise a hand in greeting and he seems to think that's charming because he smiles and slides in next to my aunt.

"Nice to meet you, Dove. I'm Emmett." He extends a hand. It's dry and warm and swallows mine when I shake it.

They order coffee, then Carlene turns to him. "Are you talking to Deja?"

He rubs a hand over his short hair and shrugs those heavy shoulders. "I've been calling…just keep getting her voicemail. How am I supposed to get through this without her?"

"How are you supposed to get through this *with* her?" Carlene stares at him even though he's looking at the table. "You know you shouldn't be calling."

The waiter ambles over with their coffees and waters for all of us. Carlene orders a double cheeseburger, onion rings, and a piece of cherry pie for later. Emmett asks for a tuna melt, and I get French toast and bacon because we never have breakfast for dinner.

"You know, I tell you things because you're not my sponsor," Emmett says to Carlene. "Sometimes I just need a friend."

She sighs. "I'm not judging you. But I've been there, and it never works out. You're the one who's going to end up suffering, not her."

"Why shouldn't you be calling?" I break into their conversation. I'd never interrupt my parents and their friends like this, but Carlene and Emmett don't seem like typical adults. I don't think they'd be talking any differently if I weren't sitting here.

"Because I haven't been sober long enough," Emmett responds without hesitation.

"Addiction can cause a lot of problems in relationships, and that can trigger a relapse—especially if you're still in the early stages of recovery," my aunt explains. "Everyone's different, but the general rule is you shouldn't jump into anything until you've been sober a year."

"A year?"

"Yeah, doesn't sound so easy, huh?" Emmett takes a long swig from his coffee cup. "I gotta wait six more months to be with the woman I love?"

"If she's the one for you, she'll still be here in another six months," Carlene says.

"Can't stand your practical ass," Emmett grumbles.

"Just trying to keep you on track like I know you'd do for me."

His eyes go down to his cup of coffee.

I look at Carlene, wait for her to keep talking about the program, but she's turned away, staring pensively out the window.

༄

My parents return after I've already gone to bed. I wake when I hear the front door banging open. My mother shushes my father and then there is soft laughter from them both.

She opens my door and sticks her head in. I pretend to be asleep, but even so, she walks over to my bed and sits on the very edge. I can feel her looking at me and I want to open my eyes, but I don't want to talk so I keep them closed. She smooths her palm over my forehead.

"I love you, Birdie," my mother whispers as she leans down to kiss my cheek. She smells like dark liquor and my father's cologne.

She sits on my bed for a moment longer, then straightens the covers over my shoulders and walks quietly out of the room.

SATURDAYS ARE THE BUSIEST DAYS AT THE SHOP: APPOINTMENTS BOOK FAR in advance, all the seats in the waiting area are full by noon, and every station is occupied.

I come down early to help get them ready for the day. Ayanna and my mother are sitting in the break room, talking quietly. The room doubles as a supply closet, and the card table is so small their knees practically touch underneath. They clam up right away when I stick my head in.

Mom says good morning and Ayanna holds her arms out for a hug. She tells me Laz isn't coming in today—something about an art festival in Old Town, but she doesn't remember who he's going with.

I grab a stack of towels and text him immediately. He's with Greg, which makes me smile. Even if I am jealous that I'm not spending my day with Booker.

I stock the towels neatly at the sinks and then go back for more to put at each station. Mom and Ayanna don't hear me coming, and just like I do with my mother and father, I creep silently to the door to listen. It's instinct since no one ever tells me anything.

"In a way, I think it's been good for us," Mom is saying. "Raymond has been so much more attentive and... affectionate."

Ew. Maybe I don't want to hear this.

But then Ayanna says, "See? Told you it wouldn't be so bad with her here."

"But what about when it all falls apart? When she breaks down and has a drink? Or uses?"

Ayanna sighs. "You don't know that's going to happen, Kitty."

"It's going to happen." My mother's voice is forceful. "It always happens. And now Birdie is going to be around to see it and—God, Ayanna. What are we doing?"

I creep backward, away from the break room door, until I reach the sinks. And then I stand there, staring at the floor, thinking about what my mother said. How can she be so positive Carlene is going to relapse? Just because she has before doesn't mean this time won't stick. Carlene sounded so disciplined when she was talking to Emmett. I really believe she doesn't want to drink or get high again. Why is it so hard for my mother to see how she's trying?

Mom's first appointment is Ms. Daugherty, who has a standing slot every other Saturday for a press and curl. She's in her late seventies now and her hair is starting to thin, but she shows up every other week without fail, passing out butterscotch candies and complaining about her adult son she calls Buddy.

I lead her back to the sinks and help her get settled in the chair. "Lean your head all the way back for me, Ms. Daugherty," I say as nicely as I can.

"How you doing, baby? You out of school yet?" Her voice is smooth as the candies she keeps in her purse.

"Just for the summer," I say, turning on the water. I test the temperature on the back of my hand before I use the sprayer to wet her silver strands. "I have two more years before college."

"You better go away," she says. "Go out and see the world. There's a lot more to it than Chicago."

"Have you ever lived anywhere else?" I reach for the shampoo and pour some in my palm, shutting off the water while I suds up her head.

She chuckles and closes her eyes as my fingers massage her scalp. "Oh yes. I moved around so much when I was young, my mama called me the Wanderer. I was born here, in the Ida B. Wells Homes. They was the largest projects they'd built for black folks, and they only let upstanding people move in then. It was a real community there— everyone looking out for everyone. The gangs started showing up right around the time I left for school.... There'd always been gangs, but never ones that wanted to destroy our homes until *they* showed up."

I rinse out the suds and squirt a bit more shampoo in my hand for round two. I never want her to stop talking because Ms. Daugherty doesn't take her cues from my mother. She says whatever she wants and she always gets away with it.

"So I decided I'd get out and see the world. Got a scholarship to Oberlin to study the flute."

"You're a musician?" This is the first time I've ever heard her talk about her younger years. Usually she's so focused on Buddy, his family, and their troubles. Nothing about her or her past.

"I was. I haven't picked up my flute in years, but I was pretty darn good back then. Played in Europe and Canada and all around the United States." She sighs, her eyes still closed. "Don't you know I ended up back here in Cabrini-Green, where the crime was even worse than Ida B. Wells? They just kept shuffling us black folk around like they didn't know what to do with us. Like we couldn't do just fine on our own. But I traveled, baby. I got out and I saw the world, and you have to do that, too. With a name like Dove, you got to fly."

I reluctantly turn Ms. Daugherty over to Mom after I condition and towel-dry her hair. My mother asks me to make a coffee run, and I'm glad that all the customers already have their own. Putting in multiple, complicated orders at the coffee shop is my least favorite part of assisting.

When I get back with Mom's black coffee and Ayanna's iced latte, the shop is full-on bustling. Every station is lined with a stylist and customer, and the front seats are filled with women patiently flipping through copies of *Ebony* and *Essence* and *Black Enterprise*.

I hold out Mom's change as I drop off her drink.

She's clutching a flat iron, getting ready to start pressing Ms. Daugherty's freshly dried hair. "Can you stick it in my purse, Birdie?"

I feel like everyone is watching me as I move through the shop. I wonder if they used the few minutes I was gone to discuss something scandalous. But what could it be? Even my mother looks somewhat amused, and she usually tries to be the good example for the salon.

I stash the money in Mom's wallet and slide it back into her purse. Then I turn around.

And I scream.

My sister is standing in the doorway with a smile so wide it's practically cracking her heart-shaped face in half.

"Mimi?" I try to say something else, but my mouth is stuck. My sister is here.

"Hi, Dovie."

She scoops me up into a hug and I squeeze her back so hard that I worry I've hurt her when we pull away.

"Miss me?" she says, laughing. I look immediately at her hair. She has a fresh fade, and it looks so good our mother couldn't say anything bad about it if she tried.

"You have no idea, Meems." I squeeze her again, quickly this time. "How long are you here?"

Behind her, our mother appears, and I understand her smile from earlier. She and Mimi may not get along all the time, but she likes having us both around. I think she feels like my sister will protect me, or that maybe I won't be tempted to get in trouble when she's here.

"Just a few days. I came for Pride. It's tomorrow."

"Will you stay in my room?" I ask, since Carlene is currently occupying hers. We have a pullout sofa in the living room, but I miss falling asleep next to Mimi. She never nodded off first, and it felt safe, having someone there. Like when my parents used to read me bedtime stories and I'd fall deep into dreamland before they got to the end.

"Actually." She pauses. "I'm staying with Ariel. She just got a new place."

"Oh," I say. But I can't blame her. Who wouldn't want to stay there instead of in a crowded apartment where our mother notices everything?

"We'll see each other every day. So much that you'll be sick of me. And"—she stops, glancing back at our mother before she continues—"I want you to come to Pride with us."

Now I'm the one with the face-splitting grin. I'm older now, but this feels just as good as when she and Ariel invited me to Lollapalooza. "You do?"

"Of course. If you want to go."

We both turn to Mom, who suddenly looks like she wishes she'd stayed with Ms. Daugherty.

"I'm still grounded."

"This is, like, the longest grounding ever," Mimi says. "And in the summer, too. Come on, Mom."

"I only have another week." My eyes are still on our mother. "Haven't I earned your trust again?"

"I don't know, Birdie," she says. "Have you?"

Yes. Except for that part about seeing Booker. And

having dinner with Carlene and Emmett. But that was only two times in three weeks. And she doesn't even know about any of it. Besides, I haven't been around alcohol at all since the night she smelled it on me.

"Mom, please. I never get to see Mimi. And I've never been to Pride. It's, like, a cultural experience. I'll be supporting Mimi and—" I stop just in time, before I blurt out Laz's name. "Please?"

I can see our mother doing the mental calculations: How much less will I respect her if she goes back on her punishment? But both of her daughters' pleading faces are too much. She can't say no, not with Mimi here. And no doubt some clients can overhear our conversation. She never wants to look mean or unreasonable in front of them.

"Fine," she says. "But consider yourself on probation for the next couple of weeks. I get to approve where you go and with whom."

"How is that any different from being grounded?"

She raises her eyebrows. "Do you want to go to the parade or not?"

"Thank you, Mom."

"Thank you, Mom," Mimi echoes.

We come up on either side of her and wrap our arms around her, creating a Mom sandwich. She's so caught off guard at first that she's stiff as a tree trunk in our arms. Then she laughs and relaxes and says, "You girls stop. Let me get back to work."

She does, but not before she kisses the tops of both our heads.

"SIT STILL," MIMI INSTRUCTS.

We're at Ariel's the next day, getting ready for the parade, and Mimi insisted on doing my makeup. Like my mother, I don't wear much. Mostly because I was only allowed to start wearing it when I turned sixteen a few months ago. I haven't figured out what works or how to apply it, so I usually just wear lip gloss—and mascara when I remember. Today, Mimi curls my lashes and rims my lids with sparkly blue eyeliner and dabs my lips with dewy red gloss.

I don't know what the point is—I won't be seeing anyone I want to impress. Laz and Greg are meeting us in Boystown, and I invited Booker, but he can't go. He texted that he wants to see me more than anything but his uncle won't let him off work.

"What's with the sad face?" Mimi asks, the mascara wand pinched between her fingers.

"Nothing."

She looks at me. "It's not nothing. What's up?"

I stare down at my hands. "I haven't told you yet, but...there's a guy."

She sets the mascara tube on the sink ledge. We're squeezed into Ariel's tiny bathroom, me on the toilet and Mimi pressed against the old pedestal sink. "Is he the reason you were grounded?"

"Yeah, kind of. I went to the party so I could see him."

"Have Mom and Dad met him?"

I look up at her. "They don't know about him. And I don't want to tell them because he's been in trouble. In juvie."

Mimi exhales loudly. "Shit, Dovie."

"It wasn't really his fault. He's not that kind of guy—"

"Well, what kind of guy ends up in the Audy Home?"

I stare at her, my mouth hanging open. "Do you hear yourself? You were the one who told me about the school-to-prison pipeline."

"I know. I'm not saying he deserved to be there, but... Well, Mitchell wouldn't end up in juvie."

"That's so not fair," I say, and I can't believe this is Mimi. She's the most open-minded person I know, and the least judgmental. She hasn't even met Booker—how can she be so sure of who he is? "Just because Mitchell is boring doesn't mean he's a good person."

I feel a little pang, like maybe I shouldn't be calling Mitchell boring. I shake it away. Just because we were civil to each other in class doesn't mean I was totally wrong about him.

"Listen, you're my sister," Mimi says. "Maybe it's not fair, but I don't want you getting in over your head because you fell for some stupid guy."

"He's not stupid." My voice is getting louder. "And I guess every girl you've ever dated is perfect?"

A floorboard creaks in the hall, and I look past Mimi to see Ariel peeking around the doorway. She looks in at us, eyes big. "Everything okay in here, Randolphs?"

My sister doesn't answer as she stuffs the makeup back into its bag. Ariel looks at me questioningly, but I just shake my head until she pads away.

Mimi zips her makeup bag and starts to leave the room. She pauses where Ariel was standing. "I dated someone my first semester who I knew was trouble. But I got involved anyway. She ended up in jail with a DUI, and I spent a good part of my savings bailing her out. She ghosted me the next week and I haven't seen her since— or gotten my money back."

"That's not going to happen with Booker and me," I say. What I don't say is that maybe I'm not as gullible as Mimi. If I got a bad vibe from Booker, I wouldn't keep trying to see him. I'm not that desperate to be with someone. "He's good friends with Laz. He has a job, and he's been sweet to me, always. And he hasn't been in trouble since then."

"I hope he's a good guy," Mimi says. "But I wouldn't be a good sister if I didn't tell you how I feel."

I stand and look in the mirror after she's left. Mimi did a nice job. I look like a better version of me. Even if I don't feel like it.

꩜

The parade stretches from Uptown to Lakeview, where Boystown is located. We can hear the music and cheers before we see the people, and I'm anxious to get to the crowds. I want to meet up with Laz, but I'm also curious about Pride. I've seen videos and pictures, but I know that can't compare to actually being here.

And it's good that Mimi and I will be occupied with something else. It's been a while since there was tension like that between us, and I hate the way it unsettles me. I only get to see her for a few days and then she'll be gone again for months—I don't want to spend our time fighting.

The cheering and hooting gets louder and louder

the closer we get, and then we're pressed up against the crowd, shoulder to shoulder, the noise almost unbearable. In the best way. I stare around in awe at the explosion of color, sound, and light.

There are rainbows everywhere, including the flag Mimi is carrying that says BORN THIS WAY in black letters. Ariel is wearing a temporary rainbow tattoo on her cheek, and I have one stamped on my arm. Colorful hats and costumes and balloons and banners surround us. There are kids running around everywhere, and I even see a couple of dogs—a golden retriever with a rainbow collar and a black Pomeranian with a rainbow-striped bow tie. Everyone looks happy as they cheer on the marchers and candy-colored floats, and the energy is contagious as it pulses through the air. I feel myself smiling for no reason other than that I'm here, in the middle of all this—immersed in a new type of joy in the city where I've always lived.

I look down at my phone to see if Laz has texted. He says they're trying to make their way over to us.

Ariel is standing between Mimi and me. She nudges my side. "How great is this?"

I nudge her back. "It's pretty great."

About ten minutes later, just as a long line of women on motorcycles roars by, I hear someone yelling my name. I recognize Laz's arm waving and the wild curls framing the top of his head. Greg is behind him, waving, too. But it's what's behind them that catches my eye—or *who* is behind them, rather.

Booker.

I stare at him as they push their way around people. He meets my eye and we don't look away. And it takes forever for them to get to us. They are moving slow as syrup, and I am on the brink of shouting at everyone to get the hell out of their way. Booker is here.

Ariel and Mimi greet Laz with exuberant hugs, squealing over how grown-up he looks now. I can tell he is trying very hard not to look at Greg, who's grinning at all the attention. Booker walks straight to me and squeezes my hand. I get the feeling he would have kissed me if Mimi weren't here.

"I thought you had to work," I say, squeezing back with both hands.

"My uncle was tired of me moping around the shop, so he let me go early." He laughs. "He'll never let me forget he did something nice, but it's worth hearing his big mouth so I could see you."

"I can't believe you're here."

"I can't believe you're not grounded."

A hole is burning through Booker's back and into my chest. I pull him aside to find Mimi staring at us. She looks pointedly at our linked hands.

"Booker, this is my big sister, Mimi. Meems..." I

pause; not on purpose, but I like the dramatic effect. "This is Booker."

She nods and says, "Nice to meet you," in her politest voice.

If Booker notices the missing warmth, he doesn't show it. He grins and says he likes her hair. This earns him a tiny smile.

Laz finishes chatting with Ariel, then turns to me. He bumps my hip. "Nice tattoo."

"You want one?"

"I'm good. How does it feel to be out of house jail?"

My eyes shift quickly to Booker at the word *jail*, but he's talking to Greg now.

"She's still going to be watching me like a hawk, but at least I can walk to the corner by myself."

Laz nods and looks out at the parade. For a while. With such brooding eyes that I ask him if something is wrong.

He shakes his head, but a few moments later, his mouth opens. "You think my dad ever came here?"

A drag queen wearing sky-high turquoise heels and a gold-sequined dress strides by, her thick makeup and cherry-red wig flawless. She waves and blows a kiss to the crowd.

"Maybe," I reply. "What do you think?"

"It'd be a good place to get lost. He obviously didn't want anyone knowing."

"You should call him." I say it just softly enough that he might not hear me over all the music and whooping. But Laz hears everything.

"And say what?" He scoffs. " 'Hi, it's your kid. Who hated your guts when you came out and divorced my mom and moved away. But I'm gay, too, and hey! Did you ever go to Pride?' "

"He'll be happy to hear from you. Even if you don't know what to say."

I don't remember a lot about Laz's dad. He divorced Ayanna and moved to Florida when we were in the fourth grade. I do remember how kind he was, and that he always told Laz how much he loved him. Laz stopped talking to him after the divorce; they haven't seen or spoken to each other in seven years.

"You don't know that," Laz counters.

"Maybe you're scared."

"I'm not *scared* of him. I just didn't have anything to say for so many years, and now that I do . . . it's been too long to just call him up."

"No, I mean maybe you're scared of what he'll say. Like that you should just come out to your mom already because she'll love you no matter what."

He scowls. "You keep saying I should just do it, but you don't get it. You're not queer. And I'm her only kid."

"She's not going to disown you because you like guys."

"You think I want to watch her find out someone is a totally different person than she thought they were? Again? I can't do that to her."

"Or maybe she already has some idea and she'd be happy that you could finally be yourself around her. She'd love Greg."

"Forget I said anything." He turns away from me to watch the parade, his scowl not budging an inch.

When we get tired of where we're standing, we start to walk down Halsted. It's jammed all the way across with bodies worse than the blanket of cars on Lake Shore Drive during rush hour. I've been to some big festivals in Chicago, but this might be the most crowded one yet.

We pass a stage where an eighties cover band is playing songs we've never heard, though that doesn't stop Ariel from bopping along as we walk by. The energy of the parade still crackles through the air, but I'm starting to slow down. We need food. I haven't eaten anything since breakfast, before I even got to Ariel's. And now I'm wishing I'd listened to my mother, whose granola bars and trail mix I refused to pack in my bag this morning.

Every place near the parade is overflowing or has wait times longer than an hour for a group our size. Mimi is starting to get grumpy; she loses a bit more patience at every place that turns us away. And she keeps looking at

Booker and me like she wants to say something about us holding hands.

Ariel falls back into step with Mimi. She types something into her phone. "Hey, Fred and Kelsey are over at Sheffield's. They said there's room for us."

"All of us?"

Ariel looks up. "Oh. I guess not."

"Sheffield's is a bar," Greg says. "We won't be able to get in anyway if we don't have fakes."

Mimi and Ariel shrug. They both have them; it sounds like they pass out fake IDs like candy at college.

"I don't have one," I say, stating the obvious.

"Me either," Laz mumbles.

Booker shakes his head.

"Oh. Well, I do," Greg says. He blushes. "But I'm not gonna leave you guys. Let's just find somewhere else."

"Is that okay?" Ariel does look like she cares, but I know she'd rather go to the bar with her friends than hang out with a bunch of high school kids.

"Yeah, go," I say. "We can meet up later."

"I'll see you back at Ariel's at eleven," Mimi says, staring at me. "At the latest."

"Okay, Mom." But I stop myself from rolling my eyes.

Because somehow Mimi weaseled her way right into our mother's soft spot and persuaded her to let me spend the night at Ariel's. Mom told us to stay together the whole time, but we'll just be apart for a few hours, at the most. And I don't think Mimi is interested in babysitting me any more than I'm interested in being babysat.

Ariel digs into her pocket. "Here's my key, just in case you beat us back there. Mimi has my spare."

"Don't do anything dumb," Mimi says as Ariel drops the key into my palm.

But she gives me a quick hug. And even if she doesn't like me being with Booker, I know she isn't mad at me.

13

AFTER WE FIND SOMETHING TO EAT AND PART WAYS WITH GREG AND LAZ a couple of hours later, Booker and I walk.

The news stories about crime in Chicago aren't false, but the city is so much more than that. It is beautiful summer nights, warm but not sticky as the sun retreats for the day. It is the rhythmic chugging of the "L" as it coasts above us, the ever-present soundtrack to Chicago. It is people sitting on stoops of gorgeous greystones, stealing bites from their children's ice-cream cones. And tonight, everywhere around us are rainbows—displayed on flags, painted on cheeks—the festivities of the day still going strong.

"What's the best day you've ever had?" Booker asks as we stroll side by side.

"The best day I've *ever* had?" I pause. "I need a minute. What about you?"

"Don't laugh," he says, glancing at me out of the corner of his eye. "But it was when I was in fifth grade. My mom kept me home from school and said we were gonna have a tourist day."

"Did you go somewhere?"

"No, tourists in Chicago. I didn't get it, since we've lived here my whole life. But she said sometimes that means you miss out on the best parts of your own city."

I can't imagine my mother purposely keeping me out of school for anything. It's hard enough to convince her I need to stay home when I'm legitimately sick.

"We had breakfast at this old-school diner that's been around forever in Hyde Park." His arm brushes against mine and I tingle.

"Valois?"

He grins. "You know it?"

"Yeah, my dad grew up around there and used to take us sometimes. Best cafeteria food I've ever had."

"That's what I told my mom."

"Where else did you go?"

"The Chicago Cultural Center. The Point, so we could go see the water and the skyline, then lunch at Ricobene's."

"Oh! Please tell me you had the breaded steak sandwich?"

"You know I did!" His smile turns sheepish. "Okay, real talk, I had two."

"Two?" Even the smallest size is so huge I'm full before I even finish half.

"She used to call me the bottomless pit," he admits, still smiling. "She was always complaining how I was going to eat them out of the house, but I never went hungry. Not even when money was tight."

I know I shouldn't be jealous of Booker's mom since she's not here, but she sounds like the perfect mother. Not only would my mom never take me out of school, but she isn't the type to plan an impromptu day to hang out or approve of me filling up on messy fried sandwiches.

"At the end of the day, we went to the planetarium so we could watch the sunset. Every place we went meant something to her and—I don't know. It was dope to hear the way she talked about them. About her life."

I barely know anything about my mom's life that doesn't have to do with Mimi or me.

Our arms bump again, and this time I find Booker's hand and fold it into mine. "I'm sorry she's gone."

"Yeah, me too. I miss having her around." He exhales a long breath. "Now it's your turn."

I start talking before I overthink it. "I guess it was the day before we moved into our place."

"How old were you?"

We pass a house party that's spilling off the porch and onto the lawn. A few people are setting up a game of bags up front, and two little kids shriek with glee as they chase an energetic German shepherd around the yard.

"Eight," I say. "I'd never lived anywhere else but our little house in Albany Park, and I didn't want to leave. My parents kept saying how much better the new place would be because I'd have my own room, but I wasn't excited about it."

"You wanted to share a room?"

I shrug. "I was eight. What did I have to hide? And Mimi was my favorite person in the world. Anyway, our parents knew I was upset, so our last night in the house, we had a family sleepover. We unpacked our board games and ordered pizza and told ghost stories while we passed around a flashlight. Then we all slept in the living room—all four of us."

I haven't thought about that night in so long, but I like the way it makes me feel. The memory of being cozy and together and happy. Before my father started working so much and when my mother was a little softer and when I was allowed to play soccer and not worry about college applications. And Mimi was still here.

"I don't think your sister likes me much," Booker says slowly.

I don't make eye contact. "Why do you think that?"

Booker laughs. "I saw how she looked at me."

"It's not you. It's—"

"My past?"

We stop on a quiet corner. I have to look at him now.

"I didn't tell her much about it, but...yeah." I sigh. "She's just worried about me."

"Are you worried?"

"No," I say clearly, staring into his eyes. "But I don't know how to make my family not be worried. And... well, I'm not grounded anymore, but I don't know if sneaking around to see you is going to work much longer. You're going to have to meet my parents if we want to keep doing this."

"I'm polite around parents." He pauses. "And I clean up pretty well. I even have a suit."

That makes me laugh. "You're not wearing a suit to meet my parents. And I don't want you to think they're, like, judgmental assholes. They're not. They just want Mimi and me to..."

To be perfect. Especially my mother. But I can't say that aloud. Not with the sad look in Booker's eyes. Not now that I've made him think he's not good enough for the rest of the Randolph family.

"What if you met my aunt?" The idea just popped into my head, but I think it's a good one. Carlene is the least judgmental person in our house, and she's an adult, so that will make it seem somewhat official. Besides, I know she won't hold back if she doesn't like him.

"Your aunt?"

"Yeah, she's super chill."

He nods slowly. "So if I meet your aunt, does that mean I'll get to date you? Like, really date you—no sneaking out and lying?"

"I don't know. But it's a start. What do you think?"

"Okay," he says.

"I'll talk to her, and we'll figure out the best time to do it." And where, since he definitely can't come to the house yet.

"I can't believe I want to meet your aunt. And your parents, eventually. I must really like you, Dove."

I smile. Booker gently rubs my arm and looks at me in the soft way that I'm realizing means he wants to kiss me. I want to kiss him, too, and I wonder if I have a look that says so. I stand on my tiptoes as he leans down to meet my lips.

꩜

My mother stopped me before I left the house this morning. After she tried to convince me that I needed snacks for the day, her eyes lingered on the duffel bag strap slung over my shoulder, and for a couple of seconds, I was sure she was going to say she'd changed her mind. That I was still grounded after all, because if she's being honest, her trust in me is paper-thin.

The skeptical look passed. She gave me a firm hug and told me to have fun, stay with Mimi, and call her when we're in for the evening.

Mimi is still out with Ariel.

And I'm standing in Booker's living room, watching him pick up clutter.

"Sorry." He scoops up a trio of coffee mugs from an end table. "My old man's kind of a slob, and now that I'm working, too..."

"It's fine." I stand in place, wiping my damp palms on my cutoffs.

He stops. "You don't look like it's fine."

"No, it's not this. I just... I have to call my mom, and I'm worried she's going to ask to speak to Mimi."

"Oh. Right." He chews his lip.

We didn't think about this when he invited me over. I wasn't ready to say goodbye and I wasn't ready to go back to Ariel's, alone, when I could still be with Booker. All I knew was that as wrong as it felt to say yes the last time Booker asked me to come over, this time felt completely right. Those separate parts of me, the scared one too afraid to take risks and the brave one who gives in to what she wants—there wasn't such a fight between them tonight.

I gave in to what I craved without thinking about it too much. The longer we walked next to each other and held hands, exchanging warm gazes, the more I knew I wanted to be alone with him.

"Can Mimi call for you?" Booker suggests. "Just tell her you're in the other room?"

"No." I pause. "But my mom can't say anything if I'm at Ariel's and Mimi is still out."

He nods like he's impressed with my quick thinking.

I look at Booker and put my finger to my lips. He tiptoes out of the room with the mugs.

Mom doesn't keep me long on the phone. In fact, she barely seems interested that I've followed her instructions. She sounds almost giggly, like when I heard her coming in from the date with my father. I wonder what they're doing tonight, then quickly scrub that thought from my brain.

But I don't feel relieved after I hang up because I still have to let Mimi know where I am. And that I'm not coming back to Ariel's until the morning. I didn't even hesitate when Booker asked me to stay over. His father is a night manager for the stocking crew at a grocery store; he clocks in for work at eleven and finishes at eight in the morning. All I have to do is make sure I'm out of here and on my way back to Ariel's by then.

I try calling my sister twice and she doesn't answer,

and I have never been so pleased to get her voicemail. I hang up and send a few texts:

> At Booker's
>
> Am safe
>
> Will be back at Ariel's early

My fingers hover as I contemplate whether I should ask her not to tell Mom. It's implied, of course, but I type it out anyway. With Mimi acting so much like our mother this afternoon, I don't want to take any chances.

When I don't get a response after five minutes, I shut off my phone and stick it back in my bag.

꿈

I've never seen Booker so nervous.

He spent about ten minutes picking up the living room and kitchen, but he keeps glancing around as if he's just seeing his place for the first time, through my eyes. He also seemed embarrassed when he showed me that it was only a one bedroom.

"We moved after my mom died," he says. "And my old man could sleep through fireworks, so he gave me the bedroom and took the couch. It pulls out."

"I like your place," I say after the quick tour. We're standing in the hallway.

It's on the top floor of a yellow-brick courtyard building in Rogers Park, near the Morse stop on the Red Line. There are lots of windows and old Chicago charm, like the built-in hutch in the dining room and arched doorways throughout. The wood floors are buffed to a shine, and even under the clutter I can see that it's not dirty, just untidy.

"It's all right," he says, shrugging. "When you were talking about hating to leave your old place...I get that. Except our old apartment was better than this one. We had three bedrooms, and we knew all our neighbors."

"Why'd you move?"

"My pops wanted to get us out of the neighborhood," he says, brows furrowed. "Said there were too many dope boys and bangers. I went to stay with my grandma in Arizona the summer after I was in juvie. Before eighth grade. We'd just buried my mom, and my old man thought I needed some time away. I think he just wanted to be alone, though. When I got back, he already had this place."

"You never got to say goodbye to your old apartment?"

"Nah. It's not a big deal. I mean, I got to say goodbye to my mom. That's all that matters. But I just..." He shakes his head as he trails off.

"But what?" I slide my palm over his cheek, stopping when I reach his jaw.

"I feel like everything keeps changing and I can't do anything about it. First, I get in trouble, then my mom dies, then my dad moves us to the other side of town. And he made me quit playing football, even though it's the only thing I've ever really liked and been good at."

Just like me and soccer.

Booker sighs. "I can't wait till I graduate and can do what I want. At least then I'll have some control over things changing."

"I feel the same way," I say softly.

"I never thought I'd meet someone like you, though. That was a good change," Booker says. And then, before he kisses me: "I'm glad you're here."

A block away, the "L" coasts along the tracks, and the steady chugging winds through the open windows as we kiss. Booker's fingers graze my hips before he pulls away and asks if I want to watch a movie.

When I first started dating Mitchell, I didn't know that "watching a movie" was code for "ignore the movie and make out the whole time." I didn't find out until Julia, one of my soccer teammates, asked about my weekend and I reported that Mitchell and I had watched a movie in his basement. She wiggled her eyebrows and asked if it was fun.

"It was fine, I guess," I said, shrugging. "Kind of slow at the beginning, but it picked up toward the end."

"Sounds successful," she replied with a smile.

I gave her a weird look. "Successful?"

"You and Mitchell. You hooked up, right?"

"What? No! I meant the movie."

But the heat was already creeping up my cheeks as I realized what everyone assumed we'd been doing. I was embarrassed that I hadn't known—why hadn't Mimi told me about that?—but a part of me was also embarrassed that we *hadn't* been doing what they thought. Watching a movie with Mitchell meant we actually watched the movie.

I wondered if maybe he was just nervous, so after that first time I tried to initiate the make out myself. I curled up next to him on the couch, leaned my head on his shoulder, threaded my fingers through his as we'd done before. I kissed his cheek, and then I started to *really* kiss him. Mitchell kissed me back at first, but then he pulled away suddenly; his face and neck were a deep red as he excused himself to go to the bathroom. When he returned a few minutes later, we sat on opposite sides of the couch and, once again, watched the movie. We didn't touch again until he hugged me good night at the front door.

I never did understand what happened with Mitchell that evening—he wouldn't talk about it, and our making out never got much further than touching under our clothes—but I very much hope Booker isn't interested in watching the movie.

He leads me back to the living room, where we settle on the couch and he scrolls through a collection of films on his laptop. We're both in the mood for *Jurassic Park*, though I am pretty sure we won't be paying much attention.

Booker places the laptop on the coffee table and relaxes into the couch cushions, wrapping an arm around me. I tuck my legs under me and lean against him, resting my head on his shoulder. This feels good, just being here with him; we have all night, but I know time is going to fly by like it always does when we're together. And I don't know when I'll get to be alone with him again, so I'm contemplating how soon is too soon to make the first move when he gently pulls me toward him. Our lips touch, soft and slow.

We move languidly. Booker's mouth travels along my collarbone, then he moves to my shoulders, sliding the strap of my tank top aside to kiss every inch of my flushed skin. He pauses, and I take the moment to lift my arms. He removes my tank top easily and then, for the first time, I'm sitting in front of him in my bra. It feels strange, being so close to naked with someone. It feels good, too, especially when I see the want in Booker's gaze.

I straddle him and his hands come to my hips, holding

me steady. When I lean in to kiss him, they slide down and around to my ass. He squeezes and then moves one hand up to the small of my back. The longer we kiss, the hotter my skin burns, and I wonder if it's possible to contract a fever from making out.

My legs begin hurting after a while and I pull back. His eyes are lust-drunk, peeking at me through lazy lids.

"What's wrong?" he asks.

"Nothing, but maybe we should...move to your room?" My heart pounds wildly, and I wonder if he can feel it. Or hear it.

"Are you sure?"

"Yes." I kiss the tip of his broad nose. "I feel weird doing this where your dad sleeps."

I love the sound of his deep laugh. "Fair enough."

Booker has a four-poster bed with an elaborate headboard made of cherry wood, and I wonder if it used to belong to his parents. I slip out of my sandals and shorts while he strips down to his boxers. It's dark, with just the faint light from the front room filtering in. I step toward the outline of his body and touch his chest, sliding my hands over his smooth skin. We stand on the soft rug for a while, just kissing, until he scoops me up and lays me on the bed like a princess.

I lose track of the time, what day it is, what we did earlier. All I know is Booker: his skin, which smells like salt and the lingering scent of deodorant; his hands that explore the dips and curves of my body; his mouth and tongue, which do the same.

"Are you okay?" he checks in with me when we're lying face to face, skin to skin.

"I'm fine. I'm good." I swallow. "But I'm still not ready to have sex."

"I think we should wait, too," he says simply.

"You do?"

"I think you can tell I want to be with you." He looks down at his waist and smiles sheepishly, slipping his fingers through mine. "But I don't want to rush you...or this. I want to do everything right with you. And I only want to do it when you're ready."

I kiss his cheek. "I really like you, Booker."

"I really like you, too, Dove," he whispers, burying his face in my shoulder.

I WAKE TO WARM SUNLIGHT STREAMING THROUGH THE CURTAINS AND
Booker shaking my shoulder.

I stretch slowly under the covers and smile, remembering last night. "Good morning."

And I don't notice the slight panic in his eyes until he mutters, "We forgot to set an alarm."

I sit straight up. "What time is it?" I search for my phone until I remember I turned it off and left it in my purse. In the other room.

"Eight thirty." Booker grimaces, holding up my tank top. "My old man brought this in from the living room."

Shit.

And by the way his father is banging around in the

kitchen, he's not happy about it. There's no way to sneak out of here without talking to him. He's already seen me.

"Does he hate me?" I ask as I start to get dressed.

"Nah, but I'm gonna hear it as soon as you leave."

"I'm sorry." I pull on my top and walk around to meet him on the other side of the bed.

"Don't be sorry. You're worth it. Even if I am going to get the 'don't be messing around with those girls' talk as soon as you leave."

I narrow my eyes. "*Those* girls?"

We haven't talked about it, and now I wonder how many girls Booker has been with before me. How many his father has met. And if I'm the only one whose tank top he's found in the living room.

Booker coughs. "His words, not mine. I told him about you, but all he knows is I met a new girl I like. He doesn't know how *much* I like you. Not yet."

"No time like the present, right?" I say with a weak smile.

Booker pulls me close. Then he leans down and kisses me, morning breath and all.

❦

Besides sharing the same dark brown skin, Booker's dad looks nothing like him. I'm five foot four, and he's only a few inches taller. He wears wire-rimmed glasses, and has a salt-and-pepper goatee and close-cropped hair to match.

152

He's listening to a talk show on a small, beat-up radio that looks as old as Booker and me. I stand in the kitchen doorway just behind Booker as I wait for him to introduce me, shifting my weight from foot to foot.

"Pops, this is Dove." Booker's voice sounds normal, but I see the tension in his shoulders as he steps aside.

His father cracks an egg into a bowl before he slowly turns around, wiping his hands on a dish towel hooked to his belt. He doesn't turn down the radio.

"Hi," I say with a wave, but he's not charmed like Emmett was. He doesn't even crack a smile.

"Dove?" There's no emotion behind his voice, and I guess he really doesn't know how much Booker likes me. Or maybe he just doesn't care, after he found us in bed together.

"Yes. Dove," I say.

He looks at me for a few seconds as if he's studying my face. Then he nods, turns around, and says, "You're welcome to stay for breakfast, Dove."

"Oh, thank you, Mr. Stratton. But I should probably be getting home—"

"I insist," he says in a tone that I know not to argue with.

The backs of my knees are damp.

Booker raises his eyebrows at me as he mouths *Sorry*.

I find my phone and turn it on, and to my relief, I have

only one message from Mimi. She texted back last night, three hours after I messaged her, and all it says is Okay. I don't know how to read that, and I don't have time to analyze it now. I text that I'll be back at Ariel's soon, then go help Booker set the table.

His dad scrambles eggs and fries potatoes. Booker makes toast. I sit at the table and sweat. Mr. Stratton doesn't turn off the radio until we're all sitting down with full plates.

"Tell me about yourself, Dove," he says before taking a huge bite of eggs doused in hot sauce.

"Oh." I glance at Booker. He gives me an encouraging smile. "Well, I'll be a junior in the fall, like Booker. I go to Behrens Academy. I used to play soccer. I'm in SAT prep this summer."

And whatever you think I am, I'm not.

He nods, finishes chewing, and slurps coffee from a travel mug. "Who are your folks?"

"Excuse me?"

"Your folks," he says, waving his fork in the air. "What do they do?"

"My mom owns a hair salon in Logan Square—"

"With Laz's mom," Booker cuts in.

"And my dad is a doctor." I feel like I'm on trial; like if I say the wrong thing, this could all fall apart in an instant.

"What kind?" Mr. Stratton asks.

"Sports medicine."

He nods and keeps chewing.

When it doesn't seem like he's going to ask anything else, I take a bite of potatoes. "These are really good." And I'm glad, because Booker's dad seems like the kind of guy who would immediately know I was lying.

"Good," he says. And that's the last word he speaks until we're done eating. Even after he and Booker go back for seconds. I wish one of them would turn the radio back on.

I'm not sure I've ever met someone like Booker's dad. I don't think he hates me, exactly, but I don't think he likes me. And I'm not used to that. I'm well mannered, I know how to make small talk, and I'm an overachiever. I'm a parent's dream.

Is this how Booker felt around Mimi? I'd like to think my parents would be a little friendlier, but I'm pretty sure their tone would change as soon as he talked about being in juvie. Which would have to come out, eventually.

I exhale when Mr. Stratton takes his plate to the sink. And I'm calculating how fast I can get out of here when he says, "Booker, why don't you let me and Dove have a little chat?"

Oh, god.

Booker frowns. "Pops?"

"Plenty to do around here, Book. Trash needs to be taken out, you could throw in a load of laundry, or clean up that bathroom."

"Yes, sir." Booker ties up the trash and makes himself scarce.

I look at his father as the back door closes. "I'm sorry, Mr. Stratton. I know I shouldn't have stayed—"

He leans against the counter, arms folded. "My son is too young to be a father."

"What?" My mouth drops open.

Mr. Stratton frowns. "I don't know how much you know about him, but…he's been through some things. He's doing good now, though. Even without his mother here. He's doing real good, and I don't need him getting some girl pregnant."

"He's not—I mean, we're not—" I stop and take a breath. "We haven't done that. You don't need to worry."

"I worry about him every day." He sips from his travel mug. "Your parents don't mind that you're seeing him?"

I swallow. "I haven't told them yet."

He nods. "I see."

"Are you going to?"

He looks at me with a raised eyebrow.

"Tell them?" My voice goes higher.

"I'm not gonna go telling your business. We don't know

each other like that. I just don't want my boy distracted. He can't afford to go down the wrong path because of drama with some girl."

I hate the way he keeps saying *some girl*, like Booker and I just met last night. Like we don't have feelings for each other. I stare down at the green plastic place mat. "I really like him, Mr. Stratton. And I don't like drama."

"Good." When I look back up at him, I think I've passed whatever test he just gave me. Not with flying colors, but you can't ace them all.

I push back my chair and stand. "Can I help clean the kitchen?"

"No, I'll leave that for Booker." His face relaxes a fraction of an inch. It's not a smile, but it's not a frown, either. "Go on home to your folks."

A COUPLE OF DAYS LATER, CARLENE ASKS IF SHE CAN BRAID MY HAIR.

She's spending a lot of time at the school to get her certificate, but she wants to practice goddess braids. "I haven't done them in a long time."

"So I'm gonna be your guinea pig?"

Carlene shrugs. "Hey, kid, you offered, remember?"

I don't mind. I've been cycling through puffs, twists, and twistouts for months now. I'm ready for something different.

She already has the hair we'll be using, so after dinner, we sit down in the living room. My father is still at work, and Mom just went to Ayanna's to do paperwork for the salon.

Carlene perches on the edge of the couch while I sit between her legs. She runs a hand softly over my hair. "It's so nice and thick."

"Mom says I got the Randolph hair."

"Well, your dad isn't in danger of losing his anytime soon." She begins parting my strands with a pintail comb. "You know, I used to sit with your mom just like this and do her hair when we were kids."

"Really?" I can't picture it.

"All the time," she says. "Our mom worked so much that she didn't really have time to do our hair. She did what she could for us, but she was tired all the time, and I had to pick up some of the slack. So I learned to do hair by practicing on Kitty. And then I got good."

"Did you really teach Mom everything she knows?"

"Yup," Carlene says. "Of course she's built on that over the years, but I taught her the basics. She picked it up right away, especially braiding. But she likes the other stuff better now—the cuts and color."

"Carlene, can I ask you something?"

I swear, she pauses for longer than she should. "Yes, of course."

"Do you think Mom and Dad have been acting weird?"

"Weird how?"

"Like, happy."

She laughs. "That's weird?"

"No, they're just usually so busy they don't spend a lot of time together. And after you..."

"After I what?" She reaches for a piece of hair that closely matches the rich black of mine.

I stare at the wood grain of the coffee table. "Never mind."

"We're gonna be here for a while. Spill it."

"They were weird after you got here, but not good weird. It was...well, like they were freaked out."

"I don't know if anyone wants their newly sober sister showing up out of the blue," she says. "Ray and Kitty have been good to me."

"I know," I say. "But then all of a sudden it was good weird. They went on a date, and she and Dad *never* go on dates."

"Be glad they're happy." She begins braiding—tightly—and I suck my teeth. "Are you tender-headed?"

"Maybe a little." It's a weakness, being the tender-headed daughter of a hairstylist. I like the way braids look on me, but sometimes it's not worth the pain.

"Well, you get that from us, not the Randolph side." She pauses until she's halfway down the braid. Her fingers move quickly, and I concentrate on the rhythm so I won't think about my throbbing scalp. "Our dad left when I was five and Kitty was three. Our mom wasn't the same after that, and she wouldn't let herself be happy again, either. I think she was more scared of finding someone she loved than being alone for the rest of her life…which she was. She didn't trust that she wouldn't get her heart broken again."

"Were you ever married?" It hits me that I don't know much about Carlene's life before she got here. Everything seems to be about her being sober or not sober.

"No," she says. "Thank god. Who knows who I would've ended up legally bound to?"

"You never wanted kids of your own?"

"That's a personal question, you know."

My cheeks flush. "Sorry."

"*I* don't care, but you shouldn't go around asking people that." She's quiet for a moment. "I did have a baby once, a while ago. I lost it."

"Oh." A miscarriage. I feel a peripheral sadness, like her emotion is lacing itself into the air. Like I can feel what she must have felt all those years ago.

"It was for the best. I would've messed up a child real good." She finishes the first braid and drapes the long end over my shoulder.

I finger the end of it, admiring the tight weave. "You could still have one, though. Or adopt. Right?"

"I'm almost forty-five. That's not too old, but…I don't know if it's in the cards for me."

We sit silently for a while, listening to the sidewalk traffic below: A group of young guys bumbles along, clowning each other mercilessly; a homeless person pushes their cart, the wheels squeaking and dragging methodically down the pavement; a car horn blares and a voice shouts out their window for someone named Sandy.

"How was Pride?" Carlene asks, stopping to turn my head this way and that so she can examine her work so far.

"I loved it. You didn't want to go?"

"Oh, I wanted to go, but I've had a lot of fun at Prides in the past. Too much. I was afraid it might trigger me. Did you have a good time with Mimi?"

I sigh. "At first, yeah. But, well…can you keep a secret?"

"Oh, I'm *too* good at keeping secrets, girl. But you should only tell me if you're comfortable with it. You're not in trouble, are you?"

"No, no. But there's a guy. And my parents don't know him, so I've kind of been sneaking out to see him."

I tell her all about Booker—how we've liked each other since the first time we met, how I've never felt this way about anyone, how he has been nothing but sweet to me every time we are together. And how we had such a beautiful afternoon during Pride that turned into a beautiful night.

"So what's the problem? He sounds like a dream," Carlene says, dipping into the bundle for more hair. "Almost too good to be true. Why not just introduce him to your parents?"

"Because *he's* been in trouble. He had…an altercation with one of the coaches at his old school and got expelled and sent to juvie."

"The Audy Home? Shit." I can tell Carlene is making a face without even looking at her.

"He's not a bad guy, he just had a bad moment. His mom was sick and the coaches were being hard on him."

"Well, in my experience, people only use the word *altercation* when they're trying not to tell you how bad something really was." Carlene pauses. "She'd kill me if she knew I was telling you this, but your mom and I once got the cops called on us for an *altercation*."

I turn around to look at her. "What? You and *Mom*?"

"I was…" Carlene clears her throat and looks away from me as she speaks. "I broke into her house and was going after the secret stash of money she had. But if I'd been in my right mind, I'd have known she never would have kept her money in the same place anymore. Not after I'd already stolen from her once. And I thought she was at work, but she was taking a sick day and heard the window break before I even made it all the way through. It was a mess by the time the cops showed up—Kitty swinging at me with a baseball bat, and me running around screaming at her with bloody legs from the broken glass."

"When was this?" I ask, picturing the house in Albany Park.

"Oh, it was before you and Mimi were around, thankfully. A fucking mess," she says, shaking her head. My ears perk up at the F-bomb, and I can't help but smile. She didn't censor herself around me like my parents always do. "Anyway, this kid is out of trouble now?"

"His name is Booker. And yes, he's doing great now. His dad even made him quit football because he's worried about all the concussions. But that didn't matter to Mimi. I told her about him and she judged him right away, before she'd even met him. And then...the funny thing is that his dad seemed to feel about me the same way Mimi feels about Booker. Like I'm a bad influence."

Carlene hoots. "You? A bad influence? Do I gotta go knock some sense into that man?"

"He wasn't mean. Just...*curt*," I say, repeating the word she used to describe my mother.

"Well, I know the feeling," she says. "I didn't make friends with many parents when I was your age. Except I *was* a bad influence."

"Did Mom ever do anything bad? Anything...rebellious when you were growing up?"

"Probably the most rebellious thing your mother ever did was turn in her homework late. She was a good kid. Like you."

"I don't feel like it lately," I say.

"Why? Because you've snuck out a few times? Had a couple of drinks?" My aunt pauses. "I'm not saying that stuff is okay, because you *are* still a kid, even if you think you're not. But I know how you feel. I know how stifling it can be to grow up with someone who expects you to be perfect all the time."

I stay quiet because I am so surprised at how much she gets me. Even though we have such different lives, she hasn't forgotten what it was like to be my age or to grow up in a home where outward appearances matter more than how you feel inside.

"You gotta live, Dove. Not as much as I did, but you can't live your life to make someone else happy. It will never be good enough for them. Or you."

"You give good advice," I say after a moment.

"I wouldn't go that far. I've just been around long enough to learn some things. And I don't want you to miss out on being a teenager because of your mother's fears." Carlene clears her throat. "But tell me: Why do you like this guy so much? Booker. Not *because* he's a bad boy, right?"

"But he's not, Carlene. He's sweet, and his temper got away from him. He's never been in trouble before or after that."

"And you don't think he's going to snap again?"

"No, I don't." I look at her over my shoulder. "And I can't explain why I like him. I just do. It's, like, that chemistry everyone talks about. I didn't have that with Mitchell, but I feel it with Booker. I understand it now."

"So, what happens next? You think your mom's gonna be okay with you dating him?"

"I know she's not." I clear my throat and turn back around. "That's why I was wondering if you'd meet him."

"*Me?*" Carlene's fingers never stop moving, just like a professional.

"You're family. And you won't judge him like my parents. But maybe you can convince them it's okay for me to date him. I mean, if you like him."

Carlene doesn't respond right away.

"You really care what I think, kid?"

"Why wouldn't I?"

She guides the thin handle of the comb down my scalp, gently creating another part. "It's just nice," she says. "That you care. I'd love to meet your not-quite-boyfriend."

"Future boyfriend?"

"I like your optimism."

IT'S GOOD NOT TO FEEL SO NERVOUS WALKING INTO MY NEXT SAT PREP course, but it's still a little strange knowing I'll see Mitchell.

We didn't talk about anything real when we were together, so why did both of us decide to open up the last time we saw each other? In a classroom, no less.

He's there early, sitting in the same spot as last time, in the desk next to mine. I slide into my seat and give him a quick smile. But as soon as I look away, I can't figure out what's different about him. And I don't want to look again, but it's bugging me, to feel like something so close is so out of place.

He brushes invisible lint off the front of his shirt and I look over as a reflex and—that's it! His shirt. When he wasn't in his Behrens Academy uniform, Mitchell normally wore button-down shirts—short-sleeved in the summer and long in the fall and winter—and colored polo shirts any other time. But he's wearing an actual T-shirt, a black one with graphics on the front. I squint at it. *Star Wars.*

"New shirt?" I ask, trying to hide my grin.

His own smile stretches the length of his face. "You noticed?"

"I don't think I've ever seen you wear a T-shirt. Like, ever."

"I haven't, unless they were undershirts."

I unzip my bag and grab my workbook. "What gives?"

"It's stupid that I have a dress code even when I'm not in school, and I finally told my parents," he says, unable to hide the pride in his voice.

I stare at him. "Your parents had a problem with you wearing *Star Wars* shirts?"

"You've met my parents—they have a problem with everything." He rolls his eyes.

"I guess I never noticed," I say, trying to think back over the times I was around them. Like my parents, they were big on manners and doing well in school and preparing for the future. But I never knew they monitored what he wore—I thought he *liked* looking like he was always on his way to a job interview.

"*Star Wars* isn't intellectual, T-shirts are sloppy, and obviously everyone will think I'm a goddamn slacker if they know I like both of those things. You didn't know?"

My parents have their rules, but that would be extreme even for them.

"They're just—" he starts, but Jared walks in then, with his surprisingly deep voice, and Mitchell shakes his head like he'll finish later.

After class, neither of us rushes to gather our things and get the hell away from each other, and that feels good, too.

But I freeze when Mitchell looks over and says, "Want to grab lunch?"

Shit. It was only a week ago that he was saying we didn't have to be friends, so why is he asking this now? Maybe all that honesty was a mistake. Is he trying to get back together?

"Um." I slip my pencil and eraser back into my bag and wish we were still going over the basic geometry sections with Jared. I'm no longer grounded and my mom didn't drive me today, so I don't have a good excuse. "I, um—"

"Not like a date," Mitchell says quickly, holding up his hands. "And feel free to tell me to go to hell. But I'm hungry and you seem like maybe you don't want to kill me, so…"

"Okay," I say before I can think about it too much.

Maybe because I'm so thankful that he wasn't asking me out; I don't think there'd be any coming back from that for either of us. "Sure. But please, god, can we not go anywhere near Navy Pier?"

"Well, what I'm thinking of isn't too far from it, but I swear it's a thousand times better than anything on the pier."

He won't tell me where we're going, and normally that would bother me, but for some reason it feels fine today. I think I'm still trying to get used to this new Mitchell, the guy who proudly wears geeky T-shirts and talks about his feelings.

We walk side by side to the train station, and I almost run into a tree when Mitchell reaches into his pocket and pulls out a vape pen.

"What are you doing?" I look at the people around us, at the buildings we pass, at the sky above us, as if we're on a hidden camera show. This can't be Mitchell. Not Mr. We're Too Smart to Go to Those Drinking Parties himself.

"Dude, just act normal. Everybody vapes. And you can't smell it," he says before he takes a long drag.

"Is that weed?" I ask in a low voice.

"It's not a cigarette." He holds it out to me as we jog up the steps to the "L" platform. "Want a hit?"

"No, I'm good. It's the middle of the day," I add, and instantly hate how it sounds. Judgy. Like my mother.

"And? It helps me relax. Sometimes people need to do that during the day, too."

We swipe our cards and push through the turnstile, then walk down to an empty spot on the platform. Mitchell takes another hit and slips the vape back into his pocket.

"When did you start doing that?"

"After we broke up," he says, his olive skin flushed. Mitchell always gets the "where are you from?" question from people and he likes making them squirm before he tells them his mom is white and his dad is half black and half white.

"Thanks a lot," I say.

He laughs a bit. "No, not because of you. It was a couple of months after we broke up. I've always wondered about it, and I felt like I was losing my fucking mind studying for final exams, so I decided to try it."

"How'd you do on the exams?" I crane my neck to look for the train when I hear it rumbling in the near distance, but I can't tell which direction it's coming from.

"Aced them." He frowns when I look at him. "Why?"

"Every single time I wanted us to go to a party with Laz, you said we were too smart for it."

He blushes again. "I did?"

"Don't even start with me, Mitchell. You know you did."

He sighs. "Do you have to keep reminding me of what a prick I was? But this is medicine, not a party drug." He throws his hands in the air when I stare at him. "Seriously, Dove. It helps with my anxiety."

The train whooshes down the tracks on the other side of the platform, sending a tunnel of wind through the air.

"*You* have anxiety?" Mitchell never seemed anything but cool and calm when I was around him. Probably the most nervous he seemed was during those few minutes on the Ferris wheel.

"Yup," he says, reaching for the vape pen to take another hit.

We end up at Portillo's for lunch. It's predictably packed inside, so I creepily watch people eat, waiting for a table to open up, while Mitchell orders for us at the counter. I scramble across the room when a couple finishes their meal and stand inches away from the table until they get up and dump their trash.

Mitchell comes back with two trays. I got what I always order, the Italian beef with sweet peppers and crinkle fries. Mitchell got a beef and cheddar croissant.

"That smells amazing." I lean down to inhale before I reach for my wallet. "How much do I owe you?"

"Nothing," he says, already unwrapping his lunch.

"Mitchell—"

"I didn't do a lot of nice things for you when we were together. Let me buy you lunch."

We did always split the bill wherever we went, but I thought it was normal. Neither of us had jobs. But now that I think about it, Booker has paid for everything when we were out: frozen yogurt, a snack at one of the food booths at Pride when we were wandering around trying to find a place to eat, and then our real dinner after that. I know he doesn't have a lot of money, but he's never let me pay, even though I offered each time.

"Thank you." I look down at my still-wrapped sandwich. "But... this isn't a date, just to be clear."

"Loud and clear," Mitchell says, laughing. "What, are you seeing someone or something?"

And there it is, that hint of superiority that used to sit on the edge of every sentence. Like I've just been waiting around to go to lunch with him. Like he can't believe I could be with someone else besides him. My heart is beating fast and angry, and I make myself take a couple of deep breaths before I answer.

"I am, actually. He goes to school with Laz. We've been seeing each other all summer."

Which is really only a few weeks, but it sounds more impressive to say all summer.

"Oh." Mitchell nods. "Cool. Good for you."

But it's not the *good for you* that people mean when they're actually happy for you, typically followed by a smile. It's dismissive and he's smirking. And the most annoying part is that he's not acting like this because he's jealous. There are no feelings between us—if they were ever there to begin with.

He's acting this way just to be a dick.

I slowly peel the paper away from my Italian beef as I try to calm down. Whenever he'd annoy me like this before, I'd do something to distract myself so I wouldn't start yelling about how condescending he could be. Like testing his knowledge of random facts.

"What do you know about CTE?" I looked it up after Booker mentioned it, but I can't even remember what the letters stand for.

Mitchell wipes his mouth after chewing a big bite. "Chronic traumatic encephalopathy?"

I nod. Of course he knows the name off the top of his head and pronounces it perfectly.

"It's a brain disease," he says. "Brain degeneration. First found in boxers back in the 1920s, but the last few years doctors have been focused on football players. It can show up in anyone with repeated brain trauma, though—like military vets or people who've been physically abused.

They can only diagnose it after death, but there are all kinds of symptoms: aggression, depression, anxiety, bad judgment, memory loss, dementia...."

"How do you know all this?" I don't think Mitchell has played a sport that wasn't mandated by a PE teacher.

"When I hear about something I don't know, I look it up." He shrugs like I should already know this. "Why are you asking about it?"

I pause, not wanting him to dismiss my...whatever it is with Booker. But I have to admit, the more I looked into CTE the more uneasy I felt. Did the football he played have something to do with him snapping on his coach? Would he have gotten worse if his dad hadn't made him quit? He sounded like he thought his dad's concern was silly, but maybe he was right to make him stop playing.

"The guy I'm seeing used to play football, but his dad is worried about CTE and made him quit." I squirt ketchup into a pool on my sandwich paper and swirl a fry through it before I pop it in my mouth.

"Probably a good call," Mitchell says. "They don't know enough about it, but it's a pretty nasty disease and totally avoidable in that case."

"Except avoiding it means he doesn't get to do the thing he loves."

"Well, yeah." Mitchell takes another bite, chews, and looks at me. "You're really into this guy?"

"I am, yeah." I take a deep breath. "Can I ask you something?"

He nods as he takes a sip of his soda.

"Why did you stay with me so long if you weren't interested in me?"

He frowns. "What do you mean?"

"You...you never seemed, like, *physically* interested in me." I lower my voice even though it's so loud in here someone would have to be sitting in our laps to hear us. "Whenever we fooled around, you didn't seem like you wanted to be there. With me. Like, ever."

Mitchell's face is instantly engulfed in flames. Honestly, it's so red it makes me feel bad, and when he doesn't say anything back, I take the biggest bite of my Italian beef that I can manage because I'm embarrassed now, too. For him, and a little bit for myself for asking in the first place.

He drinks from his soda until the dregs of it slurp loudly in his straw. He shakes the ice in his cup and tries again until nothing more will come out. Finally, he looks at me, watching as I chew. "It wasn't you, okay? And I..." He looks down and then back at me again. "It wasn't you, Dove."

"Okay," I say, watching his skin fade back to its normal shade.

We finish our meals without talking and I don't feel good about it.

It seemed like Mitchell and I were forging some sort of post-breakup civility, weird as it was, and now I wonder if that's been totally squashed by my question.

I DON'T SPEND A LOT OF TIME WITH JUST MY FATHER, SO I'M SURPRISED and pleased when we find ourselves alone for dinner a couple of nights later.

"Where is everyone?" I ask when I walk out to the living room to greet him. I yawn, still groggy from my nap.

"Clearly not sleeping like you," he teases me, tweaking the end of a braid. "Your mother is still downstairs, working on a late appointment. I don't know where Carlene is, but your mom said we're on our own tonight for dinner. You cooking?"

I give him a look. He and Mom are both good cooks; I didn't get that gene.

"I had to try." He laughs. "How about I fire up the grill? We've got those rib eyes I picked up the other day."

"I can make a salad," I offer. It's just about the only thing I *can* make, but it's something.

Dad seasons the steaks, then goes up to the roof to heat the grill. I toss together an easy salad of chickpeas, cherry tomatoes, red onion, and feta cheese that Mom showed me how to make, set it in the fridge, and take the stairs up.

It's still light out, and the air is warm and breezy on the rooftop. I kick back in one of the lawn chairs, watching my father fiddle with the grill.

"Is this the first time you've used it this summer?"

He groans. "Don't remind me. Someone's gonna take my title of master griller if I keep this up."

"Master griller?" I giggle. "Okay."

He smiles. "How you been, Dovie? I miss you."

"I'm good. Glad I'm not still grounded."

"Me too, but I'll deny it if you ever tell your mother." He slides the steaks carefully onto the grill.

"Dad?" I sit up, folding my legs. "How long do you think Carlene will stay with us?"

He looks over at me, surprised. "I don't know. Do you not like her being here?"

"No, I love it. I was just wondering. It doesn't seem like Mom really wants her here."

He eyes the steaks, then walks closer to me. "Kitty and Carlene have a complicated relationship. They always have."

"Because of Carlene's drinking?" I'm not sure why I'm asking, as if I don't already know this. I guess I'm hoping my father will tell me a story, like Carlene did the other night.

He hesitates. "Because of a lot of things, Dovie. They're sisters."

"Mimi and I are sisters and we're not complicated." Well, not really. She didn't say anything else about Booker before she went back to Milwaukee, but I also knew she wouldn't like it if I brought him up.

"Everyone's different." He checks on the grill.

"Then how were things complicated for them? Did they fight all the time?"

Dad looks at me and sighs. "They're getting along pretty well now. Are you trying to jinx it?"

"Nobody ever tells me anything," I say. "You all still treat me like I'm a baby who can't handle the truth."

He sits down across from me, arms folded on the table as he leans forward. "Carlene lied. All the time. So much that Kitty and I knew not to believe a word that came out of her mouth. I saw and heard about some pretty bad fights between them"—he shudders, and I wonder if he's thinking of the baseball bat and broken glass—"but there's one night I'll never forget. It was just so sad."

"What happened?"

Dad points his chin at me. "Don't repeat this, please. I don't want to dredge up any old feelings."

I cross my heart and lock it with an imaginary key. Tuck it away in my pocket and wait.

"Carlene showed up needing a place to stay. We hadn't seen her in about a year. Mimi had just turned five, so you weren't even two yet. Your mom didn't want her around, but she never could tell Carlene no back then. Kitty would bite my head off if I even said the word *enable*." Dad sighs. "She told us she was sober, that she was going to meetings. Neither one of us believed her, but Kitty wanted to. She really wanted her to be doing the right thing. Carlene lied a lot, but she also manipulated your mother."

"*My* mother?" I can't imagine Mom letting anyone manipulate her into anything. She's the strongest-willed person I know.

"Well, that was the time Carlene talked Kitty into letting her come to the dinner party Kitty was having for her best friend's birthday. It was a small group, but almost all their friends worked at the shop she was at then, and her boss would be there, too. She was nervous about hosting and wanted everything to go right and—well, I told her not to let Carlene come, but she thought if she showed that she trusted her, Carlene would have the motivation to stay sober."

I cringe. "How bad was it?"

"Awful. She was forty-five minutes late, showed up completely drunk, and ended up spilling red wine on two of the guests. She also insulted your mother's boss and got a second-degree burn from the stove when she was trying to 'help,' so I had to spend the second course doctoring up her arm."

"That really happened? All in one night?"

"All within an hour," he says, getting up to poke at the grill again.

I stand up, too, needing to move around after that story. "I can't believe she's the same Carlene as the one I know."

"It was hard to watch," he says. "I've always liked Carlene, but she turned into a different person when she was drinking or using."

"Do you think addiction is a disease?" I ask. I realize there's no easy answer, but I want to hear what my father believes.

"Yes," he says after a pause. "I do, Dovie. I think it's a really cruel disease, because when your aunt was going through a relapse, it was hard for me to remember that. All I kept thinking about was how if it runs in families, why was she the only one causing problems?"

What if Mimi or I have the gene? When would we know? Does something cause it to happen, or is it lying there dormant, waiting to be kicked into action? Is that why Mom was so angry when she smelled alcohol on my breath—because she was worried I started a cycle I won't be able to stop?

I'm glad my father is looking down at the steaks and not at my face, where I'm sure all of my worries are written.

"Still," he goes on, "like I said, I don't want to jinx it. And Carlene seems to be doing real good this time. Better than she ever has."

I walk around the roof, trailing my fingers over the lights strung along the railing. "What was Mom like in high school?"

I already know the answer to this—I must have asked him dozens of times, usually in front of my mother—but I like hearing him talk about what she was like back then. Sometimes, when I look at everyone else's parents, I can't believe mine are still together. Nobody takes high school relationships seriously, but they've been in love since they were my age. Could I fall in love with someone like that? I look up at the sky and smile.

"Your mother was exactly the same person then as she is today. Serious. Driven. A little bossy, which means she gets things done." My father uses tongs to lift the edge of a steak. "The most beautiful woman I've ever seen. And one of the most generous."

"What about you?"

He shakes his head. "Me? I was a knucklehead, through and through. The stars must've been aligned the day I asked Kitty to go out."

I go down to get the salad and dishes while he flips the steaks one last time. The meat smells delicious, and I'm practically ravenous when Dad cuts into it.

"Hey, do you want to come to a game in a couple of weeks?" The master griller finally retires his tongs and takes a seat at the rooftop picnic table. "I'll be working, but I have a couple of extra tickets. Front row. You can bring a friend."

"Of course." Booker immediately comes to mind, but I don't know if I'd want to be on a date in front of my dad, no matter how cool he is. I'd have to figure out how to introduce Booker to my parents within the next couple of weeks without letting on that we've been seeing each other all this time—and hope that my mom didn't do her own research on his family before the game actually happens. "I'll ask Laz. He always loves a Bulls game."

"It's a plan, then," my father says.

I nod, wiping my mouth. "The steak is so, so good, Dad."

"Yeah? The master griller still got it!"

He pumps his fist in the air and I roll my eyes, but I can't help laughing, too.

Mom comes home just as we're done cleaning up the kitchen.

I wipe my hands on a dish towel and kiss her hello, then grab my phone. I heard it buzzing while I was stacking plates into the dishwasher. I stand in the doorway while Mom opens a bottle of wine and pours two glasses. I notice her look at the bottle for a moment before she slides it back on the counter, flush against the wall.

I pull up my texts.

> Thinking about you

> Couldn't wait to say g'night so ... hi

"Who're you talking to, Birdie?" My mom isn't asking in a nosy way, more like conversational. She must think it's Laz.

But it startles me so much that I don't even think to lie. "Booker."

"Oh?" She stops on her way to the living room, glass of wine in hand. She doesn't look upset, just confused. "Who's Booker?"

"He's, um, Laz's friend." I hesitate before I go on. "And he's my friend, too. I met him through Laz."

Dummy, of course you met him through Laz if he's Laz's

friend. She's totally going to know he's something more to me.

Maybe it's the long day or maybe it's just that my mother really doesn't think I would date someone without having her meet him first, but she doesn't seem to notice my nerves. Or the way I look when I think about Booker.

"And his name is *Booker*?" She takes a sip of wine and nods. "Interesting."

"He really likes basketball, so I'm going to ask him to go to a Bulls game with me. Since Laz gets to go all the time." I look over at my father so I won't lose my nerve. "Is that okay, Dad?"

"Yeah, sure," he says easily, turning off the light above the sink. He picks up his glass of wine and then he's next to my mother. "Any friend of Laz's is a friend of mine."

Mom smiles and they go into the living room, turning on the TV to the singing competition Dad pretends to hate but clearly keeps up with week to week. I lean against the doorframe and watch them curl up on the couch.

"Hard day?" my father asks, pressing his lips to the top of Mom's head.

"*Long* day." She sighs. "My feet are killing me."

Dad pats his lap and she swings her legs over for a foot rub. Gross.

Is it that easy, though? I just pretend like Booker is my friend and I'll get to hang out with him, no questions asked? It can't really be that easy—but if it weren't, my mother would still be standing here, asking me questions. And if this does work, how long will I be able to keep it up?

I have no idea if Booker likes basketball.

I swallow and look down at my phone. I start typing.

> Want to go to a Bulls game with me?

> Front row seats

"DO WE ALWAYS HAVE TO COME TO MONTROSE BEACH?" I GRUNT AT LAZ AS we lug our things across the sand.

"What's wrong with Montrose? We've been coming here forever," he says. "Too good for it now?"

"No, just lazy, now that our parents won't drive us." I stop. "How about here?"

Laz glances around to make sure we're not too close to anyone else, and far enough from the dog beach that he won't be tempted to stare with longing. His terrier mix, Peaches, died a couple of years ago, and he was devastated. Ayanna won't let him get another dog because she says she doesn't want to be stuck taking care of it when he goes to college.

"Fine with me," he says, and drops the cooler next to him.

We have been coming to Montrose Beach since we were kids, but this is the first time we've brought alcohol. Greg bought some booze with his fake ID and slipped Laz a bottle, so he made us drinks this morning. Vodka mixed with sparkling mineral water in his sports bottle, and vodka with cranberry juice in a plastic bottle for me. They give tickets if people are caught openly drinking on the beach, but Laz says we'll be fine and I decide to let myself have fun and believe him.

We spread out our towels and slather on sunblock, looking around. It's the middle of the afternoon on a Tuesday, so it's not as crowded as the weekend. But there are kids galore—building sandcastles, running circles around their parents, and screaming their heads off. Plenty of people are swimming and splashing in the lake, snapping pictures by the water, or sunbathing on the sand.

Chicago's winters are usually so long and horrific that we take whatever chance we can to get outside when the weather's decent. There's no way we'll get hit with a freak snowstorm now, like in the spring, and it's not unbearably hot and humid. Yet.

"I am so glad to be here and not stuck in a classroom studying statistics with Jared," I say, rubbing in a thick spot of sunblock on my ankle.

Laz takes a couple of long swallows from his bottle. "Who's Jared?"

"My SAT prep instructor. But did I tell you Mitchell is in my class?" I sip my vodka juice.

"And he hasn't bored you to death yet?"

"He actually..." I pause, not wanting Laz to make fun of me. But it will come out eventually, so I go on. "He seemed kind of cool for a minute."

Laz snorts. "Mitchell? Cool? You feeling okay, Dove?"

"I mean, not *cool* cool, but...cool for Mitchell. He's wearing T-shirts—"

"Not *T-shirts!*" Laz fake-gasps and leans away before I can flick his shoulder.

"That's a big deal for him. He smokes weed now, too, and we had, like, a couple of normal conversations."

"And?"

"And...I asked him why he never seemed attracted to me," I say.

Laz's mouth drops open. "You just straight up asked him that?"

"In different words, yeah."

"What'd he say?"

"Nothing." I sigh. "Except that it had nothing to do with me, whatever that means."

"Huh." Laz scratches the back of his neck. "Maybe he's gay."

"I don't think so," I say, even though that thought crossed my mind, too. "I don't know why, but I don't."

"Yeah, I don't get that vibe, either," he says. We are quiet for a while, then Laz lies back on the towel, his brown skin gleaming with sunscreen as he stares out at the water. "Remember that time the lifeguard had to come get me?"

"You mean *save* you? How could I forget?"

He folds his arms behind his head. "How old were we?"

"Nine."

We were fighting over whose turn it was to get buried in the sand when Laz got mad and said he was going in the water. We'd taken swimming lessons, but neither of us was good enough to go far without supervision. That didn't stop Laz from jumping right into the lake. He said he wanted to swim around the bird sanctuary to the harbor, where the boats were docked. Which was silly, because the harbor is only a short walk from the beach on the other side—but he was determined.

He was so confident when he started out that I thought he might actually do it. But then I watched him slow down, and suddenly it looked like he was barely holding himself up at all. I ran down the sand and screamed for Ayanna, who screamed for a lifeguard. A teenage girl with a long red ponytail rescued Laz. He looked sheepish as she paddled them in, but relieved when Ayanna squeezed him tight in her arms.

My stomach was twisted in knots the rest of the day. It was the first time I realized bad things could actually happen to us—the first time I understood Laz and I weren't utterly invincible.

"My mom yelled at me so much that night," he groans, sitting up to take another drink. "I was grounded from playing video games for two weeks."

I match him, taking bigger sips from my juice bottle. I think I'm starting to feel the vodka, which seems to be even stronger combined with the heat beating down from the sun. "It was kind of dumb. You could barely swim."

"Yeah, but if that hadn't happened, I might not have taken lessons again, and then I wouldn't be the bomb water polo player I am today." He shrugs. Pauses. "You know, that was right after my dad left."

"I remember."

Ayanna normally would have been watching us, but she was a shell of herself after Mr. Ramos left. She always looked empty; confused when one of us spoke to her. One night I overheard Mom telling my father that she'd asked Ayanna if she wanted to take a leave from the salon, but Ayanna said no, that she needed to keep her mind busy. She's not sad all the time now, but I don't know if she ever got back to her old self or if the new Ayanna became our normal.

Laz turns his head toward me. "I looked him up the other day."

"What did you find?" I ask, trailing my fingers through the warm sand.

"Nothing I didn't already know." He shrugs. "He's married to some guy named Javier. I think he's Cuban."

"Does your dad look the same?"

"Mostly. He's kind of got a stomach now." Laz takes a breath. "I know he did everything right. He was honest with my mom and divorced her, but...I don't know, Dove. It feels shitty to see that he's moved on so easily. Shouldn't he still be upset about leaving us? About leaving *me*?"

"Just because he's smiling in pictures doesn't mean he's not upset," I say. Then: "He called you every week for five years. You never called him back and—"

"*I know.*" He shakes his head. "Dove, sometimes you act like everyone's family should be as perfect as yours."

I scoop my legs up to my chest and rest my chin on my knees. My forehead is damp and I suddenly feel woozy, and I'm not sure if it's because of the vodka or the sun or what Laz is saying. "We're not perfect. You know that."

"Where is the lie?" Laz sits up, balancing on his elbows. "Even when your aunt comes back from rehab, it just works out. She's going to AA meetings, getting her hair license....It's like everything still wraps up with a bow, even when shitty things happen."

"Just because my mom wants to act like we're perfect

doesn't make it true." My voice is shaky and my heart is thumping hard, like there's something bubbling under the surface—something that makes me want to tell him to shut up, something I know isn't right. But I don't understand why.

"Well, it sure looks like it from over here." He gazes out at the water for a while, swigging so hard from his bottle that I don't even try to catch up this time.

MY FAMILY IS LOW-KEY WHEN IT COMES TO JULY FOURTH.

We don't go down to see the fireworks at Navy Pier or head to the beach like half the city. The salon closes for the day, and my father usually has minimal appointments. Carlene's school is closed, so after her AA meeting we grill out on the roof. One of Laz's water polo teammates is having a party, but I decide it's easier to just stay in. At least I know I'll see Booker at the Bulls game soon.

"We're heading out of town this weekend," Dad says as I crunch down on a potato chip. "Your mom and I."

I finish chewing. "To see Mimi? I want to go."

"No, this is a trip just for us," Mom says. "But we are going to Wisconsin. Your father's taking me on a nature retreat."

"A nature retreat?" I look at them both. "Did you book the wrong trip?"

Carlene squeezes mustard on her hot dog. "Will the woodland creatures sing and dress you in the morning?"

I snort.

"Very funny, you two." My mother purses her lips, but I think she's trying to hide a smile. "It'll be good for us to get out of the city. Have some quiet time together."

"I don't care how peaceful it is—I'm not meditating," Dad says before he bites into his burger.

"We'll be leaving on Friday after breakfast and come back on Sunday afternoon," Mom continues. "Birdie, I already checked with Ayanna and you can sleep over the whole weekend."

I frown. "Why do I have to stay at Laz's?"

"Because you're only sixteen and we're not comfortable with you staying by yourself. Don't you want to be with Laz?"

I glance at my aunt, who's staring down at her plate. "But if Carlene is going to be here, why can't I just stay at home?"

"It's not Carlene's responsibility to take care of you." Mom pauses, her eyes sweeping over the table before they land on me. "And you've stayed at Laz's before—what's the problem?"

"I want to stay here. In my own bed. Their pullout couch is lumpy, and Ayanna gets up early and makes so much noise." I take a deep breath. I want to present my case calmly. "Carlene wouldn't have to babysit me. If I hang out with anyone, it would be Laz."

"I don't mind," Carlene says easily, even though we've been talking about her like she's not here. "I just have to go to a couple of meetings. Otherwise, I'll be around."

My mother sighs. "But what if you're not?"

"I will be, Kitty."

The silence at the table is louder than the multitude of fireworks popping and sparking in the distance. I look at Dad who's looking at Mom who's staring at Carlene.

"Kitty," my father says softly, "Dovie is sixteen. She's not a baby. If something happens, she knows what to do."

"Nothing is going to happen, Ray," Carlene says through gritted teeth.

His voice is just as tight when he says, "I'm on your side."

And I am so grateful for my father in that moment. Three against one is so much easier than him teaming up with my mother.

"Come on, Mom," I plead. "I'm not that young. In a couple of years, I'll be living on my own. You can call me every hour if you want to make sure I'm okay."

"We won't have reception anyway," Mom mutters. She sighs again, then looks warily at Carlene. "You don't mind sticking around and looking after things?"

"I already said I didn't, Kitty. She's—Dove is my niece. I won't let you down."

Mom stares at her for a while and something passes between them. Something I can't identify, but it unsettles me all the same.

Still, my mother nods. "Fine. Birdie, you'll stay here. But I'm still going to have Ayanna check in on you a few times, just to make sure everything's okay. Carlene, I expect you to be here every night."

"You got it, warden." My aunt salutes her and digs into her hot dog.

My parents leave for their trip three days later, while I'm cleaning up the breakfast dishes. Carlene and I watch the car pull out of its spot around back and head toward the expressway.

She looks at me. "What time will Booker be here?"

As soon as my parents announced their trip, we decided I should invite him over. Strike while the iron is hot, Carlene said.

"I don't know. Six? Seven?"

"Want a new set of braids before he gets here?" she asks, eyeing my head.

I run my hand over my newly loose hair. I took down my goddess braids last night, but I liked them. A fresh set would be nice. I nod.

"So," she says slowly, "maybe I could do them down in the salon."

My eyebrows wrinkle. "Are you suddenly allowed to work in there now?"

"No, but what's the harm if she's not here?" Carlene looks at the clock on the microwave. "The shop doesn't open for another couple of hours. I can give you a good wash and get most of it done before then."

"But Ayanna won't be here for another hour and a half."

"Don't you know where your mother keeps the key?"

I do. And I'd never hear the end of it if she knew I used it to break into the shop. But maybe Carlene is right— what's the harm? We'll clean up the station when we're done, and a little shampoo and conditioner isn't going to break their budget. I wonder if my mother was right when I overheard her talking to my father—is Carlene rubbing off on me? I never would have done something like this a couple of months ago, but now...Well, it's easier to see that my whole world won't fall apart if I break a rule or two or three.

Still, the guilt vibrates in my fingertips as I turn the key in the lock. I close the door quickly behind my aunt and make sure the sign is still turned to CLOSED. Then I go straight back to the sinks and sit down, but Carlene takes her time walking through the shop, her eyes traveling over every bottle, hair tool, and chair leg. I hold my breath when she looks at the cash register, remembering her story about stealing from my mother. There's no money in there now, but even if there were, I know Carlene wouldn't do that. Not now. Except maybe I wouldn't be holding my breath if I were actually sure of that.

"I think we should get started," I say when she pauses by my mom's station, looking at the framed picture of me and Mimi propped on top. Before Mimi cut her hair short. "Ayanna isn't going to be happy about this."

Carlene sucks her teeth, holding the bundle of hair she brought down. "Do I look like I'm scared of Ayanna?"

But she does come over then. I lean my head back and close my eyes. She turns on the faucet, and the warm needles of water are so soothing I almost fall asleep as they soak into my hair. Then Carlene is shampooing my tight curls, massaging my scalp like I did Ms. Daugherty's, and I have to stop myself from sighing with happiness. I almost forgot how much I like someone else washing my hair. And Carlene is good—not so rough that her fingernails are scraping up my scalp, but not so soft that I'm worried she's not getting the job done.

I didn't turn on the music when we came in, and we

don't talk, so it is completely quiet as she washes. And I'm okay with that. We've developed a comfortable silence around each other that I've come to like. It never feels like we need to be saying anything just to fill the space.

She wanders around more as she lets my hair absorb the coconut conditioner for a few minutes. "You know, I always thought your mom and I would have a shop like this. We talked about it."

"You did?"

"The only thing I know how to do is hair, and she's good at it, too. It just made sense that we'd do something like this together."

I lift my head to look at her. "What happened?"

"Well, it's so much work to start a business. Kitty couldn't do it herself." Carlene pauses, takes a breath. "I guess I thought she might wait for me to get it together, but then she met Ayanna. . . ."

That was ten years ago. I lower my head back to the sink. I hate thinking of Carlene wasting all that time. I wonder what the salon would look like if she were co-owner. I guess my mom wouldn't know Ayanna, which means I wouldn't know Laz, which makes me think my life would look a whole lot different, too.

"It's probably for the best," Carlene says, walking back over to check on my hair. "Kitty has done good. She didn't need me."

But I remember that's what she said about not having kids, too—*It was for the best*—and I wonder if she actually believes that.

"You ever think about doing hair?" she asks, changing the subject.

"I can't. Not like you and Mom. Even Mimi is way better than me. She just doesn't like it."

Carlene pokes gently at my conditioner-soaked curls. "Well, good. You're probably going to be a doctor or lawyer or something. Can't have you wasting away at a salon."

"Civil engineer," I say, smiling. "Mimi's going to be a doctor."

"See? You're smart. You don't need to know how to do hair."

"Mom's one of the smartest people I know, and her whole life is hair," I say. "You're smart, too. Doing hair is a skill, right? Otherwise you wouldn't have to be in school to make sure you're good enough."

Carlene doesn't say anything, but she squeezes my shoulder before she picks up the sprayer to rinse my hair.

Ayanna walks in just as Carlene is picking up the blow dryer. She's early, even to open up the shop. She stops in the foyer with her coffee and sighs. "Carlene, what are you doing? You know Kitty would kill you if she walked in right now."

"Kitty is halfway to Wisconsin for her nature retreat," Carlene says, utterly unfazed. "The only way she'll know is if you tell her."

Ayanna sighs again and looks at me in the mirror. "You know better, too, Dove."

I shrug, staring back at her. "I'm just an unwitting hair model."

She shakes her head as she walks past us to the break room. "Don't forget to use cool air. Her hair can't handle all that heat."

Carlene purses her lips and takes a deep breath before she nods at Ayanna.

Ayanna finishes her coffee in the break room and grumbles her way around the salon as she gets it ready to open, but she lingers by our station to watch Carlene braid. My lips are pressed tight as I try to pretend like my scalp isn't on fire.

"Those look real nice," Ayanna says after a couple of minutes.

"Thank you." Carlene's fingers don't miss a beat.

"You did her last set, too?"

"Yeah, I don't want to be messing around at that school any longer than I have to, so I'm trying to get them perfect."

Ayanna leans in. "They look pretty damn close."

Carlene glances at her. "Want me to hook you up?"

"Oh." Ayanna runs her fingers through her thick straight hair. "I haven't worn braids in years. Probably not even this decade. Won't they look too young?"

"Come on, Ayanna. You fine as hell. You've always looked good with any style."

And I think I can count on one hand the number of times Ayanna has been visibly flustered, but I swear, her brown skin flushes a bit. Honestly, she looks like she's trying not to giggle. "Stop that."

"I'm serious," Carlene says. "Look, let me do them for you sometime, and if you don't like it we'll take them right out."

Ayanna cocks her head to the side. "Are you trying to bribe me so I won't tell Kitty you broke into our shop?"

"Maybe. Is it working?"

"Maybe." Ayanna clears her throat and looks at the clock over the front desk. "My first appointment is in ten minutes, and I don't want anyone telling Kitty you were working in here. Can you move this operation upstairs?"

We do, cleaning up the station and sneaking out back just as the bell above the front door jangles.

BOOKER BRINGS FLOWERS AND A SWEATING PINT OF FROZEN YOGURT, AND they are the best gifts anyone has ever given me.

"I got black cherry," he says as I greet him at the building door. "That's what you had when we went that time. And I know the flowers aren't fancy, but—"

I wrap my arms around his neck and my lips are on his before he can say another word. We text every single day, but I haven't seen him since the Pride parade, and *finally*, I get to kiss him. We're in the staircase that leads up from the building door, a long cubicle of privacy before we get to the front door of the apartment. He pulls away, smiles at me, and then kisses me again. I want to wrap my entire body around him, but we have to stop kissing at some point so he can go up and meet Carlene.

"New braids?" he says as we part.

"Do you like them?" I spent so much time trying to figure out what to wear—eventually deciding on my shortest, softest cutoffs and a gauzy white tank with embroidered detailing across the chest—that I almost forgot he'd be seeing my new braids, too.

Carlene wove in tiny, precise plaits among the thicker ones this time and my scalp is still screaming, but they look so good I keep going to the bathroom mirror to stare at them.

"Yeah. I do." He slides the end of a thick braid between his thumb and forefinger. "They're real dope."

"My aunt did them. Are you nervous to meet her?" I ask as we walk up the stairs together.

Booker laughs a little. "Should I be?"

"I don't think so. Carlene seems tough, but she's really kind of soft underneath."

My parents would be waiting in the living room like the receiving line at a wedding, but Carlene is still bumping around in the kitchen. She came home from her AA meeting with two paper bags of groceries and said she was going to cook for us. She ordered me to stay out of the kitchen and wouldn't tell me what she's making, but it started smelling good about twenty minutes ago.

"Booker's here," I call out, still unsure if I'm allowed in the kitchen.

I guess not because Carlene walks out, wiping her hands on a dish towel. She smiles up at him as she says, "So, this is the famous Booker. I'm curious, what are your intentions with my niece?"

Booker's forehead puckers. "Uhh...ma'am?"

"Carlene!"

"I'm kidding," she says with a laugh. "I just wanted to see how he'd react. Good manners. I'm Carlene."

Booker looks thoroughly unsettled, his eyes shifting from me to her before he says, "Nice to meet you. I brought these."

"Good flowers, too." She takes the bouquet he hands over. "Shasta daisies."

They are a gorgeous deep purple with a yellow center, and I think he brought them to butter up Carlene, but it still feels like a milestone, a guy bringing over flowers. Mitchell didn't have to suck up to my parents—his GPA did all the work for him.

Carlene takes the flowers and frozen yogurt to the kitchen and tells us we're not allowed in until dinner is ready.

I give Booker a tour of the apartment, even though it means walking him past the embarrassing line of childhood photos in the hallway. Mimi's cover one side with mine taking up the other.

Booker leans in to stare at them, grinning. "This is you?"

The photos are one of my mother's favorite projects, and she never misses a year, so there are framed pictures of me since I was a baby cascading down the wall.

"That's me." I tug his arm so we can move on, but he doesn't budge.

"You look exactly the same. Always been a cutie," he says, which makes me flush. "What happened to that gap in your teeth?"

"Braces. Come on," I say, pulling him along.

I keep my room pretty neat, but I'm glad I spent some extra time on it today because Booker looks at everything. He studies the old pictures of Laz and me, looks surprised and impressed at all my soccer trophies, and stops to examine my dresser top full of jewelry.

"Why don't you ever wear earrings?" he asks, staring at the line of necklaces and bracelets.

"What?"

He walks over and rubs his thumb and forefinger lightly over my earlobe. "Your ears are pierced, but you never wear earrings."

"Oh. My mom pierced them when I was a baby, but she only lets me wear studs, so I usually don't even bother." I shrug. "Studs are boring."

My parents' bedroom door is closed, but Carlene's is open and Booker sticks his head in. I check it out, too. I haven't been in here since Carlene first moved in, but it still looks mostly like Mimi's room. Carlene's few belongings—shoes, her backpack, and long bundles of hair for braiding—are stacked neatly on the floor and desk. It smells like Carlene now: a little bit like cigarettes but mostly like vanilla and jasmine.

Carlene announces dinner is ready and when we get to the dining room, she's already placed the serving dishes on the table, which she also set. She's done everything tonight, but she looks almost energized from the task. I wonder why she hasn't cooked for us before now.

"It's chicken and mushroom marsala," she says, instructing us to sit down as she serves. "I haven't made it in a while, but it used to be my specialty."

Booker nods approvingly at the heaping spoonfuls of chicken, roasted potatoes, and sautéed Swiss chard she loads on his plate.

"You look like you can eat," Carlene says, stopping only when his plate is bursting at the sides.

"Haven't turned down a meal yet. Thank you, Ms. Carlene."

She smiles at the formality but doesn't correct him. I take about half of what Booker has, and after Carlene serves herself, we all dig in. It looks and smells delicious, but I've never tasted Carlene's food and I'm nervous for her. I know she wants Booker to like it, but I think she might want to impress me, too.

"Hoo boy," Booker says after he finishes his first bite of chicken. "Dove didn't tell me you could cook like this."

Carlene squints at him, her fork paused in the air. "You trying to flatter me?"

"This is real good, Ms. Carlene. For real, I haven't had food like this since my mom died."

"Come on now."

He takes another bite, chews, and nods hard. "This tastes like home."

It *is* very good, and as I tell her so, I wonder why my mother has never mentioned Carlene can cook. I keep hearing about all the things she's done wrong, but no one wants to talk about what she's good at.

My aunt dips her head as if she's embarrassed, but she smiles a little after her first bite, like she's impressed herself, too.

Dinner is easy with Booker and my aunt. Her questions are light and fun, like she's just trying to get to know him—like he's any other guy I would bring home to meet my family. I hold my breath whenever the subject changes, but she doesn't say anything about his time in juvie, and of course he doesn't bring it up, either. He definitely scores more points when he asks for seconds.

"Anybody ready for dessert?" Carlene asks when we've finished eating. All the dishes and our plates are left with only scraps—there's not even enough for leftovers. "That frozen yogurt might be calling my name."

"See!" I say, lightly swatting Booker's arm. "People *like* frozen yogurt."

"That must run in y'all's family," he teases. Then he groans, leaning back as he rubs his stomach. "I'm too full."

"Me too," I say.

We all take our dishes to the sink, even Booker, who refuses to be treated like a guest. Carlene won't let us help her clean up, though.

"Go hang out," she says. "I got this."

"What's that door?" Booker points across the room.

I look over. "That goes up to the rooftop deck."

He shakes his head in disbelief. "You have a *rooftop deck?*"

"Let's go up," I say, crossing the room to open the door.

Carlene says my name as I turn on the light in the staircase. I turn around.

"Can I talk to you for a minute?"

She doesn't sound upset, but it makes me anxious anyway, that she wants to talk to me without Booker. "Sure," I say, then turn to him. "It's just right up there. I'll be up in a minute."

He takes the steps two at a time, then I hear him say

"God*damn*" when he opens the door at the top and steps outside to the stars.

I look at Carlene as the upper door bumps closed. "What's up?"

She picks up a green potholder from the counter and begins fiddling with it. "Look, I know you're going to do what you want to do anyway, right?"

I frown. "What?"

"You're sixteen, and if you're not hooking up here, you're going to hook up somewhere else." She sighs. "So you might as well do it in the safety of your own home."

"Are you telling me to have sex tonight?" My skin burns, saying the words aloud.

"I saw the way you two were looking at each other," she says, waving the potholder at me. "I'm just saying, if the inevitable is going to happen anyway, he might as well spend the night."

"I'm not hooking up anywhere. We…we haven't had sex yet."

"But you're going to…?"

"I don't know. Maybe. We came close once, but I wasn't ready then."

She squints at me. "Wait. Are you a virgin?"

"Yes. Mitchell and I never had sex. Even after a year and a half. But I want to with Booker, so…" My eyes slide away from her. I didn't think it would be tonight—I didn't know *when* it would be, just that it would probably happen. But now that I have the green light, it feels possible. It feels like we have to take advantage of getting to spend an uninterrupted, approved evening together. I don't know when the next one will be—or if there will be another one at all.

"Are you on the pill?" Carlene asks.

I shake my head. My mother has never even mentioned it; we had the sex talk back in fifth grade, but she never talked about the future, as if she was positive I'd never be having sex while I was still under her roof. And then, when I was older, it's like she knew Mitchell and I would never go that far, even though she seemed to have our whole romantic future planned from the second we met.

Carlene clears her throat and it sounds too loud in the quiet kitchen. "I can take you next week," she says. "To get a prescription...if you want."

"Oh."

"I'm not encouraging you to have sex," she says. "But I know how Kitty can be about these things, and I'm trying to be realistic. Before you have to have another conversation—a harder one."

"She'll know if we go to my doctor," I say. "They'll send a bill."

"Then we'll go to Planned Parenthood. Even better."

She pauses. "If you do end up sleeping with him tonight, promise you'll use protection."

"I promise." I hope Booker has something with him. If we decide that's what we want to do.

"Good girl. Now go on up there and keep that boy company. You want some tea?"

"Maybe later." I put my hand on the doorknob but turn to Carlene before I head up. "You like him? Even knowing what happened with him and his coach?"

"I like him a lot," she says. "Just about everyone I roll with has a past, Dove. So do I. I can't judge people based on their mistakes. Not when they can see how they've hurt people and are trying to grow. He's trying to grow, right?"

I nod. "He's in therapy and he had to take anger management classes."

"Then that's the best anyone can do."

Carlene's words follow me up to the roof.

Booker is standing by the railing, illuminated by the string of white lights woven through the slats. He looks over his shoulder when he hears the door shut behind me. "Man, I can't believe you get to live here. Look at this," he says, gesturing to the night sky, the moon, the glittering lights of the sky-high buildings in the distance.

I smile as I come up behind him and wrap my arms around his middle. "We can stay up here as long as you want. And…can you tell your dad you're spending the night at Laz's?"

He turns to look at me, his mouth quirking up in a soft smile. "We gonna have another sleepover?"

"Yes. If you want." I gaze down at my feet shyly, but Booker cups my face in his big warm hands, gently forcing me to look up.

His lips brush against both my cheeks, then my mouth.

"Yes," he murmurs before he kisses me again. "I want."

21

BOOKER LOOKS TOO BIG FOR MY BEDROOM.

Or maybe it's just that there's a boy in here—a boy that
I want to kiss—when my parents aren't home. It still feels
a bit like this might blow up in my face, like Mom and
Dad will return tonight with no warning and ground me
for the rest of my life. Or that Ayanna will drop by unex-
pectedly and call my parents and, when they get back, I'll
be grounded for the rest of my life. But the apartment
is quiet, other than the sound of the TV from the living
room, where Carlene is eating frozen yogurt and watching a movie.

And here, right now, it's just Booker and me.

"You sure it's okay if I stay over?" He looks at me as he
leans against my dresser, hands stuffed in his pockets.

The only light is from my bedside lamp; it sends long shadows stretching across the room.

I'm sitting on the edge of my bed with my palms pressed to my knees. "Carlene won't change her mind."

Booker bites his lip as he looks at me. "No, I mean… is it okay with you?"

"Yes, of course…"

…but I'm nervous. Not just that my parents will come back early, but that I'm finally ready to have sex. Maybe that would have happened with Mitchell, too. I'll never know. It scares me that what I want is so clear, because I know it's something my mother wouldn't approve of. But I'm doing what I want and I'm not second-guessing it, and that feels huge. Still, I wonder if this is normal, how we seem to be on the same page less and less, or if there's something about this summer that's speeding along the separation.

"But?" Booker says.

"No *but*. I want you to stay." I pat the bed.

The mattress sinks under his weight, and for a few moments we are so quiet I can hear him breathing.

"Booker?" I take a deep breath. "How many girls have you been with?"

"Two," he replies without hesitating. "Tasha was my first everything."

"Your first girlfriend?"

He nods.

"Why'd you break up?"

"She moved. Only to Evanston, but she had a new school and new friends, and then we just stopped making time for each other."

"Do you miss her?"

Booker shrugs. "I don't think about her a lot, I guess. Not anymore. I don't really want to be friends with my exes. Too much drama."

"Who was number two?" I don't know why I'm asking this. I don't want to think about Booker with other girls, but it's hitting me that there's still so much we don't know about each other. Shouldn't you know more about someone you decide to sleep with? Especially the first person?

"A girl named Cicely." He looks down at his hands, like he's embarrassed. "She's a couple years older than me. A friend of the family. She was around a lot right after my mom died, so..."

"Right," I say. Tasha and Cicely. I don't know anything about them, but I feel like they couldn't have liked Booker as much as I do.

"What about you?" he asks.

"Nobody. I'm a virgin."

"Weren't you with that guy for a while?" Booker sounds especially curious, and I guess he's realizing there are still lots of things he doesn't know about me, too.

"Mitchell? Yeah, but we didn't sleep together. We barely did anything." I pick at a stitch on my summer quilt. "He's in my SAT class, which is kind of strange. It was definitely the right decision to break up."

"He's in your class?"

I nod.

"This whole time?"

"Yeah, I couldn't believe it when he showed up the first day. Pretty much the last person I wanted to see." But my heart thumps heavy. I guess it noticed how Booker's voice changed, too.

"Oh."

I put my hand on his. "What's wrong?"

"It's just kind of weird that you didn't bring it up." He sounds...not angry, but definitely unhappy. Annoyed. "You get to see him more than you see me."

"I'm not *seeing* him. We're just sitting in the same room. I mean, we went to lunch once, but trust me, there's nothing there. He's still so condescending."

"Sounds like a great guy," Booker says, but I don't like the sarcasm.

"Are you mad about this?" I pull my hand back. "I didn't choose to be in that class with him. And it doesn't matter that he's there, because I don't like him. I like *you*. I'm here with *you*, Booker."

He lets out a long, loud breath. Touches my hand and

then takes it in his. "I know. I'm sorry. My counselor says I get—because of juvie and my mom dying and my dad moving us out of the place without telling me, I guess I have abandonment issues or something. I never think anyone or anything good is gonna stick around. Like you."

"I like you so much, Booker," I say, staring into his eyes so he won't doubt what I'm saying. "There's no one else, okay? I wouldn't do that to you."

He nods, warmth radiating from his gaze. "Okay. And…I'm really sorry. I don't want to be that guy who's bringing his own shit into things and making it weird."

"Thanks," I say.

He slides his thumb around and around my palm. "You know, the day after he met you, my dad left a box of condoms in my room."

"Oh my god." I'm embarrassed for him—even more than when I was talking to Carlene about the pill. Which wasn't all that embarrassing, actually.

"Yeah. An enormous box," he says, making the shape with his hands. "He didn't say anything about it, so I didn't, either."

I look at him. I'm weirded out by how honest we're being, but I guess it's a good kind of weird. "My aunt wants me to get on the pill…if we're going to do this. Be doing this."

"Are you going to?"

"I think so. My mom would murder all of us if she found out."

Booker frowns. "Doesn't she want you to be safe?"

"Yeah, but to her, the safest thing is not having sex at all."

Booker clears his throat. "I know we might not get to be together once your parents find out everything about me. But I like you so much, too. I really want you to be my girl, Dove. It already feels like you are, but I never asked and...would you? Be my girl?"

"I'm yours," I say almost before he is done asking. I know that what I'm feeling for him is new, but it's so real it makes me think my chest is going to crack open. I thought someone would've been able to explain this feeling to me by now, but it is so specific and so vague all at once, there is no way to truly capture it in words. All I know is I am blissfully happy when I look in his eyes, and I want everyone to know it—especially him.

He reaches behind me to turn off the lamp on my nightstand, and the immediate darkness startles and then calms me. We take our time with each other, letting our eyes adjust as we slowly touch.

Booker's hands slip under my tank top, gently squeezing the small of my back and then sliding up my torso and over my breasts before he pulls the top over my head. I peel off his shirt and undershirt as one, then lean in to kiss him. And then we get into a rhythm, trading kisses for a discarded pair of shorts here, unbuttoned jeans there.

When we are down to our underwear, we hear Carlene's footsteps coming down the hall and freeze. Maybe I was wrong and she did change her mind and is coming to stop us before we go through with this. But then the bathroom fan turns on and the door closes and Booker and I breathe a dual sigh of relief.

I look at him curiously as he hops down from the bed to rummage in the pocket of his jeans. He fiddles with his phone for a few seconds and by the time Carlene is out of the bathroom, Booker has queued up a playlist. Jazz, which I wasn't expecting but don't mind.

It loosens me up. I feel less self-conscious with the music playing, and I don't think too much about what we are doing, just that it feels good. Booker takes his time getting to know my body, and I let him. I tremble at the newness of his fingers between my legs and sigh with pleasure when he leaves them there.

His body feels new to me, too. I haven't seen him totally naked until now, and I am shy and also more than ready to touch him. He groans softly as I hold him in my hand and buries his face in my neck as my fingers glide up and down.

Eventually, when Booker has kissed me everywhere and my heart is beating double time, he asks if he should get a condom. I nod and lie back on the bed, watching him move around the room, utterly at ease. He rips the package open, slides on the condom, and climbs back into bed, hovering above me, his eyes shining even in the dark.

"You are..." he begins and then stops, his fingers brushing my forehead.

"What?" I ask, my heart pulsing even faster, my breath quicker.

"Beautiful. Amazing," he whispers before he kisses me again.

Sex isn't very comfortable. At least my first time isn't— even though Booker is slow and careful: in the way he touches me and, once he's inside me, the way he moves.

This is the closest I've ever been to another person, and I wouldn't want it to be anyone but Booker. He takes off the condom and wraps it in several tissues when we are done. The space next to me is cold when he gets up, and I miss him until he is back again. He spoons me from behind with his warm body, brushing my braids aside to softly kiss my neck.

"Was that okay? Are you okay?" he asks, his lips against my skin.

"Yes and yes," I whisper back, snuggling into him.

"Man, I hope your folks like me." Booker slides his palm lightly across my stomach. "I'm falling for you, Dove. You're..."

Like before, he pauses, but this time I wait for him to finish without prompting. The music is still playing, my room filled with the sweet, longing wail of a saxophone.

"You're my perfect day," he murmurs, holding me tighter.

∼ℓ

I doze off in Booker's arms but wake about an hour later. I have to pee.

I slowly slide away, trying not to wake him, and open the door, listening to see if Carlene is still up. The TV is off, but light spills from the kitchen doorway and after a few seconds, I hear voices. I slip down the hallway, stepping over the squeaky patch of hardwood.

"Glad you called, Carl."

Emmett is here.

There's the sound of a glass or mug plunking down on the table, but Carlene doesn't respond before he speaks again.

"You don't sound good. Don't look so good, either."

"Don't worry about me," Carlene says after a pause. "I'm not gonna do anything stupid. Do I want a drink? Yes. But god, Kitty would be so smug if I fucked up. Just like she thinks I will. I know it's not about her. Not really. But I can't give her that satisfaction. And if that helps me stay away from the bottle..."

I lean against the wall of Mimi's pictures, staring at

photos of my own face across the way. I know I shouldn't be eavesdropping, but I want to know what has Carlene so upset—what made her call Emmett over at midnight.

"So what's wrong? What happened?" Emmett sounds genuinely concerned, and I am dying to see my aunt's face, to see what has him so worried.

"It's almost like it's too good to be true. I'm here, getting to spend all this time with her, and she's wonderful. Just such a great person, you know? But it can't last forever. This situation."

Wait—who is *she*? Does Carlene have a girlfriend she hasn't told me about? Even after she's kept my secret about Booker and met him?

Her voice is faint, but she presses on. "And the closer we get, the more Kitty seems to resent it. Like she thinks I'm going to take her away."

A coolness passes through my body, but it's not a breeze coming through the hallway. Carlene isn't talking about someone she's dating. She's not talking about a friend, either.

"You need to tell her, Carl," Emmett says, his voice hoarser than normal. I can picture him sitting at our kitchen table, shoulders hunched low as he speaks. "How would you feel if someone was keeping something like that from you?"

Carlene takes a while to answer. So long that I realize

I'm holding my breath as I wait for her to speak. Then she finally says, "I can't. It's part of the deal, Emmett."

I'm here, getting to spend all this time with her...

...Kitty seems to resent it. Like she thinks I'm going to take her away.

I stare at the pictures across the hall, at my seven-year-old gap-toothed smile.

And I don't know what's going on, but I am pretty sure the *she* and *her* Carlene is talking about is me.

WHEN I GET HOME FROM MY NEXT SAT CLASS, MOM IS IN THE KITCHEN, making lunch.

"Want some, Birdie?" she asks over her shoulder. "It's just the leftover pasta salad from last night, and I roasted some asparagus."

"Yes, please," I say. "I'll set the table."

"This is nice," Mom says when we're sitting down a few minutes later. "We don't get to eat lunch together very often."

I swallow a bite of pasta. "When did you even start taking real lunches?"

"Touché." She smiles. "I'm trying to remind myself to slow down a little. The shop is doing well, and you're growing up so fast. I don't want to regret being at work too much and not spending enough time with you and your father."

"What about Carlene?" I say tentatively.

"Carlene?"

"Don't you like spending more time with her, too?" I hope it's not obvious that I'm digging for information, but I'm still trying to figure out what Carlene was talking to Emmett about the other night.

"Well, sure." Mom sips from her water glass. "But you're my baby."

"Mom." I just barely stop myself from rolling my eyes.

"It's true, Birdie. Deal with it," she says, smiling.

"What's your favorite memory of Carlene?"

Her smile wavers. "What do you mean?"

"I keep hearing how she's done crazy or bad things, but I want to know what you like about her. What's a good memory of you and her?"

"Oh, Birdie." Mom shakes her head, smile gone. "I can't think up something like that on the spot. She's been around my whole life, more or less. The memories all start to blend together."

If that's what happens when you get older, I never want to have another birthday. I can't remember anything about being a baby, but I would be sad if I'd forgotten all the great times I've had with Mimi or Laz.

"Really? You can't think of *one* good memory?" I bet she'd be able to tell a dozen bad stories if I asked for them.

Mom chews a couple more bites of salad and starts to cut a spear of asparagus, then sighs and sets down her fork. "When I was twelve, I was in the school talent show, and I was so nervous. I had just learned to play the piano the year before, and it was the first time I'd be playing in front of people who weren't my instructor or other people's parents. I'd only just had my first recital, but your grandma insisted that I enter the show. I was so shy and tried to fight her on it, but she wouldn't let me back out. She said she wanted to get her money's worth out of those lessons."

"I didn't know you played the piano! Do you still remember how?"

"Oh, I'm sure I'd be terrible. I haven't played in years," she says, waving a hand in the air. "Anyway, I practiced and practiced and finally felt pretty good about it, even though Carlene would cover her ears like she was dying from noise pollution every time she was home. She teased me so much about piano, and it only got worse when she found out I'd be in the talent show. So, the night of the show came and it turns out our mother couldn't get off work to come see me."

I'm leaning forward on my elbows, riveted. My mother rarely talks about anything in the past, so I am truly fascinated.

"I was so upset," Mom says. "Everyone else's parents were going to be there except for mine. And we were one of the few black families at the school, so it looked even worse. There was always that group of white kids who loved making jokes about absent black fathers, and my mother not being there, too, just gave them more fodder. But there was nothing I could do about it, so when they called my name, I went up. And I wasn't going to look into the audience because the last thing I wanted was to be reminded that there wasn't a friendly face from my family. But then someone kept whispering my name loudly from the front row, and finally I couldn't ignore it anymore. I looked down from the stage and there was Carlene, sitting between two families."

"She showed up for you?"

"A total surprise. She didn't even put her hands over her ears." Mom smiles. "And she clapped the loudest. Gave me a standing ovation and cheered until the principal made her stop."

"That was sweet of her," I say, smiling back.

"It was. She...Carlene *is* a sweet person. I haven't

forgotten that. But her substance abuse has caused real issues with us and made her do some really hurtful things. And it's hard to forget that, too." Mom looks at me. "I'm glad you like her, Birdie. I know it means a lot to Carlene."

Mimi video calls a few minutes after Mom goes back down to the shop.

The place is empty, but I run up to the roof anyway. My sister is walking on a pathway along the Milwaukee River, the water moving in a sparkling strip behind her.

"Hey, Dovie. Finally, I caught you. How's it going?"

"I have news," I say, practically before she gets out the last sentence. We've been playing phone tag ever since Booker stayed over, and this was too big to text her. I feel like I'm going to burst from holding it in.

Mimi rolls her eyes. "Please don't tell me you're grounded again."

"Would I be smiling like this if I were grounded?"

"Fair enough. What's up?"

"I'm, um, a woman now." It sounds so corny I can't help giggling as I settle into one of the rooftop chairs.

"What? You had sex?"

I nod, still grinning. And I'm afraid to look at Mimi because she knows who it was with, and I already know how she feels about him.

She stops walking and sits down, too, on a bench

facing the water. All I can see behind her now is the concrete edge of a building.

"Oh, Dovie."

"Don't make me feel bad about this. I like him so much, Meems. More than I've ever liked anyone."

My sister smiles softly at me. "You really do, don't you?"

"I really do."

"Then I'm happy for you, Dovie. You deserve someone who makes you happy." She clears her throat. "Are you on birth control?"

"Not yet, *Mom*."

"I'm your big sister—I have to ask. But you were safe, right?"

"Yes." The sun is beating down hot on the roof, but I don't want to bother with putting up the umbrella. "And Carlene is taking me to get on the pill this week."

"Does Mom know about this?" But Mimi laughs before I can answer. "Of course she doesn't. I think the only part she liked about my coming out was that she didn't have to worry about me getting pregnant. She sure didn't know how to give me *that* sex talk."

"Well, she hasn't talked to me about it, either. Not since elementary school."

"I don't know what she's going to do when you're out of the house and she has no one else to boss around."

"There's always Dad."

Mimi laughs again, her teeth bright in the summer sun.

"Meems, do you ... know anything about our family?"

Her smile fades a bit. "What do you mean?"

"Like, something I don't know but should. Something Carlene and Mom know about. Do you know it, too?"

"Dovie, you're talking in riddles."

I don't know how much I should tell her. I haven't stopped thinking about what I overheard Carlene say, but I'm also starting to wonder if I imagined it. It was late. I was blissed out from being with Booker, and I had just woken up. Maybe I didn't hear what I thought I did.

"What are you talking about?" she says when I don't respond.

I could ask Carlene. She's been honest with me since she got here. She probably wouldn't lie. But what if she does? What if she gets mad at me for listening in on her and Emmett? Or what if she pretends that she never said my mother acts like she's afraid Carlene is going to take me away? It's so bizarre I must have imagined it. Why would Carlene take me away from my mother?

"Never mind," I say.

"Dovie—"

"It's nothing. Really."

Mimi nods and starts talking about a coffee shop in

her new neighborhood that will be great for studying at when school starts back up.

Maybe I was too tired to remember exactly what Carlene and Emmett said the other night. But I don't think I imagined the relief that passed through my sister's eyes when I dropped the subject.

"I'M GLAD YOU LIKE BASKETBALL." I LOOK UP AT BOOKER.

"Are you kidding? I could hate it and I still wouldn't pass up the chance to sit front row at a Bulls game. Or next to you."

He smiles down at me, and it takes every ounce of self-control not to stand on my tiptoes and kiss him. I'm pretty sure I see the same look in his eyes, and I think about abandoning all the rules I gave him tonight (no unnecessary touching, no looking at each other too long or a certain way, and definitely no kissing) and going for it. We are standing outside United Center, sucked into a sea of fans wearing red and black and white. No one would give us a second look.

But we're waiting for my father, and he's supposed

to meet us in exactly this spot, and I really don't feel like taking my chances. Not when everything is finally good again with my mother.

"But are you a *Bulls* fan?" I ask Booker.

"Yeah, but only 'cause of my old man. He basically worships that dude," he says, nodding toward the bronze statue of Michael Jordan. Tons of people are gathered around the base of the fence that surrounds it, cheesing and throwing up peace signs in selfies and imitating his slam-dunk pose. "He was living here during all those championships. Said the city was fucking crazy."

"My dad, too. Honestly, I think Jordan is part of the reason he went into sports medicine." And then I see him, my father. He's walking fast with his medical bag in hand, looking for me. I wave my arms until he sees me and nods, heading right toward us. "No cursing around him, either," I mumble to Booker.

"What do you think I am? Some kind of animal?" he murmurs back good-naturedly.

"Hey, Dovie, sorry I'm late," Dad says, giving me a quick hug and kiss on the cheek. "Got held up at the office."

"It's okay. Dad, this is my friend Booker. Booker, this is my dad."

My father looks up at him with a friendly smile and pumps his hand heartily. "Good to meet you, Booker. Heard you're friends with my main man Laz."

"Main man? Oh my god, Dad," I say, putting my hand over my face.

But Booker takes his utter dad-ness in stride and gives him a big grin and handshake back. "Good to meet you, too, Mr. Randolph."

"Please, call me Ray," Dad says, shaking his head. " 'Mr. Randolph' makes me feel old."

"You *are* old," I say, and he squeezes me to him in a tighter hug, laughing.

On the way in, Dad quizzes Booker in just the right way. Not too many personal questions, so Booker doesn't have to navigate around talking about his mom or juvie. Dad doesn't dwell on school too long, and he asks him about sports, but when Booker says he had to quit playing football, Dad moves right along to the next thing. I never really noticed how affable my father is. He's good with people in general, and I've never seen him with patients, but he must be good with them, too.

Our section of seats is crowded with silver-haired dudes. *Suits*, Laz would call them. Even though they're not actually wearing suits, it's obvious that they normally do. All of them are wearing belted jeans with tucked-in shirts and all of them are on their phones. They barely glance up when we sit down.

"You're good? Need anything?" Dad asks once we're settled.

"We're good," I say.

"Order whatever you want when the waiter comes around." Dad presses his credit card into my palm. "I'll be down on the court if you need anything, but... please don't need anything."

"This is real dope, Mr.—Ray," Booker says. "Appreciate it."

"Good to have you here, Booker. Enjoy the game," my father says before he jogs the few feet down to the court.

"Damn." Booker sits up in his seat to look around the arena, from the players warming up on the court to the people sitting up in seats so high they look like pins. "I can't believe how close we are. I can't believe how chill your dad is."

"Only because he thinks you're my friend," I say, looking pointedly at his hand brushing my knee. "If he thought we were on a date, he would not be so chill."

"You think he really believes there's nothing going on between us?" Booker looks at me, head cocked to the side in amusement.

"He's my *dad*." I watch my father shake hands with some people down on the court and bump fists with a couple of the players. "I don't think he notices stuff like that. Besides, I told him you were a friend."

"Yeah, and Laz told me Greg was just his friend and

I could see that lie from miles away. Some stuff is just obvious."

"Well, I hope it's not obvious because I want to keep seeing you and—"

"And they're going to hate me if they really get to know me?"

"That's not what I meant," I say softly.

"I know." He glances at the court to make sure my dad isn't looking and quickly threads his fingers through mine. "I guess I just don't want to pretend to be your friend when we know it's more than that."

My arms break out in goose bumps. The good kind. But even if he did manage to win over my parents, I remember: "Your dad doesn't like me."

"He was in a mood," Booker says, sighing. "That had everything to do with me and nothing to do with you."

He's already apologized for his father interrogating me and lecturing me on babies, but I'm not mad. Just embarrassed. It was mortifying, sitting next to Mr. Stratton with my peeling rainbow tattoo and crumpled tank top that he found in the living room, trying to convince him I'm not the type of girl he needs to worry about.

"Are you sure?"

"My old man's about eighty percent bark. He was caught off guard. He'll come around."

"Does he know you're with me tonight?" I realize we're still holding hands and quickly drop my fingers from Booker's, looking guiltily toward the court. My father is talking to a player who towers over him in his warm-ups, not even looking our way.

"Uh, no. Like I said, he'll come around." Booker leans back in his seat, staring at the court. "He'd probably be happy I'm watching basketball. Do you know that dude stomps around and makes so much noise every time I put on a football game, I can't even watch it at home anymore?"

"He made you stop playing *and* you can't watch it?" Wow. I thought my mom was bad for making me quit soccer, but she doesn't mind if I watch or go to games.

"He thinks football is evil. He keeps reading up on that CTE thing and swears everyone who's ever played is gonna end up with severe brain damage." Booker rolls his eyes. "That's, like, NFL-level shit. I haven't even played since seventh grade."

All this time, I thought I was the one who had to follow the most rules, but it turns out Booker's dad is pretty strict himself. More than my mom, it sounds like. Still, I think about what Mitchell said, how Booker's dad's decision was probably the right choice.

"Sometimes I wish—" Booker starts, but then closes his mouth and looks down at his lap.

"What?" I ask, afraid he won't go on.

He swallows and looks around before his eyes land on mine. "Sometimes I wish I could get my own place and stop having to listen to his lectures and just do my own thing, you know? But then... then I remember he's the only person I got now. And I feel bad."

A shrill whistle sounds on the court, punctuating his sentence.

"I know what you mean," I say. I think about that sometimes when I'm mad at my family and wish I could start over with a new one. How I have only one sister, one father, one mother, and they can't be replaced. And at least I still have both of my parents. "Don't feel bad. Sometimes I think parents exist just to drive us crazy ninety-eight percent of the time."

"Word."

"And I know it's not the same, but... you have me." I keep my hands squeezed together in my lap even though all I want to do is touch his face, his lips, his strong broad shoulders that don't look so strong right now. "I'm not going anywhere."

"What if we can't figure this out, Dove?" Anyone looking at him would think he's gesturing to the court, but I know he means us. Our relationship that can't actually be a relationship.

"We will," I say with more urgency than I've felt in a long time.

After the game we stick around and wait for Dad to finish up on the court. The Bulls lost to the Rockets, so all that red and black and white is trudging out of the arena with a lot less fanfare than when it arrived. The suits around us are standing up now, arms crossed as they talk to each other in low voices.

"What'd you think of your first NBA game?" I ask, turning to Booker. I'm sleepy and, without thinking, I rest my head on his shoulder.

He must not be thinking, either, because he puts his arm around me and pulls me closer. "Would've been better if they won, but watching them lose in person is still better than watching it on TV."

"Want to see if you can meet any of the players?" And then I remember my dad and sit straight up, shrugging off Booker's arm.

He looks hurt for a moment until I nod toward the court. Dad is facing us, but he's bent over, fiddling with his medical bag.

"Right," Booker mumbles. Then he says, "Nah, I'm not too into meeting my heroes. Especially on a night when they lost."

"Good point."

Dad makes his way up to us a couple of minutes later and I stand, stretching. He offers Booker a ride home, even though it's out of the way. Booker politely declines and says it will be easier to take the bus, and after a couple more offers, my father says okay. We all walk out together, me between the two of them. They should be standing next to each other, though, because they talk the whole time—about the game and the Bulls' scoring this season and the legacy of Jordan.

When we have to part ways outside, I wish that I could make my father disappear, just for a minute or two. I want to kiss Booker goodbye so badly. The few touches we snuck in over the evening weren't enough for me. I want to feel him against me; *need* to feel his warm lips against mine.

But that's not going to happen. My father is very much standing here and is very much ready to go. When I look at Booker, I see my want mirrored in his eyes, which makes the whole thing even more frustrating.

"Thanks again for the ticket, Ray," Booker says. "I don't know how I'll repay you, but I really appreciate it."

"No need to repay me," Dad says with a tired smile. "Thanks for coming. Get home safe."

"See you around, Dove." Booker gives me a quick pat on the shoulder, followed by a smile. Then he sticks his hands in his pockets and takes off toward the bus stop.

I don't realize I'm still watching him walk away until my father clears his throat. I look over at him. "Ready to go?"

"Yes. And I'm wondering how long you two have been seeing each other," he says in an even voice.

My heart plummets to my knees. "What?"

"Dove, I'm your dad, but I'm not blind. I saw the way you two were looking at each other from the minute I got here." He sighs. "You know your mother isn't going to like this."

"What, that I found a guy I like?"

"No, that you tried to pass him off as a friend. I don't like it much, either," he says, his lips tight. "Why wouldn't you just tell us? All we ask is that you introduce us to someone you want to spend time with."

"I don't know," I say in a small voice. "Maybe I just wanted him to myself for a little bit. He's different from Mitchell."

"What do you mean?"

"He just... They're different in a lot of ways. And I thought you and Mom might not like that since you were so into Mitchell."

Dad blinks at me. "We know every guy you date isn't going to be just like Mitchell. And I like Booker. He seems like a nice kid. But if you want to date him, you have to follow our rules and let us get to know him, too."

"Okay," I say, eyes glued to my shoes.

"I won't say anything about this to your mother, but you're going to have to tell her about Booker if you want to keep seeing him. And no more sneaking around and lying to us, Dovie. Understood?"

His tone isn't mean, just firm. But it's still more than I usually get from my father, and I feel bad for upsetting him. Even if I don't exactly feel bad for what I did.

I look up at him and nod, even as my heavy heart keeps sinking, all the way to my toes. "Understood."

THE NEXT DAY, CARLENE AND I GET OFF THE BLUE LINE AT DIVISION AND walk the short distance to the clinic on Milwaukee Avenue.

I'm anxious, even though I have no real reason to be. I always get nervous before I go to doctors—always afraid they're going to tell me something I don't want to hear. Carlene looks at me, her hand poised to open the door.

"You okay, kid?"

I nod, not quite looking her in the eye. We were quiet on the train; the Blue Line is above ground for the stretch we rode, so I stared out the window the whole time and Carlene seemed fine with that. I've felt strange being around her since what I overheard last weekend, and I'm not quite sure how to deal with it. I can't just ask her what she meant...can I?

"Hey." She taps my shoulder so I have to look at her. "You've been pretty quiet the last few days. Everything okay?"

"Mhmm."

Carlene frowns. "Things all right with Booker?"

"It's great," I say.

I'm supposed to see him again tomorrow. We only had to wait a couple of days this time. Someone from Laz's school is having people over, so I pulled the movie lie again. I won't drink this time, but I have a right to be around people.

I think this is the last time I'm going to lie about who I'm with, though. Now that Carlene and my dad have both met Booker and liked him, the only person left is my mother. And after the night Booker and I spent together, I know I'll have to work up the nerve to introduce him to her soon. I like him too much to keep him a secret.

Which means I should be more excited about seeing him again, but I can't stop thinking about my mom and Carlene and what's going on with them.

"You nervous about going in here? It's not so bad," Carlene says. "Nobody will be mad that you're having sex. You don't even have to go through the pelvic exam for a few more years."

"Okay." My eyes slide away from her, toward the door.

Carlene's mouth opens, like we're not done here, but

she doesn't say anything else. Just grabs onto the door handle and motions for me to go in.

There is paperwork and waiting, and then I'm in a room with a doctor. Carlene asked if I wanted her to go in with me, but I said I was fine. And when I'm in the room, away from her, I feel some of my anxiety melt away.

Dr. Davis is a black woman—which surprises me, and then I feel stupid for being surprised. My father is a black doctor. But I'm still not used to seeing that—especially women—and it makes me feel more comfortable. She was a black girl once, too. She is tall with dark skin and thin, manicured dreadlocks pulled back in a bun.

She looks over my forms, and her voice is warm as she asks about my health and sexual history. Carlene only mentioned the pill, but Dr. Davis says I can get a shot, or a ring that I'd have to put in and remove every month. She explains the pros and cons of all three, and I decide I'm most comfortable with the pill right now. Our conversation is brief, but she makes sure to tell me everything I might need to know, like that I should take it at the same time every day and that I have a better chance of not getting pregnant if my partner uses a condom each time.

"Do you have any questions?" she asks after she's scrawled the prescription.

"I don't think so," I say.

"Well, if you do, here's my info." She produces a white

business card from the pocket of her scrubs. "Call me if you need anything. And sometimes it takes a couple of tries to find the right pill, so call me if your body doesn't seem to be adjusting after a few weeks and we'll look into it."

"Thank you." And I don't expect it, but a little thrill goes through me as she presses the prescription into my hand. It's not even the actual pill, but it makes me feel a bit more grown-up than I did when I walked in here. A little less tethered to my mother's expectations. A lot more independent.

"Thank you, Dove."

"For what?" I ask, even though she's already opened the door.

"Oh." Dr. Davis hesitates, unsure whether she should say what she's thinking. "I'm always happy to see girls your age taking care of their health."

Then she breezes out of the room before I can say anything else.

"How was it?" Carlene asks when we're walking down the street to the pharmacy. She stops for a moment to light a cigarette.

"Not bad, like you said. My doctor was a black woman."

"I *saw* a sister walk out just before you did! I didn't know she was the doctor." She sounds as excited as I was to see Dr. Davis.

"She was nice."

Then we're quiet again, passing a long line of brick buildings with awnings that display the names of restaurants, liquor stores, and coffee shops, all mixed in among apartments and offices. The air is thick with July humidity, and today the clouds are so heavy in the sky that I wonder if we might get a summer storm before Carlene and I make it back home.

"So," she says as we wait on the corner for the light to change. "When are you going to have your mom meet Booker?"

I shrug. "I'm not sure. I have to figure out a good time." She noticed how out of it I was at breakfast this morning and waited till both my parents were gone to ask what was up. I told her about my dad meeting Booker and calling me out.

Carlene sighs, exhaling smoke with it. "I don't know if there's going to be a good time. You need to get it over with and tell her about him, kid. I'm glad you trusted me enough to meet him before she does, but you can't keep sneaking around like this. Kitty isn't stupid, and Ray won't stay quiet forever."

"I'll tell her," I say, patting my shorts pocket to make sure the slip of paper with my prescription is still there. "I just need a little more time."

"Okay," she replies, only mildly satisfied. Then she turns

to me. "Kid, what's going on with you? Really? You can talk to me, you know. About anything."

I try to swallow, but my tongue and the roof of my mouth are suddenly dry as sand. I pull my water bottle from my bag and take a long drink. Carlene waits, even as the light changes and we're clear to cross the street.

I tuck the bottle back into my bag and swallow again. That's better. I look at Carlene's flip-flops instead of her face. "I heard you talking to Emmett."

She sounds confused. "When?"

"The night he was at our apartment...When Booker stayed over."

"Okay," she repeats, and when I look up, her eyebrows are squeezed together. "What did you hear?"

"You said...that you'd been getting close to someone. A *her*. And that Mom is afraid you're going to take her away."

Now I can't look away from Carlene—I want to see exactly how she's processing this. She blinks once, twice, three times. Drops her cigarette and leaves it still burning on the sidewalk. Steps back until she runs into the base of the WALK sign. She stands in place, her breath so heavy I can see her chest rise and fall. She doesn't speak.

"Were you talking about me?"

"Dove—" she starts weakly.

"Why would Mom think that? Did something happen

when I was little?" Did she try to kidnap me or something when she was high? Is that why Mom is so protective of me around her? Why she and Ayanna didn't want me anywhere near her when she was in the shop so many years ago?

"Dove, I—I can't." Carlene's voice is so thick she can barely get the words out. She pulls her phone from her pocket and starts tapping wildly at the screen. "Not now."

"What are you doing? What do you mean you can't? So it *was* about me?"

"I'm sorry, I—I need to call my sponsor." And then she turns her back and starts walking away from me.

Leaves me standing alone in Wicker Park like she's never seen me before in her life.

25

LAZ BUMPS MY SHOULDER WITH HIS AS WE WALK.

I look at him and blink.

"You okay?" he asks, checking both ways before we cross the street.

Greg is a few feet behind us, looking at his phone.

We're in Edgewater, heading to the party. I've been to this house before, but it was over a year ago and I don't remember who lives here.

"Yeah, I'm okay." I offer a weak smile.

"Uh, you're obviously not." He stops at the edge of the yard. "What's going on?"

"Is it all right if we don't talk about it?" I pause. "I'm not doing that thing where I say I don't want to talk about it but I really want to talk about it. I don't. It's family stuff and . . . it's complicated."

"Yeah, of course," Laz says, his eyes serious. "You know I get that. But if you change your mind, I got you."

I nod and we head up to the front steps. I'm glad Laz didn't push me because I don't really feel like talking about how Carlene has been missing since yesterday afternoon when she left me on the street. I told Booker about it, but only over text. It's different talking about it in person. It makes it more urgent, more real.

Last night my mother said not to worry, that Carlene probably had some things to take care of for her school or AA meetings. But I never told her how Carlene ran off, just that I hadn't seen her since the afternoon. And I didn't mention what we had been talking about, which is exactly what made her disappear.

Mom didn't seem so relaxed this morning when we woke up and Carlene still wasn't there. When she was opening up the salon, she kept looking at her phone and over at the door too many times. And later, she was so distracted that she didn't even stop her clients when they started talking about politics—which she *never* allows. Even Dad looked unsettled, and I know we were all thinking the same thing: Is this where Carlene relapses? And if she has, how do I tell my parents that it's all my fault?

When we walk in, a few people are sitting in a circle, talking. Everyone has a drink in their hand. Laz and Greg wave to them, then steer us directly to the kitchen. A girl with a shiny, swinging bob is making drinks at the counter. Greg says hey to her, proudly holding out a bottle of cheap rum while Laz peruses his options on the counter and in the fridge.

I'm not drinking anything tonight, so I look around at who's here. The kitchen is getting a lot of foot traffic as people head in and out from the backyard. I recognize a few people from the last party I was at, but nobody that I've talked to. I hope Booker gets here soon. I don't feel like making new friends right now, and I don't want to be the third wheel to Greg and Laz all night.

My eyes scan the room a second time and come to a screeching halt when I get to the corner with the china cabinet. What in the actual hell is Mitchell Simmons doing here? Standing with a red cup in hand. The same Mitchell who never wanted anything to do with parties is now standing in this kitchen talking to actual people and looking happy as a pig in shit.

I stare at him so long he feels my eyes on him and turns around. He looks just as surprised to see me, then gives a shy grin and waves. We haven't talked much in SAT prep since our lunch at Portillo's, but we say hi and sit next to each other. Still, like every time I see him, I'm dying to ask the same question that has been sitting on the edge of my tongue since our lunch: What did he mean when he said our lackluster make outs had nothing to do with me? I give him a wave and small smile in return, and he turns back to his friends.

My phone buzzes against my hip and I pull it from my pocket right away, thinking of Carlene. But it's Booker. He's here. Finally. I tell Laz I'll be right back and head out front to meet my boyfriend.

∿

I feel better with Booker here.

Outside, he kisses me under a tree, his lips lingering until I pull away and wrap my arms around him, resting my head against his chest.

"Heard from your aunt yet?" he asks.

"No. Not yet."

"Sorry," he says softly. I press even closer to him. I like feeling and hearing his voice at the same time. "We can go somewhere if you want. Just sit and talk. Or sit and not say anything—whatever you want."

"You wouldn't mind?"

"I'm only here to see you." He squeezes my hands. "Can I get something to drink first?"

"I'll go with you."

I briefly consider telling him Mitchell is here, but I don't want to make it into a big deal. He won't even know who he is if I don't say anything.

Booker says hey to Laz and Greg, who tell us to meet them outside before they walk out to the backyard, clutching plastic red cups. Booker rubs his hands together as he looks at the spread of bottles.

"Should I make something new?" he asks.

"Like what?"

"I don't know." He shrugs. "Something that isn't rum and Coke."

I lean against the counter, watching him. "I thought that was your drink."

"It is, but don't you get tired of black cherry all the time when there are so many other flavors of frozen yogurt?"

"Not really," I say, shrugging. "It's been my favorite since I was a kid."

"How does this taste?" Booker asks a couple of minutes later. He hands me the drink he's been working on.

I forget I'm not drinking tonight and take a sip. The strong taste of hard liquor hits me right away. I haven't had any alcohol since I was at the beach with Laz, and it feels like my first time all over again. It also feels good to have something to concentrate on besides the fact that my aunt is missing. But when I take a longer drink, Carlene's face flashes through my mind. What if she's doing the same thing right now? All because of me? And I think again about my mother's freak-out the last time I drank—how she's worried I'm going to turn out just like my aunt after a few sips of alcohol. I push away both of those thoughts as I swallow, but it's hard to get past the giant lump in my throat.

"It's good," I finally say to Booker. "Will you make me one?"

"You sure it's not too strong?"

I shake my head. Maybe it is, but that's what I want now.

"Have that one. I'll make another," Booker says, lifting a cup from a tall stack on the counter. When he's finishing up making his drink, he says, "Should we try to find an empty room in here? Or maybe take a walk?"

"We could just go outside and find Laz and Greg," I say.

"You don't want to go somewhere and talk?" There's concern in his eyes, like he doesn't want to let me down.

"Um, maybe later." But I don't want to talk. Not really. Because I'm worried that the more I talk about Carlene, the more upset I'm going to get that we still haven't heard from her.

"Oh, I'm not good enough company?" he says, raising an eyebrow. But he's teasing, and then he drapes his arm over my shoulder as we walk out back.

My drink is, in fact, too strong.

I've been steadily sipping since we sat down on the grass in a circle with Laz and Greg, and when I try to get up half an hour later, my legs wobble every which way like Jell-O.

"Oh my god," Greg says, cackling. "You are such a lightweight."

"This is, like, my third drink ever," I snap. "Of course I am."

But I laugh along with him as I plop back on my butt, and then Booker and Laz are laughing, too. Booker puts his hand on my knee and rubs.

The sun has been down for a couple of hours now, but the air is still thick and warm. If there were a breeze, it would be perfect. Booker is squinting at the air, concentrating hard on something I can't see. Maybe his drink is also too strong. I lean on my elbows but that takes too much concentration, so I lie all the way on my back in the grass.

Booker suddenly clasps his hands together. "Got it!" He settles down next to me, palms still cupped.

"What are you doing?" I ask, turning to lie on my side.

"I caught a lightning bug," he says. "First one I've seen all summer."

He holds his hands down to my face and I peer

through his fingers, see the bug blinking on and off like a tiny lantern.

"Pretty," I say. "Now let it go."

He does, and the firefly flits away from us and into the night.

Booker lies next to me, his hand sliding over the curve of my hip.

"Get a room!" Laz yells, his voice sounding farther away than it is.

"Man, shut the hell up," Booker says, but then he grins at me. "Want to go find someplace ... ?"

I run the tips of my fingers up and down his arm. Now I do want to be alone with him because I know there's not going to be much talking. "Yes."

"Be right back," he says, hopping up and heading toward the house before I can ask what he's doing.

Laz follows him, saying he needs another drink, and leaves Greg and me alone.

"You guys are pretty cute." Greg shakes the ice around in his cup.

"So are you and Laz." I look up at him from the grass. "Is he your boyfriend?"

"I guess so. Unofficially."

"Does it bother you that he's still closeted?"

Greg shrugs. "Just with his mom."

"But that doesn't bother you?" The alcohol is making

me say too much, asking for answers that Greg doesn't owe me. But I can't stop my lips from moving.

"It's not up to me to decide who he tells," Greg says after a pause. "He'll do it when he's ready. And it's nobody's business but his."

"He's my *best friend*. Everything is my business."

"Maybe this one isn't, Dove." Greg's tone isn't unkind, but it is serious enough to shut me up.

Footsteps cut across the grass toward us. "That was fast," I say without looking up.

"Hey, you guys want a hit?"

I sit up immediately, my gaze landing right on Mitchell. He's holding his vape pen and passes it to Greg, who takes a couple of puffs and says how good it tastes. Greg tries to give it to me, but I shake my head. I've been curious about weed, but I don't know if right now is the time to try it. I'm already so buzzed.

"I wanted to say hey in the kitchen." Mitchell takes the pen back and slips it in his pocket. "Then I turned around again and you were gone."

"I can't believe you're here," I say.

He laughs. "I do have friends, you know."

"I didn't mean... I just... You never used to go to parties."

"Fair enough."

"And who do you know from Laz's school?"

"This dude Tyler invited me. We're neighbors."

"I've never heard you talk about him," I say.

He shrugs. "Well, the old Mitchell wouldn't have hung out with him."

"Yeah, and the old Mitchell wouldn't be caught dead at one of these things. Now you're drinking *and* vaping? I know the booze doesn't help your anxiety."

"You're doing a very good impression of my mother right now," he says, giving me a look. "Are you about to lecture me on my shirt, too?"

"Ha ha." I give him that same look back.

Greg's narrowed eyes are ping-ponging back and forth from me to Mitchell. "What's going on here?"

"We used to date," I say, and it doesn't sound as wild to me as it once did. I guess we were both different people then.

"Yeah, for a little while," Mitchell mumbles, looking down at his feet.

"For a year and a half," I say.

Behind Mitchell, I see Booker and Laz walking back to us. And Booker is looking right at Mitchell. Frowning. Mitchell follows my gaze and steps back, making room for them.

"Laz, what's up?" He's grinning like they were once the best of friends.

"Uh, not much, man. What's up with you?" Laz sticks his hands in his pockets, not even giving Mitchell the chance to go in for the bro hug he so clearly wants to give him. Mitchell was never really nice to him and always implied that Laz wasn't very smart because he was so focused on sports.

"Just sharing the wealth," Mitchell says, brandishing the vape once again. "Want some?"

Laz hesitates, then raises his shoulders like *fuck it* and takes the pen.

Mitchell smiles, but it fades as soon as he looks at Booker. Who is still staring at him.

"Hey, we haven't met. I'm Mitchell." He appears only slightly nervous, considering Booker towers over him like a tree and doesn't look entirely friendly.

There's some sort of commotion coming from the back porch, but I'm too invested in my new boyfriend meeting my old boyfriend to pay attention to what's going on.

"I'm Booker," he says, but I notice that *he* noticed Mitchell's name. He remembers that he's my ex. And I wonder how he's going to take it.

Mitchell nods, then looks at me for clarification, like *This is the new guy you were telling me about?* I give a slight nod.

"Nice to meet you, man," Mitchell says.

He offers Booker his vape pen, but Booker declines.

And I have to admit, I'm glad. It's good that they're being cool with each other, but they don't need to be *friends*.

"Uh, guys?" I didn't notice Greg had wandered a few feet away, toward the porch, but now he's back, clearly panicked. "I think the cops are here."

And now the scene around us comes into sharp focus. People are dropping their cups and bottles, anxiously searching for ways out of the yard that don't exist. Every time someone passes we hear the word *cop* or *police*. Suddenly the music inside stops and we're the only ones still standing here. Then the back door flies wide open and a cop steps out onto the porch.

"Let's go," Booker says, grabbing my arm. "Now."

Greg's eyes never leave the porch. "Maybe we should just stay here. Maybe if we don't run, they'll let us off with a warning."

"And maybe you're real fucking white." Laz glowers. "Should we split up or all go one way?"

"Jesus Christ," Mitchell breathes, terrified.

He's not the only one.

The cop hasn't seen us yet, but his flashlight is sweeping across the lawn, and if he leaves that porch he'll be able to shine it right where we're standing.

We run.

The night, the yard, my friends are a fast-moving blur,

like when the "L" switches to express mode and flies down the track. Trees rustle. Fireflies wink. Grass swishes. And we keep tripping over discarded cups and bottles as we tear across the yard.

"Hey!" the cop yells, moving swiftly off the porch.

Booker stumbles and almost falls, but I pull on his arm as hard as I can to keep him up while Laz pushes us from behind. "Go! *Go!* We'll split up when we make it around front."

The cop is still behind us, still yelling. I know I shouldn't, but I glance back once. He's running, too, and red-faced. We've crossed the entire yard now and are rounding the corner, almost to the gangway, that tiny strip of space between houses that just might get us out of this situation.

I haven't run this hard since I played in a soccer game, and with the adrenaline coursing through me, I think I could run forever. Maybe even all the way back to Logan Square, if I had to. Booker is still ahead of me, first in line, pulling me along so fast it feels like we're actually flying.

"Come on, come on, come on," Laz huffs. "We're almost there."

I guess Greg is still behind him, and Mitchell, too, but I don't dare turn around and check. We can't afford to lose a second.

I can see the tree limbs in the front yard, and the sidewalk, and we *are* almost there and—

"Going somewhere, folks?"

A big white hand slams into Booker's chest, sending the chain of us toppling backward like a stack of dominoes.

26

THE POLICE STATION IS FREEZING.

That deep, dank cold that seeps into your bones, the result of too much air-conditioning, ancient metal furniture, and windows that never open.

We are being detained until our parents get here, but they haven't let us call anyone yet. I'm sitting on a padded blue chair next to Greg. Mitchell is behind us; he looks sick with anxiety. Everything is blue in here—shades of pale, navy, and a really ugly turquoise. All of them make my stomach hurt.

I can't stop the tears. They keep rolling down the side of my nose and into my mouth. My mind is a constant replay of them handcuffing Booker and Laz, putting them in the back of the same squad car. The one with the cop who stopped us.

"Handcuff *me*!" Greg said loudly as we watched. "Why won't you guys handcuff me?"

But we all knew why.

And I loathed Greg in that moment—hated him for knowing he could shout something like that without getting the shit beaten out of him. Or worse.

One of the officers frowned and then finally decided to frisk him, something they'd done immediately to Booker and Laz but took their time to do with us. I'd never seen Mitchell's skin pale to that shade and I wondered if he was smart enough to drop his vape back in the yard. The cop's partner made Mitchell and I raise our arms and spread our legs as she lightly patted us down. I was petrified, my whole body shaking the entire time she touched us. I flushed with embarrassment and rage, but it was nothing like what that other cop did to Booker and Laz. Their frisking seemed to last twice as long as it should have.

And now we are here, sitting in a room with guarded doors, cops staring us down, and loud, drunken people in lockdown rooms to the rear. A section of desks sits in front of us, but none of the uniformed people behind them are paying attention to what we're doing.

Greg shifts in his chair, making the vinyl squeak.

"Wonder where they took them?" He glances back at Mitchell, who shrugs.

I don't respond. The more I think about Booker and Laz being shuffled off to a different part of the station, the more I think I'm going to vomit on this cold linoleum floor. What if they lock them up just to "teach them a lesson"? Or see Booker's record and punish him even worse because he's been in trouble before? I double over, clutching my stomach.

"Hey," says a voice in front of us.

We look up to see the female cop who brought us back to the station. She is short and white with cool blue eyes. She doesn't smile, but she has the least threatening face of all the officers we've dealt with.

"Time to call your parents," she says, nodding toward a phone on one of the desks.

Greg clears his throat. "Can you go first? My dad is going to kill me and I'd like to cherish these last few minutes of life."

I could say the same for my mother, but better to get it over with. I follow the officer to a desk; her name tag says WILSON. She points to the phone, tells me what button to push for an outside line, and steps back a couple of feet.

I should call my parents, but I keep thinking about Carlene. It's probably foolish to think she could help me when she's been missing since yesterday—especially when she left me standing on the street with no explanation. It's possible she never wants to see me again. Or that she's not sober enough to take a call. I swallow and look at Officer Wilson.

"I don't know the number by heart."

She sighs. "You don't know your parents' number?"

"I need to call my aunt. My parents are working late, and it's better if I call her." I stare right in her face as I lie.

"Fine. Get it from your cell phone, but put it away again after that. No games, calls, or texting."

"Thank you." I pull up Carlene's number with shaking fingers, then slowly push it into the station phone.

As it rings, I think how silly it was to try her first. Mom, Dad, and I have all tried calling her, over and over again, and each time it goes to voicemail. If she's relapsed, she probably won't pick up. And even if she is fine, she might not pick up from a strange number. All I'm doing is buying time until I have to call my parents. And, like Greg, I'm afraid if that happens this is going to be my last night on Earth.

I don't have many more rings left until it will go to voicemail.

I pull the receiver from my ear, getting ready to hang up, when I hear: "Hello?"

"Carlene?" My voice has shrunk to almost nothing.

She doesn't sound any different than normal, but she pauses. "Dove? Where are you?"

"I'm, um, at the police station."

"What?"

"I wasn't arrested," I say quickly. "I'm with my friends. I need you to come pick me up."

"Oh, Dove."

"I'm sorry, Carlene. And I'm sorry about yesterday. I promise never to bring that up again if you'll come get me. Will you please come get me?"

I'm not dumb enough to think this is a secret we can hide from my parents—not with Laz in handcuffs—but I don't want them to see me here. I don't want to see the look on my mother's face as Officer Wilson tells her I was at a party with bottles and bottles of alcohol. Don't want to face that disappointment in here, with these sad blue walls and musty smell and people in uniforms who are walking around laughing and joking, like they're not in the midst of ruining some people's lives.

"I'll come get you," Carlene says after a long, labored breath. "Give me the address."

I head back to my seat after I hang up. I glance at Mitchell. He's leaning forward with his elbows on his knees, his head in his hands.

"How'd it go?" Greg asks, standing up as I sit down.

"My aunt is coming." And she's not drunk or high, and I don't think she's mad at me.

"Is that better than your parents?"

"For now."

"Wish me luck," he says before he walks over to Officer Wilson's desk.

"Hey," comes Mitchell's voice from behind me.

I turn to look at him. "Are your parents going to kill you, too?"

"At this point, they might as well round us all up and do it at once," he says. He tries to smile, but I can see the fear behind his eyes, thinking of what his parents are going to say when they find out he's being detained.

I try to laugh at his joke, but I'm feeling the same thing.

Mitchell starts and stops like he's going to say something. He does it a couple more times, then clears his throat. "Listen, I…what we talked about at lunch that day…"

"It wasn't the right place to ask you that," I say. "Sorry it was weird. I guess I was just so shocked that we were talking again and—"

"I'm glad you asked," he interrupts me.

"You are?"

"Yes…and no." He looks down at his hands. "I've been thinking about it, but I'm not sure how to put it into words."

I stay quiet, wondering if he's going to find the right ones to explain whatever it is to me. I never thought Mitchell had trouble effectively communicating his feelings—I just thought he didn't want to.

"I think you're pretty," he says bluntly. "I always have."

I smile because I'm not sure what else to do.

"But I didn't really want to kiss you, or have sex with you, or any of that stuff." He hesitates. "It was fine when we fooled around a few times, but that's it. Just fine. Not something I really wanted to be doing."

He's not making me feel great about myself, even though he started it out on a positive note, but I keep listening because I think I owe him that. He's being honest and explaining what happened with us, and that's all I've wanted since we broke up.

"It's not just you, though," he says. "I mean, at first I thought it was, but I realized I've never wanted that. With anyone else. You were just the person who people expected me to have sex with, so I didn't understand it was an everyone thing, not just a Dove thing."

"Okay..." I think I know where he's going with this, but I don't want to say a word until he's finished.

"I looked it up," he says. "And it seems like I might be somewhere on the asexuality spectrum."

Even though that's what I thought he might say in this moment, it never crossed my mind before now. Which makes me feel stupid. And I am embarrassed that he didn't feel comfortable enough to say something or try to figure it out with me while we were together.

"So, surprise, I guess," Mitchell says, playing with his hands now.

"Thanks for telling me," I say. "You didn't have to."

"I know, but you were my first real girlfriend, so I figured you deserved to know." He looks at me sideways. "You really had no idea?"

"I know a couple of people who identify as ace, but we're not good friends," I say. "And I know it's different for everybody. And...maybe I'm just self-centered, but I thought it was about me the whole time."

"You're not self-centered," he says. "I didn't understand it and it drove me crazy sometimes, and—I don't know. It just feels like I'm under so much pressure constantly, and that was one more thing to add to the list. Don't laugh, but my weed guy called me out on being a dick for no reason and kind of helped me see the problem."

"Your weed guy?"

He gives me a look like I should keep my voice down and I glance around, hoping no one heard me. It's hard to believe, but for a few minutes I forgot where we are.

"Yeah, I have a toxic relationship with my parents. They expect me to be the best at everything all the time and it's been building this pressure in me and I'm, like, always on the verge of exploding. And it's hard to go against them, because I do want MIT and I know their pressure helps keep me on track. But I also just want to be a normal teenager sometimes."

"Wow." I make a face. "That guy told you all that?"

He looks down at his feet. "We figured it out together, I guess. I know I'm fucked up, and I'm trying not to be such a prick, but... it still comes out. So... I'm sorry about that, too."

"You don't need to apologize for figuring out your sexuality," I say. "That's normal."

"Well, I haven't figured it out yet," he says. "I mean, I don't know where exactly I fall on the spectrum. Or if I'm on it for sure. But it's nice to know there's something that explains what I've been feeling. And that other people know how it feels, too. Thanks for being cool about all this."

"Thanks for apologizing for being a dick sometimes," I say. Even if I do get why he acted the way he did.

The front door of the station swings wide open and a small dark-skinned man strides in, wearing khakis and a short-sleeved button-down.

Booker's dad. Does that mean Ayanna is on her way, too?

I watch him talk to a man at a desk up front, away from us. He uses his hands a lot, and his face is pinched behind his glasses. He listens to the man for a few moments, then starts talking again. I can't hear what they're saying, and maybe that's a good thing.

Greg slides back into his chair. "Oh, shit, that's Booker's dad, isn't it?"

Mitchell looks over at him, too, as he walks up to make his phone call.

I nod. It's only a matter of time before he sees me, and something tells me he's not going to be pleased or surprised. "How'd it go with yours?"

"Lots of screaming and blaming before I could even explain why I'm here." He stretches his legs out in front of him. "As was expected."

The man at the desk must tell Booker's dad to take a seat because he turns away from him, frustration in his eyes as he looks at the empty chairs around us. I quickly drop my head, but it wasn't fast enough. There aren't enough of us in here to hide.

I look up when he stops next to me. "Hi, Mr. Stratton."

"I told you my son couldn't afford to get in trouble again," he says. "Why is he sitting in some room in handcuffs?"

"It's not her fault, Mr. Stratton," Greg offers. "We were all there. I told them to handcuff me, too. Booker and Laz weren't doing anything we weren't. They wouldn't listen."

Mr. Stratton ignores Greg, still staring at me. "I hope all this fun was worth it. Tonight is the last time you'll be seeing Booker. I told you I didn't want any more trouble and now they got my boy in cuffs again. He was doing good until you came around."

"I'm sorry," I whisper, but he's already walking away to find the seat farthest from me.

"It's not your fault," Greg says, putting his arm around my shoulders. "Don't listen to him, okay, Dove? It's not your fault."

Greg continues to comfort me, but I can't stop shaking and my eyes fill with tears again. No matter what Greg says, it does feel like my fault. If I'd just gone off with Booker like he suggested when he got there, maybe none of this would have happened. Maybe we could have slipped out of the house easily, and then he never would have been handcuffed and pushed against a wall and frisked by a strange red-faced man with a chip on his shoulder.

Carlene shows up about ten minutes later, smelling like jasmine and cigarettes. Officer Wilson says they're letting me go on a strict warning since I've never been in trouble, but that if they catch me at another party with alcohol, I'll get a citation or worse.

"I'm sorry," I say to Carlene when we're standing outside the station.

"It could've been a lot worse than a warning," she says with a shrug.

"I mean, for this, too, but I'm sorry for the other day. Are you okay?"

Carlene puts her arm around me. "It's okay, kid. I'm all right. My sponsor kept me on track. I didn't mean to get upset like that in front of you."

But she doesn't offer to talk about what was bothering me—what's *still* bothering me, even if it's been pushed to the back of my mind for the past few hours.

"Are you back at the apartment?"

"I stayed with Emmett last night, and I called Kitty after I talked to you. I didn't tell her where I was going," she says. "But I let her know I'm all right."

"Will you come back with me?"

Carlene hesitates.

"I don't want to be alone when I tell them. And I have to tell them. Before Ayanna does."

"I got you, kid. I can't tell you how many times I had to go home and face my mother after something like this," she says, linking her arm through mine. "I'll even spring for a cab to get us to the apartment."

MY MOTHER IS SITTING ON THE LIVING ROOM FLOOR, BACK PRESSED TO THE couch as she paints her toenails a shiny bronze.

She looks at Carlene for a long time, as if making sure she's really her sister and not an imposter. I wonder if she'll believe she's sober. I wonder if she will even care about what Carlene has been doing once I tell her where I've been.

"What are you doing home, Birdie? I thought you and Laz were going out for a bite after the movie?" She screws the top back on the polish and stands, careful not to smudge her toes.

"I, um." I look at Carlene, who nods as if to say *Go on, you can do this.* "Something happened. I'm okay, but I need to tell you something, and I don't want you to freak out."

Mom frowns hard. "Birdie, what's going on?"

"Is Dad here?"

"Raymond! Come in here!" Mom calls, and a few seconds later, my father comes running down the hall.

"What's wrong?" He looks around the room. He's in pajama pants and a black undershirt, and he's wearing his glasses, so he must have been reading in bed.

"I don't know. That's what Birdie was about to tell us."

I take a deep breath and stare at the floor. "I went to a party tonight with Laz. We were drinking. The cops came, and…and they took me, Laz, and some of our friends down to the station."

"They *what*?" my mother shouts.

"I wasn't arrested. They just held us until someone could come get us." I breathe in and out again; it doesn't make this any easier. "But Laz and our other friend—they put them in handcuffs. And they're still there."

"Did they fingerprint you? Make you fill out any forms?" my father asks, walking over to stand next to my mother, who is seething.

"No, they gave me a warning. But I don't know about Laz, or Booker—" His name comes out before I can stop it.

And my mother doesn't miss a thing.

"Booker? The friend who went with you to the game?"

I can tell my father is staring at me, waiting to see what I'll say next.

"Yes." I lick my bone-dry lips before I speak again. "But he's actually, um...he's my boyfriend."

"Your *what*?" Mom's voice is getting louder, and it's making me want to stop talking forever.

"I was going to tell you about him, but there wasn't a right time and—"

But her rage has already shifted to her favorite target: Carlene. "And you just think you can go pick up my child from the police station without telling me? You think that's okay, Carlene?"

"Kitty, don't start." Carlene's voice is firm. "She called me. What was I supposed to do? Leave her there?"

My mother stomps across the room until she's standing inches from Carlene's face. "You were supposed to call and tell me, since I'm her *mother*. What is wrong with you?"

"What is wrong with *you*?" Carlene yells back. "Your *daughter* doesn't even want to tell you she has a boyfriend. She's *sixteen*. This is normal high school stuff and you're acting like she committed a goddamn murder."

"Did you know that she has a boyfriend?" Mom asks her. Then she looks at me. "Did you tell her about him?"

"Yes," I whisper, wishing I could vanish on the spot.

Mom's face falls in a way that makes me think this is the ultimate betrayal in her book—confiding in Carlene before I told her.

"Why would you do that, Birdie?" she whispers back.

Carlene doesn't give me a chance to answer. "Yeah, I knew about him. He's a good kid, but she's afraid you're going to think he's not good enough, so she was scared to introduce you to him."

"I don't understand," Mom says, still staring at me with a face so full of hurt it makes me want to look away. "Why were you scared for me to meet him?"

"It's a long story," I say. And is it even worth telling, since Booker's dad made it clear that I won't be seeing him again anyway?

"You're too hard on her, Kitty," Carlene says. "She's also afraid to talk to you about sex, but don't worry—I've got that covered, too."

"I've talked to you about that, Birdie," Mom says, defensive.

"Not since she was a *child*." Carlene glowers. "What planet do you live on where you think teenagers aren't going to have sex just because you don't want to talk to them about it? She's on birth control now, FYI."

I hate how they're talking about me like I can't hear them.

If this were a movie, my mother would be breathing red-hot flames. "This is so like you, Carlene. I put myself out to help you yet again and you just keep crossing the line. And you know what? I'm done. I don't want you in my house and I don't want you around my daughter."

"You can kick me out, but that won't make her stop liking me." Carlene is right in my mother's face, nose to nose, her finger jabbing the air. "You really can't stand how much Dove likes being around me. How we get along. Try to keep her away from me again, but it doesn't change anything. She will *always* be mine, Katrina."

The air-conditioning clicks off, plunging the room into silence. The street noise evaporates. All I can hear is her last words on repeat, and then things start snapping into place:

My mother never mentioning Carlene all those years, doing her best to bury her existence.

She will always *be mine.*

Carlene's bird tattoo—a delicate inking of a dove.

She will always *be mine.*

Carlene saying she had a baby once and me assuming it was a miscarriage.

She will always *be mine.*

And Carlene telling Emmett how my mother is afraid that she'll take me away.

She will always *be mine.*

"Mom?" I stare at my mother. But the full-on nauseating dread in my stomach makes me almost sure I'm looking at the wrong person when I say that name.

Her face is blank in a way I've never seen before. Like her insides have been stripped raw. Like her worst nightmare has come true right here in her own living room.

I turn to Carlene when my mother doesn't answer. "What do you mean? What does that mean, I will always be yours?"

My mother is a statue, but Carlene is shaking uncontrollably, her limbs a quivering mess. For the first time ever, I see tears in her eyes. The rapid trembling of her chin makes them spill over and slip down her neck.

"Mom?" I say, looking back and forth between them. "Carlene?" And then, when I still get no answer: "Dad?"

But he is frozen, too, staring at the scene before him like he's just stumbled upon a fatal accident.

I try once more. "Carlene?"

She speaks this time, but her voice is so low I can't make out one word.

"What?" I say.

Her tears are still flowing—streams of them, her eyes two broken faucets. She shakes her head again and again, but this time I hear her loud and clear: "I'm your mother, Dove. I'm your biological mother."

I bend over, grabbing my knees. But they are made of rubber. I can't stand up. I back up until my butt is just barely pressed into the armchair.

This isn't my life, this isn't my life, I keep thinking. Over and over again, as if that will make it true.

I look at my mother—at the person I *thought* was my mother. The woman who has been lying to me for sixteen years. And who would still be lying to me now if Carlene hadn't said anything.

"It's true, Birdie," she says like a robot.

"Birdie was *my* name." Carlene's voice is strong, even as she sobs. "It was my name for her, and you stole that, too."

"I didn't steal her." Mom is still using that stiff voice and it scares me. I hate it. It makes me feel like I don't know anything about her. Like I never did. "You couldn't take care of her. And I couldn't watch my niece go into foster care because of your addiction."

"Because of my *disease*," Carlene manages to snap. "You've never respected me enough to call it that. You think I wanted to give her up? You think I didn't want to be here for her?"

My father is squatting, elbows pressed to his knees, head in hands. Which he keeps shaking over and over, trying to will away what is happening.

"If you're my mother..." I start out, my voice so weak I don't know if I can go on. And the last thing I want is to talk to anyone in this room—all these people who've betrayed me. Who didn't want to tell me the truth about my own life because it made theirs easier. But I need answers. I need to know everything. "If you're my mother, then who is my father?"

"Oh, Birdie," Mom says, and then she finally cracks, too. A tear tumbles down her cheek, something I haven't seen in ages.

"Who is it? *Who is my father?*" I am screaming now, and it fills the entire room with my anger. But it's still not enough, still not the punishment they deserve for keeping these things from me. If I could, I would burn this fucking place to the ground.

"I am," comes the last voice I expect to answer. Muffled, because his head is still in his hands.

"No, my real father. I want to know who it is."

He lifts his head wearily and stands, and it appears to take every last bit of strength for him to look me in the eye. "It's me, Dovie. Carlene and I... It was just one time, and... It's me. I'm your biological father."

I don't know where to go. What I do know is I have to get out of this room. Away from these liars posing as my family.

And for the second time this evening—I run.

I TUCK MYSELF INTO THE TOP LEFT CORNER OF THE MEGABUS AND PUT my purse next to me on the empty seat, willing no one to join me.

The bus is only about half full by the time we take off, though, and the people around me immediately put on their headphones or curl up to go to sleep. The ride to Milwaukee is short, not even two hours, but I wish I were already there.

I texted Mimi and told her I'd be on the bus arriving just before 2:00 a.m. She tried to video call, then voice call, and when I didn't answer either of those, she texted back and asked if I was okay.

Yes/no

> Please don't tell Mom and Dad I'm coming

Then I shut off my phone.

I remember the way Mimi looked when I asked her about Mom and Carlene—if she knew anything that I should know, too. But I forced myself not to think about it when I bought my ticket. I don't know where else to go. Laz's place is out of the question, if he's even home from the police station yet. Booker's, too.

Mimi is the only person I want to see right now. Maybe she can help me make sense of what the hell is going on. How everything I knew to be true about my life has been lie upon lie, orchestrated over the years. And how it suddenly feels weird to call Mom and Carlene the names I've always known them by; should I be saying Kitty and Mom now?

I put on my headphones and try to sleep, but my heart won't stop pounding, my blood won't stop boiling. The scene from our apartment won't stop replaying itself, and I can't unhear the things Mom and Carlene shouted at each other. Or forget how bedraggled my father looked when he said: *I am. It's me.*

Across from me, a girl about Mimi's age is flipping through a magazine as she dips into a package of store-bought cookies beside her. She feels me watching and looks over. Smiles and holds out the package of cookies.

I manage a smile back and mouth *No, thank you.* Lean my head against the window.

I guess I do doze off, because I'm looking out the glass with confusion as the brakes squeal the bus to a stop. We're right on time and I'm here, in Milwaukee.

It doesn't quite hit me what I've done until I get off the bus and see Mimi's terrified face, craning her neck to look for me among the passengers. As soon as she sees me she runs right up, wrapping me tight in her arms.

"Oh, Dovie, what did you do?" she says, pulling back and smoothing a hand over my braids.

"Did they call?"

"Only about a hundred times." She pauses. "I had to tell them you were coming. You're a minor, and they were, like, five seconds from filing a missing persons report."

I frown.

Mimi holds up her palm, as if to say give her a minute. "But I made them promise not to come up. I told them I can handle it. Whatever it is...we can handle it."

"So you don't know?"

"Let's wait to talk," Mimi says, leading me to the parking lot. "Until we get back to my place. Are you hungry?"

"No." I am tired, but I press on. "Why do you want to wait?"

"Dovie, please." She beeps the key fob on a car that isn't hers. She's never wanted her own because she says it's easy enough to get around without one. "It's late. Let's just get back to my place, okay?"

I am so restless the seat belt feels like it's choking me every second of the ride. I still don't turn on my phone, but before she started up the car, I saw Mimi text our parents to say that I got here safely.

Her place is on the top floor of a four-story brick building that reminds me of a nursing home from the outside. Inside, the apartment is still, and she tells me to be quiet because her roommate, Sienna, is sleeping. She places Sienna's keys into a small bowl by the door.

I haven't showered since this morning—yesterday morning, technically. All I want is to wash off. And a pillow. But I'm not going to let Mimi wait until the morning to talk. She must know this because she shows me where the bathroom is before telling me to meet her back in the living room.

I pee and sit on the toilet for a while. I must be Carlene's daughter. Both of us run when confronted with something we can't process. I wash my hands and splash water on my face.

Mimi has put on a kettle for tea, and I curl up on the couch while she waits for it to boil. It's clear that almost everything in the apartment is secondhand or hand-me-down, but it's comfortable. It feels like a home. What if I lived here instead of going back to Chicago? I don't know if anyone in that apartment deserves to hear from me again.

After a few minutes, Mimi walks over to the couch with two mugs of chamomile tea, then circles back to the kitchen and returns with a plastic honey bear and a spoon. I grab a mug and hold it to my lips, blowing on the top so I'll have something to do.

"I knew," she says, breaking the silence.

I almost drop my tea. Even though it's not as much of a surprise as it should be. Even though I guess Mimi might be the worst liar in the family because I saw it in her eyes that day. Even if she wasn't quite sure what I was talking about, she knew something had been kept a secret for years that affected me.

My mouth takes a moment to start working again, but I get out my question: "For how long?"

"Only a couple of years, I promise. It was an accident." She sets her mug on a hexagonal coaster. "I needed my birth certificate for something and Mom gave me yours by mistake."

"And you didn't tell me?"

"It was right before I left for school, and I...I couldn't

believe it was real, Dovie. I just kept staring at Carlene listed as your mother, and then I showed it to Mom and she had to tell me the truth."

I scowl down into my mug. "I still can't believe you didn't tell me."

"I know. Mom made it seem like such a big deal, and I didn't want everyone to get mad at me for this thing they'd managed to keep secret for so long. But you deserved to know, and I'm sorry. I'm so sorry, Dovie."

"What happened? Were Dad and Carlene together? Like, dating?" But he said it happened only once. And he and Mom have been together since high school, with no breaks.

"I didn't get a lot of details, just that it wasn't something we talk about a lot. Or ever," she corrects herself.

"So, is Mom my legal guardian or has she just been taking care of me this whole time? Did she adopt me? Is there paperwork?" My head hurts, thinking of all the possibilities I hadn't even considered until now.

"I don't know," Mimi says apologetically. "I'm glad you're here, but I don't have any answers for you, Dovie. You're going to have to talk to them if you want to know exactly what happened."

"I fucking hate them."

She puts her hand on my arm. "I know."

"They've been lying to me every single day for sixteen and a half years. And with Carlene in our house…How could they even look at me, knowing she's my real mother?" I choke back a sob. "Mom barely ever mentioned her before she showed up. What if I never knew her at all?"

Mimi doesn't respond. I don't think she knows what to say, but she rubs my arm as we let our tea cool.

"What about us?" I ask slowly.

Her hand stops. "What *about* us?"

I look into her eyes for the first time since she admitted she knew. "What are we?"

"We're sisters," she says almost before I can finish. Forcefully. "Same as we've always been."

"But our bio moms are sisters.…So, aren't we cousins?"

She stops to think about it. "Yes, but we have the same bio dad, so…sister-cousins?"

"Sister-cousins." And then I burst out laughing.

Mimi gives me a funny look. "What?"

"Just…sister-cousins? This is, like, Mom's worst nightmare. She'd be horrified if this got out. You know if we were anyone else she'd say it was ghetto."

Mimi smiles. "Well, she'd think the word *ghetto* but never actually say that."

"True." I sip my tea.

"But, seriously, Dovie, this doesn't change anything, okay?"

"I know."

She stares at the coffee table as she says this next part. "And as much as you don't want to hear this, it doesn't change what you have with any of them, either."

"But they lied to me."

"I'm not saying that's okay, but—I think they did it to protect you. So you could grow up with the best, most normal life possible. It's fucked up, but they did it because they love you, Dove."

Maybe what she's saying is true, but it doesn't make me feel much better. Because love or not, they did it to protect themselves, too.

MIMI AND I DIDN'T GO TO SLEEP UNTIL ALMOST FIVE, AND I STILL FEEL groggy when I wake up at one in the afternoon.

She pokes her head in the bedroom as I'm stretching myself awake.

"Morning," she says. Then: "Tea?"

I nod. And I don't sit up until she returns with a fresh mug.

"So, Mom and Dad are on their way."

"What?" I take the mug from her. "They promised they wouldn't come!"

"I guess that promise was only good for last night." She perches on the side of the bed where she slept.

"Are they staying here?" I take a drink of tea; ginger this time.

"No, Sienna doesn't need to witness all this drama. They're getting a hotel. And taking us to dinner tonight."

I make a face.

"You knew you'd have to see them again at some point, Dovie," she says quietly.

I sit back against the pillow. "I just didn't think it would be this soon. Is Carlene coming with them?"

"No, just Mom and Dad." She winces after she says it this time, like she doesn't want to make me feel bad for calling them that. "If it makes you feel any better, Mom sounded awful. Like she hadn't slept and had been crying all night."

I wish it made me feel better, but it doesn't. I'm angry and hurt, and I will be for some time. Maybe forever. I don't understand how she could have looked at me every day and called me her daughter hundreds of times and never felt compelled to tell me the truth. But I haven't forgotten the pain on her face last night; how, after her tears broke, it appeared to be physically ripping through her body.

Mimi curls her legs up beneath her. "How's Booker?"

"Not great," I say, before explaining the whole story about the party and the police station and the cops putting handcuffs on him and Laz. I can't believe that was less than twenty-four hours ago.

"*Just* Booker and Laz?" She shakes her head. "Of course. Well, they didn't arrest them, did they?"

"Laz texted me last night. They both got citations, but he thinks the judge will probably just sentence them to an alcohol education class or something and drop it from their record."

"But what about Booker? He's been in trouble before."

"I don't know." I texted him, but he didn't respond, and that wasn't a shock. I almost expected his father to call me and tell me one last time to stay away from him. "I hope they don't send him back to juvie. They wouldn't do that, would they?"

"He's black and we're talking about Chicago." Mimi sighs. "Anything is possible."

⌒ℓ

We lie around and watch movies the rest of the day until it's time to get ready for dinner.

I finally take a long, hot shower, and it feels heavenly, but thinking about seeing my parents soon makes me more nervous than when I went on my first date. More apprehensive than the days I had my final exams, and even more anxious than when Booker and I first had sex. Part of me can't stop worrying they'll have even more secrets to tell me, and I can't handle that.

We meet them at the restaurant, a fancy seafood place with velvet-lined booths and a long marble bar. When I asked Mimi why they wanted us to go out instead of staying in, she just looked at me like I should know better. "If we're in public, they don't have to worry about you freaking out on them," she said. I know she's right, but it doesn't matter to me either way. I don't have anything to say to them now, and I don't think I will by the end of dinner.

Mom—I don't know what else to call her; *Kitty* doesn't feel right—and Dad are waiting up front and positively light up when they see us. I don't hug them like I normally would, and they don't make me.

"It's good to see you, Birdie," Mom says. "I'm so glad you're safe."

Dad gives me a small smile, and I try to return it, but I think it comes out as more of a grimace.

Mimi carries the conversation, chatting about living with Sienna and the classes she's signed up for next semester. I keep my head down, only looking up to order water when the server comes by, then burying my nose in the menu.

I can feel Mom peeking at me when she thinks I don't notice. I keep my eyes down until the server returns. But he has to leave, eventually, and then it's just my family and me. Pieced together in a completely different way than just two days ago.

"I'm not sure what to say," Mom begins, sipping her

coffee. She looks flawless, as usual, but when I meet her eyes I can tell she's running on fumes.

I don't say anything. Don't want to make this easier on her, no matter how beaten down she is.

"It's probably best if we start at the beginning," Dad says, rolling his cloth napkin between his fingers. "But first, we love you, Dove. We have always loved you. We will never stop loving you."

"We love you so, so much, Birdie," Mom adds, unblinking. "And you'll always be our daughter."

I nod so they'll go on.

"You know Kitty and I have been together since high school," Dad says. "And we've been committed to each other since then, but we went through a rough patch in our twenties. It seemed like a good idea to get married right after graduation, and then we couldn't wait to have our first baby, our little girl." He stops to smile at Mimi. "But we were only twenty-three when she was born, and it was harder raising a baby than we'd thought it would be."

"By the time Mimi was three, we were still struggling and living in a one-bedroom apartment in Hyde Park," Mom continues. "Your father was in med school and we were barely scraping by. I was terrified we were going to have to move in with Raymond's parents."

Dad nods. "You and me both. It was a tough time, and tensions were running high. Carlene had been living in a communal space with some people over in Iowa. She showed up out of the blue."

Mom sighs. "Which usually meant she had outstayed her welcome with friends or made somebody angry. She said she just needed to stay a couple of nights, and I knew I needed to stop helping her. She wasn't sober. But she's my sister. I didn't want to turn her away, either. She didn't have anyone else."

The server comes back to check on us, sees the looks on our faces, and turns right back around.

"I was going up to the bar around the corner to meet a friend for a drink," Dad says. "Carlene said she was going to take a walk with me to get some fresh air and come right back to be with your mom and Mimi, and . . . I guess I knew deep down that she shouldn't be anywhere near a bar at that point. Not even walking by one. But I was stressed out and I wanted a drink and I wasn't thinking." My father is twisting away at his napkin, and if it were paper, it would be torn to shreds by now. "She followed me right in and I didn't have the energy to fight with her. She was going to do what she was going to do, anyway— she always had. I couldn't stop her."

Mom and Dad both hesitate, neither of them wanting

to say what happened next, even though we all know. Mimi and I exchange a look. We're not too eager to hear it, either.

Finally, Dad says, "A drink turned into two, which turned into I don't know how many. It was foolish and beyond selfish, and I've never forgiven myself for stepping out on your mother. It was just one time, but that's no excuse. I'm even sorrier that I didn't tell her right away, but Carlene and I made a few bad decisions that night, and promising not to tell your mother was one of them."

"She left before lunch the next day, and I didn't see her again until she turned up six months pregnant, saying the baby was Raymond's." Mom's hands shake so much she can't pick up her coffee cup. Her features are so wracked with pain I have to look away from her. "I didn't believe her. I knew she'd been with several men by that point, and she wasn't always careful when she was drinking or using. But most of all, I couldn't believe Raymond would be with her. We'd been together for almost ten years at that point, and he'd known Carlene all of them. It didn't make sense to me."

"I admitted to it," Dad says, and now he abandons the napkin and puts his hand over Mom's. She flinches, the memory too raw, but doesn't pull her hand away. "And by some miracle, Kitty agreed not to leave me."

Mom takes a deep breath. "I sent Carlene away.... Told

her I never wanted to see her again, not with her bringing all those lies into my house. I still didn't believe there was any way her baby could be Raymond's, even after I knew the truth about what happened between them."

I am dizzy. All this information is coming so fast, and I'm a little shocked at how open they're being with Mimi and me. It's like all those years of keeping quiet has pushed the floodgates wide open. Mimi squeezes my shoulder.

"I didn't see Carlene again for a while. Not until you were six months old." Mom smiles for the first time all night. "And my heart just melted when I saw you, Birdie. You were the sweetest, chubbiest, most serious little baby. I loved you the minute we met."

I look down at the table.

"I also knew..." She pauses, catching her breath. "The minute I saw you, I also knew you were Raymond's. You looked a little bit like me, in that way Carlene and I look a little alike. But you were Raymond's baby. We got a paternity test to be sure, but I knew."

Our appetizer comes out then: a seafood plateau, one of those dramatic tiered platters with oysters and fish and shrimp cocktail and mussels on beds of ice. I'm not hungry—I'm not sure any of us are—but we are collectively happy to have something to do with our hands and we dig right in.

"Carlene was sticking around Chicago for a while,

staying with friends," Mom says, a piece of shrimp in hand. "But I was worried about her. Worried about you, and what kind of situations she was putting you in. We were giving her money, and I tried to talk to her about it, but she was stubborn. Said nobody was taking her baby, and that she could do fine alone. Then—"

Her voice chokes. She opens her mouth to try again but shakes her head, staring hard at the shrimp.

Dad picks up where she left off. "Then one morning, before we were heading off to work and to drop Mimi at daycare, we got a call. From someone we didn't know, who told us to come get a baby. They gave us an address and…it wasn't Carlene who called, but we knew that baby had to be you."

I stare at him. I can't believe this story is about me, that there was this whole existence with Carlene that I know nothing about.

Dad's eyes are watery. "The place was empty, except for a couple of people passed out here and there. It was dirty and abandoned. A drug house. We found you in the bathroom. Someone had put you in the tub. You were bundled in blankets, asleep in a broken car seat."

"You looked so peaceful," Mom cuts in as she dabs at her eyes with her napkin. "So innocent, and I promised myself that I wouldn't give you back until Carlene had proved she could stay sober for more than a few months at a time."

The anger inside me has been slowly melting away as they talk. It's not completely gone, but the more they tell me, the harder it is to be so furious with them. They are telling the story of how much they love me. How they loved me enough to save me from what could have been a very different life than the one I've lived all these years.

"We've had you since you were eight months old," Mom says. "And no, I didn't give birth to you, but I've never thought of you as anything but mine, Birdie. Keeping this from you all these years...well, it wasn't the smartest thing we've ever done. But we only wanted to protect you. Never wanted you to question where you come from or what you could be."

My eyes are wet now. When I look over, Mimi is crying, too. This can't be good for the restaurant, a whole family trying not to sob over a seafood plateau. My parents' plan backfired. But I don't care who sees us or what anyone else thinks. This is the most imperfect, honest moment my family has ever had, and I am not going to be ashamed of it.

"We've made some mistakes along the way," Dad says. "And we'll understand if it takes you some time to forgive us."

"But the one thing we got right is taking you in," my mother says. "You have always been such a bright spot in our lives." She looks back and forth from me to Mimi. "We are so proud of you girls. We know we're hard on you sometimes, but it's because we love you. We love you both so much."

CARLENE ASKED IF I WANTED TO GET SOMETHING TO EAT, BUT I SUGGESTED we go for a run instead. I need to cleanse the memory of sprinting across Laz's friend's yard and down the gangway like fugitives.

She is sitting on the front stoop when I get back from SAT prep, just like the first day I saw her. Only she's in workout clothes and there's no cigarette. I can tell she wants one by the way her fingers trace and tap along the steps.

"Hey," she says, standing when she sees me. She exhales like she's been holding her breath for a while. "I'm early."

"Do you want to come up while I change?"

All her things were cleared out of Mimi's room when we returned from Milwaukee.

"I'll stay down here and stretch."

I change into an old pair of soccer shorts and a tank, then meet her back downstairs. We do a few stretches together in silence. I poke my head into the shop to remind Mom I have plans with Carlene. Then we set off.

We take the same route as last time, and Carlene says hello to her friends along the way. But other than that, we don't talk. It's not the comfortable quiet from before, but it's not completely tense, either. Somewhere in between.

I am sweat-soaked and panting by the time we reach Humboldt Park. We stop at the boathouse, leaning over the railing that overlooks the water.

"I think you're getting worse at this running thing, kid," she says, laughing at how winded I am.

I try to banter with her, but I'm too out of breath and have to hold up my index finger. When I finally catch my breath, I start laughing, too.

Carlene turns to the water, her smile fading. "So, you're here. With me. I guess that means you don't hate me."

"I don't hate you." I gaze out at the water, too. Ducks pop their heads in and out, skimming along the surface so gracefully they appear to be floating.

"Kitty said you were taking it pretty well. As well as you can, considering the shitshow we hit you with." She looks at me now, and I meet her eyes. "I'm sorry, kid. I'm so fucking sorry for lying to you. For not being here.

For not being able to get a grip on this shit and raise you myself."

I swallow. "You couldn't help it. I believe it's a disease, too."

"I wanted you more than anything in the world, but… One night, I was getting high and you were with me, but you were such a good sleeper—always a good sleeper—that I forgot. And I left you in the corner all night. I passed out. Forgot you were there until someone—they had to slap me across the face to wake me up." She blinks rapidly, her lashes fluttering like butterfly wings. "And told me to take care of my baby. And I looked over and there you were, screaming your little head off. You must have been hungry or—I think you were teething, too. Maybe you just wanted to be held."

I don't interrupt her story. I just listen.

"I held you and you sucked on my finger until you fell asleep again. And you were just so forgiving. You didn't care that I was an addict. I was the only person you knew, and you trusted me." She rubs a hand over her face, but the tears she wiped away are replaced with new ones. "I knew I had to give you to someone who could take care of you. All the time. And Ray was your father, but Kitty was the person *I* trusted most. I knew she would love you as much as I did. As much as I do." She sniffles. "My friend and I moved on to a new house the next day or the day after that...I can't remember. But I had him call Kitty and Ray, tell them to come get you. I put you in the bathtub so no one would bother you until they got there."

"How did you know they would come get me?" I ask in a small voice.

"Because they knew I needed help...and they knew you needed them."

"I remember you coming into the shop once," I say, ignoring the way my chin quivers. "I think I was about eight?"

She nods. "I was so fucked up I'm surprised Kitty didn't call the police on me. I wanted to see you over the years, but she wouldn't let me. Not until I sobered up for good. And that wasn't happening, so I took a chance. But she pushed me out of there so fast I barely got to look at you. She filed for official guardianship the next week and I relinquished custody. I had to. You deserved better. You've always deserved better."

"Why did you name me Dove?" I might as well ask everything I've ever wanted to know, now that the truth is out. The questions are also keeping my tears at bay because the more she talks, the harder it is to stop them from falling.

"I did quit using when I was pregnant with you. I found a halfway house that took me in, and I got clean for the last

310

few months. Got a job, had a routine…I felt like I was a productive member of society for the first time in I don't know how long." She lets out a shuddery breath. "There was a bird book in the house. Some old battered thing, pages missing. But I loved looking at it. All those birds were calming. And the dove seemed so pure, so good. It stood for peace. The name sounded so pretty to me, and I knew that's what I wanted to call you. I don't know when I started calling you Birdie, but it stuck, and you'd look at me with your eyes all wide when I'd say it. And then…I *was* high as a kite when I got the tattoo, but it's so I'd always have a part of you. Looking at it every day made me feel better, to know I put some good out in the world once."

"What did you do all those years you were away? Where were you?" I don't mean to sound accusatory, but I think it's my right to know.

"Oh, Dove, I was everywhere. Nowhere. Out of my fucking mind." She clutches the balustrade, the skin on her knuckles pulled tight. "I'll tell you all about it sometime. But I want you to know that I never stopped caring about you. I thought about you all the time. I *always* wanted you. You are the best thing I've ever done, and I mean that."

We are quiet again, watching a great blue heron glide over the water, wings spread wide.

"Where will you go now?" I ask when the silence is too much.

"I'm staying with Emmett, but I can't keep crashing with him. I have a couple of interviews at other hair salons—just assisting, until I get my license. I can wait tables if those don't work out. Kitty told me I didn't have to get out, that she was angry when she said I needed to leave and didn't mean it. But I think it's time for me to make my own money and get my own place. Even if it's just a studio. I've been relying on her and Ray for too long." She pauses. "And I hope—well, I hope we can still have a relationship. I get it if you can't forgive me for what I did. But I want to be in your life. I want to do better for you. Try to make it up to you if I can."

"I'd like that," I say softly. Immediately. "You don't have to make it up to me. But I told Mom I'm not going to stop seeing you. So can we still go on runs and out to eat and just… talk?"

"Of course," Carlene says, tentatively touching my wrist. "Of course we can do all of that. We can do whatever you want. But… you really told Kitty that you weren't going to stop seeing me?"

"Yeah."

"How'd she take it?"

I shrug. "She just said okay… and that she wouldn't have tried to stop me. I guess she was just mad when she said all that."

Carlene looks pleased.

"Will you still braid my hair?"

She laughs, her nose stopped up from her tears. "Anytime you want."

"Carlene?"

"Yeah, kid?"

I clear my throat to make sure she hears exactly what I have to say.

"I love you, too."

GREG LEANS CLOSE TO THE DASHBOARD, BARELY DRIVING TEN MILES PER hour as we look for the address I gave him.

"It has to be right around here," Laz says. "Let's just park and walk."

We're in Bronzeville, over on the South Side, trying to find Booker's uncle's auto shop. When I told Laz I was coming down here, he said he'd come with me. Greg was there, too, so he offered to drive. I started to protest at first, but I get nervous going to new places by myself. And Laz checked to make sure Booker was working today, but what if he isn't here for some reason? At least then I won't be alone.

The shop is on a corner, surrounded by a tall wrought-iron fence. The signage that wraps around the top of the building is neon yellow and simply says LES'S AUTO in black, with the phone number printed next to it.

I thought I'd gotten over my nerves about seeing Booker, but my heart starts its familiar pound as we walk through the gate, passing a few cars that look like they've been here for decades. Different size tires are stacked up in a couple of corners, and two cars are parked inside the garage, hoods open. The air is thick with motor oil.

A handful of black and brown guys are darting around in grayish-blue coveralls, talking and laughing over the radio that plays as they work. I hang back behind Greg and Laz, wondering if this was a mistake.

Greg turns around. "Over there," he says, pointing to the corner of the garage.

My heart skips faster as I see Booker for the first time in almost a month. His broad back is turned to us as he searches through a rack of tools. And I think maybe this is enough, just to see the back of him. To know that he's still here, still doing okay.

But then one of the guys sees us watching him and taps Booker on the shoulder. Says something so he turns around. And seeing his face feels so good I want to cry. He stares for a few seconds, mouth open and eyebrows up, then puts his head down and jogs over to us.

He slaps hands with Greg and Laz, who give him shit about his coveralls until, smiling, he pushes past them and tells them to take a walk.

Then he's in front of me and I stop breathing.

"You're here," he says, then laughs a nervous laugh. "I mean, of course you're here. Hi. I just didn't expect to see you."

I look around the property. "Your dad's not here, is he? I think he'd get a restraining order against me if he had to."

Booker sighs. "Sorry about him. I told him none of that was your fault, but he's not trying to listen to me."

"It's okay. I didn't come here to talk about him. I wanted to see you, before school starts again." I take a breath. "And I'm so sorry, Booker. About the party and—"

"Dove. It's not your fault."

"I'm just really glad nothing happened to you. I was so worried."

"I know, me too. I was lucky." He grimaces. "Laz and I were both lucky."

Luck shouldn't have anything to do with it; he and Laz should've been treated the same as Greg and Mitchell—and me. But we both know that's not how it works.

I focus on one of the tires behind him. "Laz said you have to do community service?"

"Yeah, starts up in a couple of weeks. So then I get to go to school and work *and* serve meals at the food bank." He shrugs. "Could definitely be worse, though. I'm not complaining. Judge kinda went easy on me, considering."

I want to touch him so badly, but I don't know if that's okay anymore. It's been forever since we've seen each other. His dad took his phone away, so there was no way to get ahold of him. Laz stopped by his place a couple of times and updated me after they talked.

"It's still not fair," I say, clasping my hands behind my back. "Laz's ticket was totally dismissed."

"Yeah, well, Laz hasn't been in trouble before." His eyes are soft as he looks at me. "How are you doing? Been missing you."

"I miss you, too. I guess your dad hasn't changed his mind?"

"Nah. You should see my new phone. It looks like a burner. It only calls him, my uncle, and 911. I can only go to work and then back home. Wash, rinse, and repeat that shit every day." He laughs again—a real one this time, and hearing it reminds me so much of all the good times I had this summer that I can't help but smile. "And, you know, my pops went to bat for me in front of that judge."

"Is that allowed?"

"Probably not, but it was late in the day and the judge

was tired. And my old man can be pretty convincing. Might've missed his calling as a pastor or something." He shakes his head, then clears his throat a couple of times. "I don't expect you to wait around for me. If you find someone else."

I doubt his father will let him date for the rest of high school, so waiting didn't really seem like an option. But the truth is: "I'm not looking for anyone else, Booker."

He smiles shyly. Then his face changes as he remembers something. "Laz told me all the shit that happened with your family. You doing okay?"

"Yeah, things are okay." I shift my weight to my other foot, staring at the name tag sewn on the chest of his coveralls. His name looks so fancy in the thick blue script. "I think it's better that the truth is out there."

And then I can't help myself. I touch his forearm, where the sleeve is rolled up. His skin is warm beneath my fingers, and I shut my eyes for a moment, thinking of us together. He leans into my touch and closes the gap between us. Booker bends down to kiss me, and I melt right into him, savoring his thick lips on mine. Maybe for the last time.

Behind him, hoots and whistles ring out in the garage.

"Ayyyyyyyyyyeeee, Stratton!" calls someone.

Someone else shouts: "Check out fucking Romeo over here!"

We pull back reluctantly, but not before he kisses my neck, just below my earlobe.

"Carlene pierced them," I say. "That's why my mom has that weird rule about studs."

He looks at me, confused. "What?"

"You asked about my ears, when you were in my room that time. Carlene pierced them when I was still a baby, before I went to live with my parents. She just told me the other day."

I still call them that, because what else are they? Yes, technically, my mom is my aunt, but she raised me like I was her own. She's the only mom I've known for sixteen and a half years. She'll always be Mom.

"Man, your life sounds kind of like a puzzle." He touches the same earlobe as he did that day.

"It kind of is," I say, nodding.

"What are you guys doing now?" he asks, looking to the front of the property, where Laz and Greg are on the other side of the fence, their backs to us.

"I don't know. Maybe get something to eat. Maybe at Valois." He smiles at this. And then, even though he'll probably say no, I ask anyway: "You want to come?"

"I do, but . . . Is this cool?" He swallows, never breaking eye contact. "Doing this when we know we can't see each other? I feel like I want all or nothing with you, Dove."

"I feel the same way. And I don't know. Maybe it's

319

a really bad idea." I trace the stitching on his name tag. "But I'm here. And I miss you. And even if we don't get to see each other again for a year, we'll still have this day to remember."

He peers back into the garage, looking at a clock that hangs between the two cars. "I go on lunch in fifteen. Can you guys wait?"

"Of course. No rush. But." I glance toward the little window in the garage that looks in on a small office. "Is your uncle going to tell your dad I was here?"

"Nah, I think Les feels sorry for me. Says Pops is busting my balls too much. I don't think he's gonna snitch about a lunch. Give me a few minutes to finish and clean up, okay?"

He kisses me again, which elicits more hoots and whistles from the garage. I step away, embarrassed, but he slides an arm around my waist and pulls me back toward him. Holds his middle finger up to the guys behind him as he kisses me long and slow.

A COUPLE OF WEEKS LATER I STEP OFF THE TRAIN, FRESH FROM MY FIRST day of junior year.

Maybe it's best that Booker and I can't see each other right now, because by the looks of every single syllabus I received, I'm going to be buried under books for the next few months.

I was worried things might be a little weird being back in school with Mitchell instead of the SAT prep class where nobody knew us. But it's fine. We were friendly with each other but didn't eat lunch together or sit next to each other in class. I did ask him what happened after the police station and he said it helped him talk to his parents. After they lectured him on how that night could have ruined his entire life before it actually started, he told them that he was still serious about school and getting into MIT, but he needed some space from their rules and over-the-top expectations. He said they listened. And I noticed his hair is longer, curling just above his collar, which is the longest he can grow it according to the school dress code.

"Hi, Birdie."

I look up, startled to find my mother standing outside the train station.

"What are you doing here? What's wrong?"

"Oh, nothing," she says with a smile. "But you only have one more first day of school after this and I had a break, so I figured I'd walk you home. Just like we used to."

Mom has been dipping into some serious nostalgia ever since the secret came out. She talks a lot about the past now—what Mimi and I were like as babies and toddlers, stories about her and Carlene from when they were younger. It's weird, but a good weird. I can tell that she wants to stop sometimes when she's getting deep into the reminiscing, but something inside her makes her go on.

We pass the homeless woman who leans against the station every day, just like we always have. But this time, I stop. Tell Mom to hang on as I dig into my bag and pull out a couple of dollars. I jog back to the woman and stuff the money in her cup. It's not a lot, but it's something.

She gives me a peace sign with her grubby fingers, then her head drops back down to her chest.

"Oh, Birdie," Mom says with a sigh when we start walking again. "You know I prefer to give to shelters. That woman has been sitting out there in that same spot every single day for years and—"

"But that's the thing, Mom. *You* like to give to shelters. *I* want to give my money directly to people sometimes."

"She's probably just going to use it for more alcohol or drugs," she says as we cross the street.

"Maybe she will and maybe she won't. If Carlene had been on the streets, wouldn't you want someone to give her a couple of dollars if it would help her?"

My mother doesn't answer, but she doesn't fight me on it, either. "Well, how was the first day?" she asks instead.

"Not too bad. It's going to be a lot of work this year, but I already knew that." I push the strap of my bookbag higher on my shoulder. "I have class with a couple of the girls I used to play soccer with."

"Oh? How are they doing?" she says in a tone that means she's asking only to be polite.

"They're great. You know, even if I can't play at school, I could do the leagues again."

"Birdie, you haven't played soccer in three years now."

"Yes," I say, stopping to look at her. "And I miss it. I miss it a *lot*, Mom."

She stops, too, and meets my eyes. "What about school? You just told me it's going to be a tough year."

"It is, but that doesn't mean I can't handle something else. Soccer helps relieve stress. It takes some of the pressure off school. It's *good* for me, and my grades were always good when I was playing."

"But that was middle school, Birdie. You're a junior now, and—"

"Mom, I really want to do this. I don't have to be the best. I just want to play."

She looks at me for a long time, and I can't tell what she's thinking, but I know that face, and it's not her *No* face. Not quite. "I'm not promising anything, but I'll talk to your father about it, okay? We'll see what we can work out."

I squeeze my arms around her and kiss her on the cheek before we start walking again.

She comes up to the apartment to freshen up before she goes back down to the shop.

I get a glass of water and lean against the sink. I don't notice the manila envelope on the kitchen table until I've drunk half the glass.

My name is scrawled on the front in handwriting I don't recognize.

"Mom?" I call out. "What's this envelope?"

She appears a few seconds later, smiling. "It's for you, Birdie. Open it."

I slip my index finger under the flap on the back

and slide out the piece of paper inside. Carlene's name is printed in big letters; the calligraphy above it says *Certificate of Completion*, and under her name is the logo of a cosmetology school.

"She did it!" I say, grinning hard at the paper.

Mom nods, coming around to look at it over my shoulder. I can hear the pride in her voice as she says, "Yes, she really did it."

I look at the Post-it note stuck to the bottom, with the same handwriting as the envelope.

Got my 300 hours, kid!
Wanted you to be
the first to know.
    Love, Carlene

Booker was right. My life is like a puzzle now, with so many pieces to make sense of and try to fit together.

But I have all the pieces now, and every single one belongs to me.

ACKNOWLEDGMENTS

I would like to say thank you to:

Alvina Ling for being a wonderful person and editor. I am so happy to work with you.

Nikki Garcia for your sharp eye, wit, and patience.

The rest of the team at Little, Brown Books for Young Readers who support me and my work with such kindness, thoughtfulness, and professionalism: Victoria Stapleton, Kristina Pisciotta, Michelle Campbell, Christie Michel, Valerie Wong, Marisa Finkelstein, Kelley Frodel, and Marcie Lawrence. And Erin Robinson for my beautiful illustrated covers; you bring black girls to life in such a vivid, inspiring way.

Tina Dubois, because you get me. How lucky I am to have you as a friend, confidante, and my brilliant literary agent.

Tamara Kawar for assisting said agent with efficiency and charm.

Elana K. Arnold, Robin Benway, Anna Carey, Maurene Goo, Corey Ann Haydu, Kristen Kittscher, Stephanie Kuehn, Courtney Summers, and Elissa Sussman for being good friends and colleagues.

I appreciate you all.

TURN THE PAGE FOR A PREVIEW OF

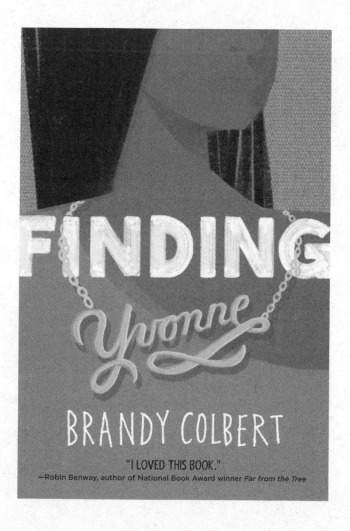

AVAILABLE NOW

1.

There are three things I know about my father: He smokes pot daily, he doesn't like to speak unless he really has something to say, and he is one of the most respected chefs in Los Angeles.

I also know that the best time to see him is at Sunday breakfast. We aren't around each other much; Dad gets home from work so late during the week that he's rarely up in time to make a proper breakfast. He usually grabs something light when he gets up, around noon, and then eats family meal with the staff before the restaurant opens for dinner. But Sundays are special. He reserves Sunday mornings for an actual meal that he plans in advance, and there's always plenty to eat.

Sometimes I want to skip it on principle alone. I shouldn't have to set aside one day a week to see my own dad for more than a few minutes. But I love Sunday breakfast, and he's usually in a good mood because he gets the day to himself, so I find myself at the table every week.

He's standing at the counter when I stumble into the kitchen this morning, coating pieces of chicken in a mixture of flour and seasonings.

"Morning," he says over his shoulder. "Coffee's on."

"Thanks." I pour a mug and stand next to the fridge, watching him. "Is Warren coming over?"

"Should be here any minute."

Which means I'll need to down this cup of coffee if I want to brush my teeth again before he gets here. I slurp steadily at the mug, but the doorbell rings before I can finish. Well, it's not like anything is going to happen with my father here.

Warren Engel is standing on the porch in jeans and a plaid button-down with the sleeves rolled up. He smiles and wordlessly reaches for my hands. I pull him inside and we stand looking at each other for a moment, his big tea-colored eyes roaming softly over me before we hug.

"Missed you last night," he says in a low voice, though Dad couldn't hear us over all the banging around he's doing in the kitchen anyway.

"Sorry I didn't make it over. The party went late, and then I just wanted to sleep in my own bed."

"It's cool. I was at the restaurant until late." Warren was promoted to sous chef at my father's restaurant a couple of months ago, a big honor in itself but especially since he's just barely twenty-one. "What's Sinclair making today?"

"Come see for yourself," I say, leading him back through the hallway. His hands trail lightly over my hips as we walk, sending warm shivers up the small of my back, but it ends as quickly as it started. We break apart when we're standing in the same room as my father.

We're not official, Warren and I. We probably would be if he weren't so paranoid about our age difference. We're only three years apart, and I don't think my father would care. He basically thinks Warren can do no wrong.

Dad is carefully placing chicken legs and thighs into a skillet of hot oil as we walk in.

"Chicken and waffles?" Warren says, grinning like the day just turned into Christmas. My father has a lot of fans, known and unknown, but I think Warren might still be his biggest.

"You know it." My father moves the skillet to a cool burner. "Want to get the waffles going? Iron's already hot, and the batter's in the fridge."

I reach into the refrigerator to hand Warren the pitcher of

batter, then grab the jug of orange juice, too. "Isn't he off the clock?"

"Happy to let you take over if you're so concerned about Warren," Dad says, smirking as he heads over to the sunroom.

Not two minutes later, the skunky scent of marijuana wafts through the air above us. Neither Warren nor I bat an eye. My father's frequent pot-smoking isn't exactly public knowledge, but it's certainly no secret around here. He says it's mostly to combat the stress that comes with owning a successful restaurant, but he also swears that he's created some of his most iconic dishes while stoned. He probably knows that I've smoked, but we don't talk about it and we've certainly never done so together.

Dad is what I call a professional stoner. He's been smoking for so long that it's hard to tell when he's high. The whites of his eyes turn just slightly pink, and sometimes he takes a little longer between thoughts, but other than that he's completely functional. Almost disturbingly so. I've seen him carry on extremely involved conversations when I know he's blazed up pretty recently.

I down a glass of orange juice while Warren tends to the waffles, creating a generous stack on a plate next to the chicken. Dad comes back in just as they're ready, and we all help transport everything to the table. I carry plates and silverware and quickly set the table as they place the food.

Eating with my father and Warren isn't like sharing a meal with anyone else I've ever known. Usually people taste a few bites of their food, declare how good it is or what it's lacking, then move on to more stimulating conversation. Warren and my dad analyze each bite, discussing which spices were or were not used and what they've changed since the last time they made the meal. Sometimes Dad gives him tips on his method, but I realized how much he respects Warren when he started asking for his opinion.

I grew up in the restaurant industry, but I don't understand food the way they do. Except for sweets. Baking makes sense to me, maybe because there's science behind it. There's so much trial and error with cooking. I get frustrated when a recipe doesn't turn out right the first time, even when I follow it to the letter.

"I was thinking about going to check out that new spot in Venice," Dad says to Warren. "The one Courtney Winters just opened up."

"Oh, that place is supposed to be the real deal." Warren wipes his mouth and takes a long drink of water. "You're going today?"

"She has a Sunday supper. What do you think?"

"Yeah, sure." Warren pauses and looks at my dad first, then me. "You want to come?"

I pour more syrup over my waffle and take a bite. Even I

can't help but stop and think how perfectly light and fluffy it is as I chew. "I don't know," I say, looking at my father. "Am I invited?"

"Of course you are, Yvonne. I thought you'd be practicing," Dad says with a shrug.

I do usually practice my violin on Sunday. It feels like a good end to the weekend. A structured start to the week. But I need a break from the routine sometimes. And now that I'm no longer taking private lessons, I can make my own practice schedule.

"Can we stop at the boardwalk?"

"Yeah, sure." Dad waves one hand in the air as he drags a forkful of chicken and waffles through a pool of syrup with the other. He's already done with this conversation, ready to get back to food talk.

The meal with them tonight will be almost exactly like the scene at this kitchen table, only they'll sample an unreasonable amount of food, and my father will go back to the kitchen to talk to the chef, and I'll have to hear everything from why he thinks the dining-room sconces are incompatible with the space to him breaking down the components of a sauce.

It's exhausting, but I know the meal will be good. My father won't try just anyone's food. And I'll get to spend time with Warren, which always makes me happy. He works such long hours that we don't get to see each other as often as I'd like.

Besides, I don't have anything else to do today. My Sundays used to be filled with violin practice, but with Denis no longer around to crack the whip, I don't see much of a point.

It's hard not to give up on yourself when the person who's supposed to believe in you the most already has.

2.

My geology teacher, Mr. Gamble, used to live in Venice Beach before we were born, and he says none of us would have survived it back then. He says the streets were full of gangs and crumbling bungalows and people addicted to crack.

Gentrification has changed a lot of that, but luckily the boardwalk has remained as weird as ever. One area is devoted to shirtless meatheads who like to lift weights in front of tourists, the aptly named Muscle Beach. Then there's the section where the skaters take turns braving the terrifying maze of concrete ramps on their boards.

But my favorite part is walking down the pavement-lined path that stretches by booths of tie-dyed clothing, shops hawking cheap souvenirs, and doctors who will prescribe medical-marijuana cards in thirty minutes. There are places to grab a drink or a bite to eat, and on the other side is the ocean, separated only by the art vendors, the street performers, and the wide expanse of sand.

Salt water and incense and competing strains of weed fill the air as I stroll down the boardwalk between Warren and my dad. My father's phone rings and he looks down at the screen, says he has to take it and he'll catch up with us.

Warren and I walk so that our arms occasionally bump into each other, but no closer than that. I think he's afraid my dad will freak out if he ever sees us touching, but I keep telling him he's paranoid. My father knows there's something between Warren and me, even if there's no label. The fact that I spend the night at Warren's place so often and Dad never says anything about it should reassure him more than it does.

"Would you ever live over here?" Warren asks as we pass a table full of heavy silver jewelry displayed on black velvet.

"I don't know." I wrap my arms around myself. The beach is always noticeably cooler than the rest of the city. It feels like we're not even in Los Angeles, the temperature has changed so much from when we left Highland Park. "It's so different. And I'd pretty much need to be a billionaire to rent an apartment."

"You're so practical." He nudges me gently. "If money

were no object and you could live anywhere in the city in your dream house—could you live in Venice?"

"I guess the beach is nice, but I like where we live better," I say. "I couldn't handle so many tourists."

"It's probably easy to avoid them when you know your way around." He pauses. "I think I could hang at the beach."

"You're not allowed to move this far away from me," I say, shaking my head. "I'd never see you."

"You mean not until you leave next year?" Warren's voice is more matter-of-fact than accusatory.

Still, it makes me wince. I've been trying not to think about the fact that there will probably be a day when we don't live in the same city. Even if I don't go to an out-of-state school, there's a chance Warren could move on himself. He could get scooped up by another chef when my father isn't paying attention. Or he could just move somewhere else to start his own restaurant, which he'll inevitably do one day.

"That's a whole year away. And we don't even know what's going to happen."

He doesn't say anything else about it, and I'm trying to figure out what to say to bring the mood back up when I hear the strings.

If cooking is my father's and Warren's thing, music has always been mine. Dad got me my first violin about a year after my mother left, when I was seven. We tried a few different activities—I guess so I wouldn't spend all my free time wondering why I suddenly had no mother: dance lessons, Girl Scouts, classes at a local children's theater. None of it stuck, but as soon as we walked into the violin shop, which was also filled with beautiful violas and cellos that seemed absolutely monstrous at the time, I felt right at home. Even the shop owner, whose deep frown made it clear that he didn't like children getting too close to the merchandise, said nothing as I walked around slowly, staring in awe at the instruments.

My elementary-school orchestra teacher, Ms. Francine, told me I had a gift for music. She didn't say I was the best in the orchestra or even the best in the violin section, but I never forgot what she said. I never told anyone, though. I had been taking private lessons with Denis for a couple of years by the time I started playing in her orchestra. I only realized recently that maybe I wanted that praise all to myself because I didn't want anyone to taint it. People are always telling my father how great he is at what he does—one of the best—but that was the first time anyone had said that to me, and I didn't want the validation taken away. Even then, I knew I had to be protective of it; I've never stood out for anything besides violin.

Coaxing bittersweet melodies from the strings of my instrument has always been satisfying, but performing has never given me the same thrill as listening to other people play.

The music is coming from a guy and a girl at the edge of the boardwalk. A crowd stands in front of them, but it's a small group. No more than a dozen people tapping their feet on the pavement, leaning closer to better hear the notes. The makeshift audience is trying to place the song, but if anyone knows it, I can't tell. Most of them stand there with bemused but pleasant expressions on their faces, as if they were unaware that such music could come from string instruments.

I put my hand on Warren's arm so he'll stop. He looks confused at first, then nods as he sees them. We stand silently, and I let the notes of the old song soar through my ears and into me. Sometimes I hear songs that I like, that are interesting or catchy enough for me to take notice as I'm doing homework or getting ready for the day. Then there are melodies that seep into me, winding through every part of my body with such intensity that I can't do anything but sit still and listen. It's not always the song itself; sometimes it's a certain variation or the musician's individual stamp that resonates. I can't pinpoint what it is about the music I'm listening to now, but all I want to do is close my eyes and let it settle into me.

Jessie Weinberg

BRANDY COLBERT

is the critically acclaimed author of the novels *Pointe*, *Finding Yvonne*, Stonewall Award winner *Little & Lion*, and *The Only Black Girls in Town*. Born and raised in Springfield, Missouri, she now lives and writes in Los Angeles.

FROM
BRANDY COLBERT

FOR TEENS

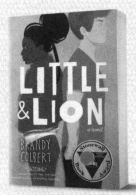

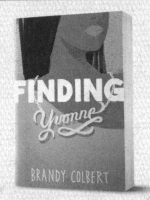

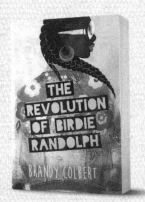

FOR KIDS

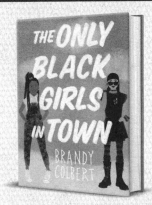

"Brandy's ability to find larger meaning in small moments is nothing short of dazzling."

—Nicola Yoon, *New York Times* bestselling author